I0647483

If after finishing this book you find that you liked it or found it worthy, the Author humbly asks that you leave an honest review on Amazon to help in making this book more widely known. He would be in your debt.

—Review of Robin's first book,
      "Dreams, Desires, And Dead Ends"

"Memorable, quirky sketches on life and love from a storyteller with potential"
                                    —Kirkus Reviews

Previous Book by Robin Chappell

"Dreams, Desires, And Dead Ends"
"Nothing Personal"

Upcoming titles
"Happily Married"
"Sometimes…"

Shadows and LIGHT

a novel by

ROBIN CHAPPELL

Book One
of the "Secret History of the World" series

ILLUMINOUSITY PRESS
Los Angeles

"Illuminousity Press, LLC" is the property of
Robert Alan Chappell

First Illuminousity Press paperback and ebook editions October 2023

Cover and all interior design work by Robin Chappell
Header Typeface: Impact
Body Typeface: New Times Roman

Library of Congress Copyrighted
Chappell, Robert Alan
"shadows and LIGHT"
1. Novel 2. Fiction I.Title

ISBN: 978-1-7374519-6-9   Paperback
ISBN: 978-1-7374519-5-2   eBook

Illuminousity Press
Los Angeles

Dedicated to my Aunt Kate;

One of my most dedicated Family and Followers.

shadows and **LIGHT**

Robin Chappell

death and dying though thought a curse
believe me when I say that there's worse
dead is gone and fled this earth
better than to stay here as a curse.
in essence dragged for power to stay
that tied here in the Red Circle Way
to live another thousand years or more
to witness all our earthly fears to grow
shadows all in the light of pain
the Light of Love to kill this day

shadows and **LIGHT**

Part I
Escaping the Darkness Without

ONE

The Silence had a deafening roar to it. As if the very earth was trembling at the feel of the sheer feral Hatred and Malice that was threatening to be given Voice.

But the only *sound* that would have been evident to the naked ear in this too, too silent night, was the ominous and rumbling Silence. Coming as if from some tremendous depth and a very great distance... from some distant star's solar system.

Almost imperceptible at first but slowly now, the low thrum was ringing up to the point where even those ears that only hear the normally Spoken Word would be questioning their own hearing.

Up from the very center of the earth, this low, shrieking, grinding groan carrying the weight of the Intent of the Deepest and most malignant Malice... was now rising out of the Void.

It began coming slowly and menacingly and then began climbing through the octaves of the unheard. Finally crashing Its Malevolent way into the felt more than heard, it continued climbing towards a mind-rending agony soon to be evident to the unprotected ears with its Fury.

A psychic avalanche building speed, it began beating every molecule of air in the clearing into deadly submission, cresting towards a tidal wave of Fury as the naked ear was finally allowed to be assaulted by its shrieking, building roar. The very earth began trembling like a coming earthquake with its echo of severing, shearing madness.

Even to the shielded defenses, it would have begun to take on a low dull hum, a murmur of madness rising like some far off wind mounting an assault on the elements of air and fire.

To the unshielded defenses...

Out of the deepest of Darknesses, a dire Chant began to be malevolently barely whispered.

Words began to rise out of this Whispering meant to gnaw at the very core of the Soul. Almost subvocal at first, They began rising through the inaudible, rising as They did to strain the lower registers of sound. They now became a hint of dire words and grave maledictions attached.

Words with the purely evil Intent of centuries of madness and malice, now pent up and being coaxed into form.

Words that were at the very heart of this Madness, harnessed to break all but the most powerful of minds into a million shards of abject terror.

Words that had been uttered only in the most blasphemous of events of pure, naked evil which were of a singular purpose. It now began shrieking Its pure hatred into the fracturing night sky, causing the very stars above to begin shivering from the Force of this feral hatred.

Words that were just now taking on a recognizable, but still utterly foreign shape. Mutterings of Power, drawn out of the very elements being rent that shape being and non-being.

Words, or sounds like words, mixed in with what seemed like a million animals grunting and squealing in sheer agony in the darkness.

Words that were guttural phrases intended to tear, twist and shred at the very notion of peace and knowledge. Words that were intended to flee shrieking from the Void, guaranteed to shear the unprotected Soul from its physical moorings.

Words flashing like raging, red, puncture wounds from razor-edged blades stabbing out against the night. For that was the Intent blazing fiercely and rising furiously out of this Darkness being called upon and drawn out to destroy all hope.

Words stoking the preternatural fire which was stabbing out against the darkness like flaming, fiery blood, pulsating with the rhythm of the rising chant.

Words that drove the Bodies circling this Madness as they swayed, blocked and unblocked the direct painful sight of the Pyre in the center there, again and again (should anyone be unlucky enough to be there as an Observer and not a Participant).

Words meant to hemorrhage the night that began driving towards Their final blasting crescendo.

Words which were now beating at not only the physical ears, but the doors of the Soul as well. Careening beyond the range of normal hearing into the White-hot incandescence of pure Hatred screaming out of the Void with a force seeking to shred physical reality into the bloodied pulp of centuries of vile Acts.

Words illuminating the rising flames of physical fire searing into the burning night.

Words feeding this hatred of all things that are free was being reflected in the Pyre that was the central Focus of this Gathering.

Words being fed by the psychic fury swirling through the assembled bodies and their energies gyrating to the inhuman Call they were creating.

Words that flashed in the growing material image of Hate Incarnate beginning to form there.

Words drenching all of those surrounding It in Its pyre of Malevolence.

Words increasing the pulsating waves of destruction of all that is whole and Good.

Words that were the rending Sound emanating from the It that now began feeding the Voices raised to It.

Words increasing Their Frenzy.

Words fusing this forest of Bodies into an even greater single focus, driven as if by a tornado of Hatred and Fear of such devastating force as to crush and obliterate Everything in Its path.

Words buffeted the Bodies being whipped into even greater heights of fury and frenzy, with the Power of Evil Itself rising to engulf, enflame, and finally...

Taking on a tangible Shape now, **IT** was Floating and rising above the assembled Furies and Frenzies, this was the very Shape of Darkness Itself, living flames that were starting to solidify.

The semblance of Horns began rising above It out of the flame drenched Darkness. Horns. And, a Body now. That the very sight of which creates sheer Madness in those even looking at this **IT** which would be beyond what most minds could handle before breaking.

IT was the Image of thousands of years of the ultimate personification of Hatred, Malice and Darkness.

IT was making Its presence physical out of the swirling illusion of Madness, to dominate all that was brought before It now.

Tornadic Spirals of fire and smoke finished building their way into this physical Embodiment of absolute sheer Terror.

Words of The Chanting were now recognizable as a language both ancient and utterly foreign, continuing its pulsating rising up through the registers of hearing and, rising like a wind of pure devastation, which were both fed and were being Fed by the Force of the Non-Being at the center.

Words having risen beyond the detectable and were now slamming forward into a screeching crescendo of pain transcending Madness. This Sound beat at and began pounding down the very doors of the Soul itself.

Words Seeking to sheer the Soul from the body. The Undefended would feel excruciating Pain beyond the belief of the mind to handle, screaming in an absolute Agony beyond Words.

Suddenly... a heavily ancient jewel-incrusted **Blade** both shining blood Red from within and reflecting the deadly Pyre's Light as well, was lifted above the frenzy for the final Act.

It had reflected in Its' Jewels the dripping malice of the bloody history of tens of centuries of human sacrifices it had been the focus of.

Almost as Alive as those frenzied hordes surrounding **IT**, The **Blade** was held high by a hand almost as old as It was, so that that

14

Blade was almost an extension of that Hand.

Lifting It above the shrieking multitude for a long madness-drenched set of beating second bleeding into centuries, The **Blade** began shrieking a blood-thirsty 'song' of Its own.

The Form in the center becoming more solid by the second, the anguished wail of madness crying out from the body of an innocent child about to be slaughtered in the middle of this madness, somehow managed to raise it's screaming, squalling Voice into piercing the Void of the Chant of Madness raised around it.

Shrieking now beyond the range of possible hearing, these **Words** of Pure Hatred were opening a **Black Hole** beyond the physical. A doorway for the Embodiment of this Ultimate Sacrilege to finish descending completely into physical Form; to witness and feed upon this act.

Unbearable now, almost even to the most protected of Souls witnessing it, The **Energy** reached its crescendo and suddenly snapped with the force and fury of an earthquake, as this Blade, plummeting, fell out of sight and found its mark.

The wailing Cry of the Innocent suddenly a shriek of pain as—

shadows and **LIGHT**

TWO

—in another dark night, far away and much later, the body of the Woman whose nightmare this had been making itself felt through the years, shoots bolt upright out of the shrieking, searing madness of that Nightmare—

Into the too, too, deathly, silent night of her present apartment.

Her mouth still fixed in a wordless shriek of terror with sweat streaming from every pore of her body, she leapt out of bed now and began tearing blindly through that present darkness, from room to dark room, frantically turning on each and every light she could find in her apartment. Until the flood of light had beaten back the darkness, and not a single bulb remained dark.

With some part of her finally satisfied, she dove back into the *safety* of her bed, finally finding herself burrowing under the sheets and blankets and pulling them up to the point where only her eyes were still to be seen. Wide from the Terror she had just re-lived.

Shivering violently from the demons threatening to rise out of her very mind, the stark Terror there was still blinding her to Itself in the present.

The lights blazing around her now and somehow feeling protected at last, the steel trap of her mind snapped loose, allowing her heart to catch up with her mind. Her heart was now hammering like a locomotive at full throttle in her chest, threatening to tear her chest apart from the pain and wrenching anguish.

Threatening to escape and run screaming off into the night by itself, she thought that she was going to die right there and then. Her soul almost sheared from her body, she began crying anguished tears of desperation for that Child sacrificed in her 'dream.'

After some time and some semblance of "reality" had begun approaching her again, her mind began working just as furiously to convince herself that what she had just experienced was 'just' a nightmare — nothing more. Yes, an all too vivid nightmare, but yes, just a nightmare just the same.

It took a few seconds to sink in however that no matter how much she desperately needed for it to be that easy to convince herself that what she had experienced was 'just a dream,' It was still there. And It was not a dream.

If she made the mistake of closing her eyes, for even just a second, the images would come flooding back, searing her soul as if she had never even woken up.

Obviously, no sleep would be coming to her again tonight. Only a silent vigil remaining shaking her in primal fear against tonight's visions.

Her eyes were still screaming wide.

shadows and **LIGHT**

THREE

It was morning once again when she finally woke up, and the shadows and darkness of the night before were gone.

Snapping bolt upright in her bed again, she groggily took in her surroundings. Although it was early, the sun was glinting through the trees that lived just outside her bedroom window, casting very different kinds of shadows on her ceiling. Soft. Reassuring. Comforting shadows that swayed silently in the unseen breeze outside.

Starting to rise and suddenly remembering the terror of the night just past, the Woman — "Kathryn. Yes. My name is Kathryn Runyon. That's my name," she said to the air.

She looked around her bedroom as if she was in some foreign place, but it seemed just as it was when she had fallen asleep the night before. Before—

Her body still drenched by the sweat from the previous night was showing through her soaked nightgown now. But she wouldn't have been aware of it, with her lungs heaving and her eyes still bulging from the terror she had just re-remembered experiencing. Nothing else mattered now.

Looking back in her cloudy memory this morning, she remembered lunging for the lamp at her bedside, snapping it on furiously...

It was all replaying in slow motion in her head now and in one fluid motion, as she remembered throwing herself off the bed and tearing through her apartment. Knowing that every light in her apartment had to be turned on, her mind had screamed. Beat back the darkness. Beat back the...

Standing and slowly pulling away from the drenched sheets, she was uncovering herself, thinking that she was unsure of what she would find.

But all she found was her still clammy nightgown. Her body was as she had remembered it from yesterday; that much hadn't changed. But suddenly she thought, could she even trust her memories now? Or her senses for that matter?

Shaking the copper-colored mass of her tangled medusa-like hair and suddenly realizing just how damp her nightgown still was, she lunged down and grabbed the bathrobe off the floor from where she'd unthinkingly dropped it the previous night.

It wasn't cold out, but she felt somehow still extremely vulnerable, as if the bath robe were going to offer her no protection. Clambering out of bed and finding her way to the bathroom, she reached blindly to her right to flip the light on...

But looked up to see that it was already on.

"Right," some part of her said. "Last night."

At least that part had been real. And finally looking up at her image in the bathroom mirror, she was stopped short by her "pale as a ghost" face staring back at her. *The dead risen indeed,* she thought to herself critically.

Running her fingers through her hair and ready to cut it all off, she now remembered having woken in abject terror, tearing through her apartment turning on all the lights, and then plunging back into her bed.

Remembering now how she had pulled the sheets up so tightly around her neck and shivering uncontrollably from the terror that wouldn't leave, she was now feeling amazed that she hadn't passed out from suffocation.

She remembered now, how with her lungs still heaving in fright even much later, that she had reached our for the phone on her bedside table, hesitating to be out of the protective haven of her covers for too long.

Fumbling with punching in the number she should have known now by heart (and should have had as an auto-dial preset by now), she had finally managed to get the number right.

Ring after ring had echoed in her ears before the line had finally clicked through. "Tommy?" she had screeched into the receiver, but found herself answered only by the mechanical voice of the answering machine saying, "Hello. I'm sorry no one is at home right now—"

Whimpering, she had carefully placed the receiver back in its cradle; like it was a newly foreign object, or some wild animal that she was afraid of disturbing.

And Kathryn— "Yes," she said once more in the present morning, remembering her name again. "My name is Kathryn."

Feeling the fear that was beginning to shred her last vestiges of sanity after this — she had reached for the phone again, hysterically dialing the only other number she thought that she could count on; that of her therapist.

Sitting up unthinking after remembering too much of what she wanted to forget, she had begun rocking violently back and forth on the edge of her bed, while she waited for her anxiety which was rising like a gale force wind to break. Before that anxiety broke her.

If she wasn't able to reach someone...

After the phone clicked through though, yet another recorded Voice began (this time a woman's) with the same, "Hello. You've reached the office of—"

This time she threw the receiver back into its cradle, not waiting to be retreating to and not wanting to be at further *risk* being outside the covers.

24

She was to the point of jumping out of her skin, now that both of her "anchors" were...

Her eyes showing almost all white now, she had settled back into her bed, clutching the covers firmly up to her eyes once again. Terrified to return to sleep and also terrified to leave the feeling of safety of the sheets as her only protection, she had been whimpering like a small child and trying very hard not to shout, scream or howl out of the remembered Agony.

And then, much, much later, she had finally managed to fall asleep, exhausted. Both from the memories and the fear that had gripped her.

Unable to keep her eyes open any longer, no matter what horrific dreams might come, she was soon fast asleep.

And here she was the next morning, supposedly rational again with the memories of the previous "night mares" receding further away, staring at her image in the mirror.

She was wondering, seeing the wreckage of the night before, whether she should be going in to work this morning at all. Or rather perhaps she should be checking herself in for observation, instead of working.

In many ways, she was no longer really sure of much of anything any more.

shadows and **LIGHT**

FOUR

The Hawthorne Hospital for the Mentally Ill was a seemingly normal mental institution from the outside. That is, if any mental institution could really be considered "normal."

It consisted of a large campus of almost a dozen buildings, many of which were still covered with the ivy planted around them from the nineteenth century when these buildings had been built. There were also a few more modern structures of quite differing styles thrown in here and there however, in and around the ancient Ones still standing.

It was a live-in facility (meaning that if you ended up here, you might be here for a very, very long time). On the outside, it looked quite the respectable New England organization that it seemed to be.

Waking with a start once again, Kathryn found herself in front of the building where she worked. Without any recollection of how she'd gotten there, except that her car was parked in the space marked with the sign reading "DR. KATHRYN RUNYON" on it.

Except that she hadn't remembered even getting into the car, much less driving it here.

She reached to turn the key in the ignition off, and suddenly felt immobilized. She continued to sit where she was, staring at the key for what began feeling like an eternity, but was in "reality," only a few seconds.

Staring blankly ahead, the engine continued to drone on in front of her. Shivering suddenly, she realized that she was already at work. Again.

Sometimes a certain amount of dissociation can be a good thing, she thought to herself rather clinically. Her clients dissociated, psychically removing themselves from whatever trauma they had experienced in their life as a coping response. So why couldn't she, she supposed? *At least this one time.*

And in reality, everyone dissociates periodically. It's called daydreaming, and seemed to be a very common human coping mechanism, a way the mind has of relaxing.

As long as it didn't last for too long. Or happen behind the wheel of a car; especially at night. This had been during the day however, but still...

This "dissociation" had been for the almost twelve miles between her apartment and here. And even though it was in broad daylight, it was still something of a shock. She hadn't ever found herself having driven herself fully unconsciously all this way before. (Or had she?)

This was new. And this was also very unsettling.

Looking back now, she realized that she couldn't remember when exactly she had checked out and gone on auto-pilot.

She had heard too many stories from her patients about "lost time" — indeed, that was one of the first clear signs that something was most definitely amiss in their personality.

But this was the first time that she herself had consciously remembered being unconscious for a long period of time. Not the least of which was while she had been driving on a highway.

The road from home was winding and could be perilous under the least bit of wet conditions. And here she had just driven it, completely without having consciously driven it.

She shivered involuntarily again at the thought. She had had no previous indications that she might be just as screwy inside as her clients. But then she sobered up again, chastising herself inside for even thinking such a thought.

The last conscious recollection that she had that she could remember, was that of standing in front of her bathroom mirror looking into her own eyes. Then she had obviously taken a long hot shower, since her hair was still soaking wet. Still also in the daze of her dissociation, she had proceeded to get ready for work in the same condition.

Some part of her having done what was necessary to start her day, had then driven her the twelve miles from home to work. Also on auto-pilot. Had then pulled her car into her precious parking space and come to a stop, then allowing *her* self to *wake up*.

And here she was — the good Doctor Runyon. Doing her best to *help* her patients make sense of their lives. Having pulled into the parking lot at the clinic before she was even fully conscious of where she was and what she had been doing.

Waking up as it were from a dream of driving, staring at the ivy covered campus she didn't remember having driven to.

Looking at herself in the rear view mirror once again before preparing to get out and go inside, she was greeted with her freshly scrubbed face of thirty-eight years looking back. She knew she normally looked somewhat on the pretty side, but had fully expected to find a very different face staring back at her from the mirror this morning.

But the face looking back at her was still her own, and she thanked whoever — *Or whatever*, the thought suddenly came to her — that had helped her arrive here for yet another day of work. Looking as if she had had a good nights sleep. She suddenly shook her head in shivering disbelief.

Maybe I did have a good nights sleep last night after all, she thought. Maybe the whole thing last night was indeed merely a bad nightmare, and she really had woken up just as refreshed as she felt and seemed now.

Part of her really wanted to believe that. Desperately wanted to believe that.

Yet part of her knew that this wasn't the case. She took a deep breath several times working to calm herself down enough to feel grounded, deciding to not look in the mirror again. Even to adjust her hair. Just in case she saw something completely different this time.

Opening the car door to get out, she found herself having walked halfway to the entrance before stopping and turning slowly. Suddenly realizing that not only was the engine still running, but she hadn't even bothered to close the driver door. Shaking her head to clear it of that realization, she began putting one step in front of the other, back to the scene of her fleeting mind set and still running car.

Reaching in and turning the key in the ignition off, she closed the door very carefully and deliberately. And turning back towards her office building, she began slowly walking once again in the direction of the front door.

Catching herself shivering again even in the warm summer air, she consciously began slowing her breathing again, before plowing through the revolving door and into the lobby. Ready to present the professional Dr. Runyon, (and not some screaming mess of a child).

Stopping at the desk to calmly pick up her ID badge, she looked up to find herself confronted by the broadly smiling face of the institutions guard, Jimmy Hagan.

But an involuntary chill raced up her spine at the glowing teeth of

31

his almost feral Smile. She had known this man for all of the years she had worked here, usually pleasantly smiling at him in return. The usual daily routine.

Except that this didn't feel routine at all this morning. That Smile just didn't quite feel right to her, and she suddenly flashed on the anthropological theory of the origin of "The Smile."

It was basically the idea that the baring of teeth in a "smile," was a still animal-like way of subconsciously saying, *Hello, my friend. Do you like my teeth? Watch out. They just might eat you.* A stark remnant of our earlier more primitive animal heritage, the theory went.

Normally, it didn't strike her as sinister. But today—

"Good morning, Dr. Runyon!" Jimmy said a little too sunnily. And concluded with, "Nice day out, isn't it?" As if he were some announcer from the Fifties or Sixties. "Nice — day..." he had emphasized. Almost as if it were a curse, with a hint of malevolence lurking not too far beneath.

Smiling tentatively back at him while the hairs on the back of her neck rising like iceberg crests, she returned his seeming greeting with, "Good morning, Jimmy," and began walking away from him.

Having been at the Institute for almost twenty years now, he had almost always greeted everyone that way. Normally she considered him just a fixture that she interacted with, and she was sometimes mentally already preoccupied with a particular patient. He was Someone she barely knew, but politely acknowledged.

32

This morning however, Kathryn felt there was something really not right. She continued on down the hallway, trying to shrug it off, not wishing to think too much about anything out of the ordinary at this point.

But it wasn't working.

With somehow heightened senses, she was also now noticing that there was a faint smell in the halls this morning. One that she couldn't quite put a finger on, but was also disquieting. It spoke of putrefaction, and of some subtle antiseptic trying but failing to mask that odor.

Known to what few friends she had as "Kat," the esteemed and much published Doctor Runyon was now feeling like an awkward teenager again, about to walk around a corner some part of her knew, but which had a feeling of some sort of attack she sensed lying in wait.

It was the queasy feeling that something was very *not right*. Indeed, had been in just about every day of her life. Some part that lately (whatever it was) had grown into some kind of monstrous thing, lurking in a very dark corner of her mind.

And it was also a feeling that, whatever that *it* was, *it* was also about to be stepping out from Its corner and would manifest in full in *reality* soon. *Whatever the hell "reality" is*, she suddenly thought.

As she got off the elevator on the fifth floor that held her office, it began to intensify. Not quite a smell exactly, she thought, but...

Kathryn continued walking down the hall shaking her head distractedly, and turned into the door that she wasn't really looking at.

33

Instinct (or something like it), had once again taken over directing her. Moving into her front office, she somehow felt as if she were almost safe inside her own sanctuary as Kay, her secretary for the last four years, began walking out.

Kay offered Kathryn her first cup of coffee for the day, smiling a Mona Lisa smile bordering on the edge of— *What?* she asked herself.

"My, you're looking fresh this morning!" Kay said fake cheerily, obviously lying now. "Did you have a really good nights sleep last night, Dr. Runyon?"

Using Kathryn's title instead of her first name didn't help her in this feeling Kat couldn't shake.

"Why, Yes," Kathryn answered cheerfully back, once again putting on her "routine" smile that she didn't at all feel. Even though she hadn't "had a good night" and felt anything but "fresh" this morning, she maintained the outward play of normal as she was passing through Kay's office on the way into her own.

Reaching the sanctuary of her inner office and closing the door, she started having an overwhelming feeling of *not quite right-ness* about Kay, even though she'd been her secretary now for a very long time.

What is it? she thought. *Why is it everything anybody says to me this morning has this dark feeling to it?* She shrugged it off once more, shaking her head and setting her coffee down precariously close to the edge of her desk. She began walking around to sit down in front of the large stack of reports that hadn't been there yesterday.

"And why are there always so many reports," Kathryn sighed, as if there was someone who had a good answer close by. *If I'd realized how much paper work was going to bury me, maybe I wouldn't have gone into this crazy profession*, she thought.

Reaching for her cup of coffee with her left (unusual) hand without looking at it, she didn't notice that even though her hand didn't reach it, the cup suddenly sprang into her grasp.

Taking her first sip, she opened the top file drawer of her desk with her right hand, once again without looking and pulling out her client log. She distractedly placed it lying open on the desk in front of her, but was still doing it largely without consciously directing her actions.

The esteemed Dr. Runyon was tending to flip back and forth between being "not there," and then suddenly snapping back to the present without any rhyme or reason. If one of her clients reported this, she would explain it to them as the "missing time" of their Dissociative Disorder, otherwise known as the sign for having "Multiple Personalities." She could diagnose it in others, but not for herself.

Her office was very sparse and sterile by most peoples' (even therapists) standards. Yes, it had all the requisite diplomas on the walls, with book shelves filled with all the books necessary for her to reference if needed. And the walls were the standard issue institutional green cinder block with the institutional curtains hiding the high windows.

She never questioned why her office was almost a windowless, prison-like cell. She was high enough (and credentialed enough) to have a screen of leaves to make it cheery in the spring, summer and fall. Instead, there was only high blocks and a high window, with the all too present institutionally green painted walls.

Finally filling out the room were the requisite file cabinets neatly labelled against the far wall, rounding out and topping off the clinical but cold look of her office. Today, it didn't faze her at all that this wasn't normal for a psychiatrists office.

There were no photos of a happy family hanging on her walls, as with most people. Her mother had died young, and she had always been both hesitant and a little uneasy about having any photo with her father in it being within eyesight of her as she worked. And being an only child, she had no photos of any siblings or their families either.

The one photo that she did have on her desk, was one of herself and her boyfriend Tom, taken by someone else on one of their many camping trips together. There were no other types of vacations that she could remember their having taken; no cruises, no visits to the various Big Cities within easy driving distance.

And not even any trips to visit his family either. Nothing but camping trips that is, when she could even drag him away from work that is. And that was hard enough.

Except for the occasional professional conference she was required to attend for her job, she couldn't even remember going anywhere outside of her job and home for most of her life. Nothing except for those camping trips, that is. She was not one to consider going on vacations as part of her yearly routine either.

Looking at this photo this morning, she was struck with an odd sensation. He had a "devilish'" expression on his face (one of the things that she liked about him), that seemed at once both open and a mask. Something about this photo this morning however struck her as odd.

She was shivering herself out of yet another bout of dissociation, when she noticed that more more than a few minutes had passed on the old 1950s analog clock (also an institutional throwback) on the opposite wall. Unconsciously reaching for the top file and opening it up to read and take notes, she poured herself back into her work, determined to not take any more notice of these bouts of disappearing time.

"Abnormal Psychology" was what her field was called, and she had specialized in the treatment of what most people knew of as Multiple Personalities, which had become to be called "Dissociative Disorders" ("DiD" being the clinical term) amongst her profession.

Up until very recent times, it also used to be called by another name — "possession." Musing to herself one day, *Maybe that's not so far off the mark as we've been led to believe*, she thought ironically, and then brushed the thought away.

Considering the content and the messengers of this form of human consciousness, possession seemed to adequately describe the phenomena she experienced on a daily basis. Although admittedly, some of her patients were in the extreme (case-wise) with this form of psychology. Lately though, "Abnormal" hardly covered it.

She had been practicing this particular brand of dealing with madness now for almost twenty years. Almost from the point that psychiatry determined that it could be "cured."

Psychiatry called that state of "being cured" "integration," when all of the various "alternate personalities" were bypassed, released and the "Core Personality" re-assumed control with a sense that one was an "individual," instead of being a "many."

Kat had ruminated on the phrase on the Dollar Bill many a time. "Out of Many, One" it said in latin. But then she also considered another form of "integration" upon reading Mary Shelley's "Frankenstein" in college. Had Shelley been a Multiple as well? Had the Monster been a metaphor for *her* feeling split into many "parts?" Like the Monster?

Dr. Runyon was beginning to wonder however, if it ever really happened though.

Or whether perhaps all of those personalities buried somewhere deep "inside" her patients didn't just all get together at some point and decide (by "committee," as one of her patients had called "Them") to "call it quits." "Let's pretend, *I'm cured*, doctor.'" That they were just going *underground* to live in whatever passed for them as some kind

38

of "peace." All the children of the devil giving up the ghost and...

Escape. If only she could...

Yes, all the paperwork was a pain to deal with. But it also represented right now a more solid sense of reality that Kathryn could cling to in all this madness. And it represented something that she so desperately needed right now... Stability.

Returning her attention to the paperwork at hand, she sighed, letting herself the occasional thought that led to darker areas she didn't want to go to.

My whole life is devoted to abnormal psychology, she once thought. *Including my own.*

shadows and **LIGHT**

FIVE

Inside one of the patient treatment rooms some time later, the now highly professional Doctor Runyon was in the middle of working with a patient dealing with a memory out of the deepest recesses of her patient's mind.

The smell of cleaning with antiseptics and disinfectants in this room helped to stabilize that sense of "professionalism." *Comforting and strange at the same time*, she thought to herself, that this "clinical" sort of smell could bolster her trembling in fear from last nights nightmares. A sense of cleanliness and orderliness to dispel the chaos of her inner life that has been bursting uncomfortably out.

Except that the "patient" believed that "she" was a *they*, and that *they* were not remembering fantasies at all, but altogether too real "realities." Which of course then Dr. Runyon must deal with as a reality too, for the patient to reveal to her what (in this case the Patient was genetically a "she") needed for their treatment.

This room was as sparse as her office, largely having only the required amount of furniture to be in it.

In the center, there was a patient table/couch with straps on it, in case the patient being treated turned violent. For her — the therapist — there was merely a simple stuffed chair and a small stand beside it for all the therapists use while in this setting.

The only other item that was there was on the wall (once again cinder block and Institutional Green) in front of the patients view, was a very large (and now quite ancient) ornately framed Pastoral Scene (to induce a sense of "calm" in the patients). The image was faded, and the frame was dulled from the long time it had hung there, the metal surrounding it almost corroded to a deep burnished black. But it still served its purpose (or so the argument ran).

And on the third wall to the left of the patient and to the right of Kat, was a large plate glass One Way Mirror with an Observation Room just beyond it. It was covering the majority of the wall, and it was hiding what she was pretty sure every patient knew was there — the Hidden Observer.

Quite appropriate in the case of Multiple Personalities she often thought, in a little (again appropriate) "inside joke" as it were that she relished. Usually it was another psychiatrist (sometimes supervising), but in this case, it held Kathryn's current Intern, Kristen.

Kathryn was sitting in her "throne" listening intently and writing notes on the steno pad lying in her lap.

This client was a former middle aged housewife who had become

42

rather obese in the last few year of her life after she had had her third child, but was now this woman of forty, looking more like a frightened and petulant child now balled up into an almost a fetal position on the couch.

Dr. Runyon was asking the woman on the table, "What do you see now, Mouse? Are there any adults around you?" after which she patiently waited for the answer.

"Mouse" was the name of this particular "Alter" (short for Alternate Personality) that was "presenting" (being out) now. It (*she*?) represented one of the shards that this particular middle-aged woman had dissociated (or broken into) you might say, for reasons that Kathryn was still trying to determine. Each of the "incidents" that her patients related, often had different Alters that went with each series of episodes.

Whereas the patient Mary was a very large woman, the Voice that came out of her when the Alter Mouse was "out" (being evident as a "separate" personality) seemed anything but. This Alters voice was that of a scared and seemingly quite small child.

Sometimes these "memories" seemed to make sense to Kat and at other times they seemed random and almost hallucinatory to her. Her job as therapist was to take all of these fractured pieces of these "alters" puzzles, and bring them together into a determination or totality of treatment. She would hopefully see the whole picture at some point, of what the emotional (and/or often sexual) abuses that

43

her clients had gone through, were resulting in this mental fragmentation.

The calm that she had begun to feel descend on her this morning in her office with her first cup of coffee, was now starting to fray around the edges as she worked with this patient though.

The experienced Kathryn Runyon, PhD, should be able to maintain her professional distance when she was working with one of her clients. But now the inner Kat (her childhood nickname) Runyon was being jarred by the shear raw emotion she had been hearing from this patient during this morning's session.

Something however, was tugging on her mind, working its way like a worm up from the depths that Kathryn had so far been able to hold at bay. Now however, she was wondering for how long she could keep whatever it was at bay.

On the outside though, she was still managing to maintain her air of professional appearance. But this was belying the inner approaching storm she felt roiling up inside, like a dark cloud filled with ominous rolling lightning cascading strange light.

This particular patient, who had up until recently been a mother, was now being a "child" herself. Thrashing around on the couch in front of her, it seemed to Kathryn as if the very hounds of hell were in pursuit. The change that each patient went through in opening to their inner pain could still be wrenching to her, even after all this time.

"Nooooooo..." Mouse began wailing. The wail was in the shrieking plaintive voice of a little girl about three, even though the patient lying on the couch was chronologically going on forty- five.

Dressed in her starched white clinical coat and wearing reading glasses perched far down on her nose, Kathryn's coppery hair was tied back into her "professional ponytail," as she sometimes referred to it as. She was taking notes while her Patient was staring madly at the ceiling, her eyes darting here and there as she relived whatever it was she was seeing inside her head.

Whispering madly, almost silently now, Kathryn had to lean in at times in order to catch what her patient was saying. "Go on, Mouse," she prompted her patient. "You can tell me."

Suddenly Mouse rose up off the couch, startling Kathryn and told her therapist petulantly, "No." Simple and to the point, this word was the second one that any child seems to learn, just after "Mama."

Shoving her glasses back up her nose, Kathryn was finding her professional patience being tested. Deciding to match stubborn with stubborn, she said clinically, "Ok. I can wait as long as you need me to." Preparing to do a battle of wits with a *three year old* however, was not what she wanted to be doing this morning.

"Can't," Mouse parried again defiantly.

This is gonna be a very long session, Kathryn thought. In a job that requires tremendous patience, she sometimes had a hard time fighting her own sense of inner screaming and need to react.

On the outside however though, she always managed to let her professionalism reign, as she asked with an almost noncommittally, "Why not?"

Laying back down, Mouse folded her arms over her chest in the child's defiance and said cryptically, "They wan let me."

Pausing to write something down, Kathryn sighed slightly before pressing further. "Who, Mouse? One of... *Them*?" she asked, referring to some superseding "Bad" Alter or group of alters that seemed to control what "Mouse" wanted to say. "Or one of the Others?" she asked, referring to other more "parental" personality Alters.

"No," the Patient said again petulantly. "Not gonna tell," was all the answer Kathryn was apparently going to get.

These "children" could be so exasperating to deal with at times. Kathryn couldn't tell whether it was just the inner child of her patient being petulant in a child's way of playing an adult, or whether some particular important piece of information was being blocked because it was too painful to deal with.

Instead of fighting with her, she told Mouse, "Ok, Mouse. If you don't want to talk," and began closing her notebook.

This was designed to let her client know that she wasn't going to be playing this game today. Sometimes, it was as if the *child* inside was being obstinate for several sessions in a row, and they weren't going to get anywhere until the "child" in the "adult" tired of the charade.

Looking up and beyond her patient to that One Way Mirror, Doctor

Runyon shook her head imperceptibly no, telling her resident who was observing there by the agreed upon hand sign, "I'm not going to get anywhere this session."

What Kathryn couldn't see however, was what was happening behind that Mirror.

Her current Resident, Kirsten Anderson was watching intently — and not just not as a student. She was supposed to be video taping the session in progress, observing and writing notes — not only observing the patient and their reactions, but also seeing how the experienced therapist deals with a live case.

Live, and not just text in a textbook. She was supposed to be learning about the process by which their mentor was guiding each client through the process to integration.

In this case however, there were no notes being taken. And the intensity with which Kirsten was reacting towards this "patient" on the other side of that glass, was not in any way a "student" frame of reference.

In her early twenties and slender with blond hair about the same length as Kat's, Kirsten normally had the startlingly ice blue eyes of a child that would remain undimmed by age or glasses.

Yet unlike Kat's professional but engaged demeanor, Kirsten had a very cold, steely stare in her eyes now, which was growing colder by the second. There was something Cold and Malevolent in this Intent.

And although the video camera was sitting on the tripod next to her, it was neither "on" nor was there even any tape in it. Instead of hand with pen to paper, this "Resident" stood watchfully alert, both of her hands palm up and placed within a hairs breadth of the glass between her and the treatment room.

And those hands had a faint and unnatural, sickeningly greenish glow emanating both around and through them. It was like an electrical charge which was building up, ready to lash out as if in a lightning storm.

"Can't," the Patient repeated again.

This is going nowhere, Kat thought, and sighing, decided on another tactic.

"All right then," she said abruptly. Speaking coldly and professionally, she commanded the client, "Let me speak to Mary, Mouse."

With her patient still sitting petulantly for a few moments, Kathryn was about to rise and signal the orderlies to take her patient away. Before she had a chance to do either however, the patient began shaking, with a visible change coming over her.

Her eyes fluttering closed, a seemingly older and more relaxed woman was now the person slowly turning to look at Kat now. "What is it Doctor?"

Unfazed by this change, Kat tells her, "I'm afraid we're going to have to end this session today, Mary." Leaning in to work some of her magic on this patient, the good Dr. Runyon continued with, "That is...

unless, you can convince Mouse to talk to me."

Turning her head slowly back to staring at the ceiling, the "patient" Mary once again became the "alternate personality" Mouse, with her eyes rolling back into her head.

With a flit of her eyes and her little girl voice again, Mouse "continued" with, "You can't talk to her neither. You'll get us both in trouble."

Writing in her notes and without looking up, Kat asks her in an equally singsongy "little girl" voice coyly, "Why?"

Mouse paused, looked over her shoulder in the direction of the mirror, and then said mock petulantly, "Can't tell," folding her arms defiantly across her chest again.

Looking back up at the mirror herself and shaking her head "no," Kat began closing her notebook. Placing her right hand on the folded arms of her patient, patting them, "Then we're going to have to be finished for now. Tell me when you want to talk."

"Wait!" the adult Mary suddenly shouted out in a quite loud voice that seemed much larger than this woman could muster, knocking Kathryn emotionally and physically back into her chair.

"I think she's ready now," Mary said, in a more normal voice.

"Ok," Kat said, slowly but skeptically, taken aback at what had just happened.

Hesitant and leaning in carefully, she asked, "Mouse? What adults do you see around you? Who is there?" she said repeating it this time much more forcefully. Often she had to do this many times before getting anything of a reasonable response out of her patients.

"Yes," Mouse suddenly screamed in her shrill little girl voice. "All roun' me. They hurtin' me."

"Ok. What exactly are they doing to you, Mouse? I need for you to tell me exactly what it is that they're doing to you."

As much an abused child as a petulant one now, she shouted, "Nooo. Can't!" The "alter" was now seeming obviously terrified.

Still not sure she had the patience for this, Kat was sighing impatiently now. "Why can't you? You know you're not there anymore. That they can't hurt you. Don't you?"

"Cause they say they kill me I tell. Tha's why," Mouse said, with a sudden innocent child-like, as well as petulant, "Isn't it obvious?" attitude.

"They can't hurt you anymore. You understand?"

Quieting down a little from her previous shrill tone, the little voice replied not really believing, "Sure?"

"Yes, I'm sure," Kathryn spoke softly, sighing. *God*, she thought. *This whole process would be so awfully tedious... if it weren't for the atrocities these children speak of.*

"Lotsa adults. BIG circle." This Alter was now obviously recounting some "ritual" she was in the center of.

"What are they doing now?" Kat said forcefully, issuing her patient a verbal command to break through whatever it was that she was hiding. When she didn't get an answer, Kat asked her again more forcefully, "What are you doing?"

Squirming on the couch, the patient was flailing her arms wildly about her momentarily, before they snapped to her sides, seeming as if they were being pinned to her by some external force. Just as suddenly, one of her hands yanked itself up, forming a set of fingers screaming in protest.

"They makin' me hold 'nife. Don wanna hold 'nife."

"Why are they making you hold a knife, Mouse? What are they going to make you do with it?"

"They wan' me kill somethin' I don wanna kill."

Sighing, Kathryn kept digging. "What do they want you to kill, Mouse? I need you to tell me what they want you to kill."

"NO! Not kill bunny!" Killing a small rabbit was one of the first things that they had a child kill apparently, in order to get them to the point where they had no moral guidance against killing something much *larger* than "just a bunny."

In the ritual killing of the rabbit or other small animal, it also wasn't uncommon for the animal to be killed being the child's own pet. Or some next door neighbors' pet stolen for the purpose. The killing of animals however, were only really a prelude to the killing of the young of the real species desired to be sacrificed: human young.

This was where the Abuse got very "Real."

"They're not going to kill you, Mouse. Ok? They're not going to kill you. You're here now, not there," Kat said, trying to calm "Mouse" down.

But it wasn't working this time. "No, they wan me kill bunny. No, I don wan do it. No!" she said as she screeched a piercing scream from out of nowhere.

"What are they telling you to kill the bunny rabbit for?"

"They not! They jus tell me to kill it. I ask why, they tell me jus kill it. I tell em I don wan kill it. They tell me I kill bunny, or they kill me. I don wanna kill bunny!"

This would all be too unreal for Kathryn to take seriously, if it weren't for the fact that most of her clients sooner or later recounted the exact same experiences. These rituals were recounted to her over and over again, in much the same progression from client to client.

The "body of evidence" surely indicated that these events were real. Even if the events recounted weren't so horrific — and detailed — repeatedly in nature. The weight of so many Patients recounting the same process over and over again would almost seem to confirm there was "Something" there.

And of course, her recurring "nightmare" was always in the back of Kathryn's mind.

In the community surrounding the controversy of what was dubbed "false memory syndrome" as the psychiatrists and other professionals had termed it, it was all obviously "created" in the mind of the child-seeming adults, therapized for this type of "illness" in growing numbers.

They had watched too many "scary stories" on TV and in theaters, and they were merely "remembering" (and recounting) what they had "seen" in reel life.

Except for Kathryn being on the front lines, it had crossed over a certain line. If she had told one of her fellow psychiatrists about her own experiences of late, they would no doubt explain to her that (as with her patients), that her "dreams" were merely a reflection of her "day job." And also her —Kathryn Runyon's — "active imagination."

And then of course, they would report her to the "proper authorities" for dismissal. And also most likely, recommend her for her own "institutionalization."

Except that it certainly was not feeling that way.

"Ok Mouse. You can stop remembering now." Kathryn was feeling exhausted for some unfathomable reason, so she decided to end this part of the session. "I want you to tell Mary I need to speak to her. Can you tell her for me?"

"Yes," the little voice said, as the body visibly relaxed once again. The eyes fluttered for a second, and then opened again with the look of an adult behind them. "Yes, Doctor?" Mary asked.

"Is that the only Alter centered around that incident?"

"No Doctor. I feel like there's more, but I can't see them. They're still hiding from us."

"Are there any of Them that you feel are present now?" she asked. The "Others" "inside" called "Them," was the name that her patients usually gave to what could only be considered to be "demonic" entities that these patients always felt sure were lurking in the background.

When one of these Alters came out, Kathryn knew that she was getting close to some core issues. And also that the presence of "Them" suggested unpredictability, as well as grave danger, although she didn't know just why.

Gladly, she had only experienced one or two of these during her years of practice. Although the first almost caused her to quit doing this line of work altogether, it had frightened her so much.

"Only the known Alters," Mary told her therapist. "This episode is less significant than usual for them to pay it any more mind than they usually do."

Less significant than usual, Kathryn thought sourly to herself. *Is this ever going to end?*

"Ok," she said aloud to her patient. "I think this was enough for this session."

"Thank you, Doctor," Mary replied, getting up off the couch.

But before walking out however, the now adult woman turned to Kathryn with a strange look in her eyes. "Doctor, there's just one more thing."

Looking up distractedly from finishing her notes, Kathryn asked her, "What is it, Mary?"

"Do you ever get bored or tired? Listening to all of us tell our stories, that is?"

Kathryn pondered for a second before responding, wondering whether Mary was referring to all of her patients, or merely all of those different "parts" of Mary that she listened to.

Staring intently at her patient, she answered distantly, "No. I wouldn't say I think I ever get bored." Silently she amended to herself, *My God, how could I?* "Why were you asking, Mary?"

"Oh, just wondering," her Patient said cryptically, and walked out being helped by the Assisting Orderlies at the door after she rang the bell. With her already being held firmly with a muscular hand from either side gripping each of her biceps, Mary seemed quite placid now.

Kathryn was left staring after her, wondering anew what all of that was about. *What really does go on inside their heads?*

Sighing in a somewhat exhausted state, Kathryn began looking over her notes, as she prepared for her next Patient.

shadows and **LIGHT**

SIX

Finishing up her last case before lunch, Kathryn was closing her notes when Kirsten opened the door from the observation, and walked ever so quietly in.

"That one patient earlier was right," she said to Kathryn without any warning, startling the older woman to look up with a Mouse-like squeak. "Don't you ever get tired of hearing all of these wild stories Dr. Runyon?" she asked innocently enough.

Recovering, Kathryn looked up from the notes and asked her, "Why? Are you having second thoughts about going into this?"

Since Kirsten was still in her early twenties, most of the time she usually acted like it. But then there were also times like these though — and more incidents had been coming up recently — when Kathryn caught her assistant seeming nothing like her age. At least nothing like Kathryn remembered vaguely she had been at a similar age.

Kirsten was now seeming both younger *and* older, and somehow both at the same time. Far older Kathryn felt, than her years would seem to tell.

Kathryn's life now seemed very different in some ways, other than anything that she had ever imagined it would be when she was in her early twenties. Here she was, hearing these fantastic tales every day, and yet she had to take a coldly clinical approach with these tales, instead of being influenced by them.

And yet she was also still not married and was without children, at an age when most of those around her had at least one, if not several children. She sometimes (when she allowed herself to), thought about that too. Her work had become everything to her.

She had her boyfriend of course, but even that seemed to be somehow somewhat off. He was the sort that many women dreamed of. Tall and strong, and yet...

Although Kathryn could tell that this resident of hers wasn't necessarily as innocent as she was always attempting to seem at this moment, she could see a difference between the two of them.

She could also feel some sort of strange similarity between them, that she couldn't quite put a finger on. Kirsten was somehow a very different person each day than the one she was the day before.

This was now impressing itself on the older woman's consciousness even more than it had in the past. She was feeling very definitely unsettled by this "young" woman.

Sometimes Kirsten didn't look like she would be able to handle even one of the more milder alters in some of her mentor's patients, much less some of the truly psychotic ones. Those were the ones that even she, the experienced and estimable Dr. Runyon, had to sometimes have strapped down and severely sedated.

And yet sometimes, Kat felt her skin crawl around this "younger woman," especially when Kirsten was just there, suddenly, like a cat can, and quite stealthily. And not particularly Kat felt, like a "house" cat, either.

"I mean, my God, Doctor. I don't know how you can be so patient with some of these — cases. How can you stand working with these people day in and day out."

Kirsten was acting just a little too animated right now, Kat thought, as if she were acting her heart out to convince her supervising doctor of her innocent nature.

"I mean, some of this is seriously creepy stuff," Kirsten said just a little too forcefully. "I think it'd give me really creepy nightmares too."

Kat stopped cold inside at this comment. It was taking just about every ounce of her professional demeanor for Kathryn to not blanch at this.

"Why are you asking?" Kathryn tried to ask, just as innocently. And pretending not to notice the all too knowing "too" at the end of Kirsten's remark.

With some part of her taking over and putting on her highly patient and professional "mentor mask," she told Kirsten, "It just takes time, that's all. You get used to it. That's what your residency here is for anyway. Getting you used to dealing with—" and using air quotes here for Kirsten's benefit, "The Real Thing, and not just the textbook description."

Stopping and folding her arms protectively over her heart, Kat continued more defensively than she wanted to, "And besides, it has to be done if these women are going to go on to lead normal lives again.

"You and I have our own nightmares as well," Kathryn added playing the Sage Elder. "It's just that these women have nightmares that appear to have taken over their entire lives."

Loosing the perkiness abruptly and becoming coldly "clinical" herself, something about Kirsten's sudden change scraped a raw nerve. "You don't mean that literally, do you," Kirsten asked once again, now way too forcefully for Kathryn to ignore.

If Kat hadn't been trying so hard to evade looking directly into her "residents" eyes at that moment, she might have noticed the slight clouding of black invading the corners of Kirsten's eyes and partially obscuring the whites, like lighting from a "storm" that was only seeking the right moment to light up and strike.

Kirsten cocked her head to one side coyly, "Oh, I don't know. It just strikes me as kind of odd that you take these obviously crazy people so seriously."

As she finished this last question, Kirsten looked up with a little more intensity than she was probably aware of. As she did, Kathryn

60

felt a very hard chill suddenly run down her back. Her mind suddenly racing, Kathryn intuitively knew that she had to choose her next few words, very, very, carefully. That how she responded was very important.

Interjecting before Kathryn could make her response, Kirsten recovered suddenly and asked her, "I mean..." all perky innocence once more rising to present, "How can you possibly take these stories seriously?"

What she wanted to say was far different from the, "I have to take them seriously," which Kathryn told her. "Whether they're real episodes or not, there is some kind of damage there that needs to be confronted, regardless of their lack of reality.

"As a therapist Kirsten, you have to treat them as real. You have to get to the bottom of any cause, no matter how layered in unreality it might be."

Curious, Kathryn thought. *Why can't I just tell her that I think that they're telling me the truth? Why is it that I feel the need to disguise what I think from this "little girl?"*

But another part of her said rumbling from deep inside, *Because this is not a "little girl."*

"Well," Kirsten said, just a little too girlishly, "I was just wondering. I mean, we studied all about Dissociation and Multiple Personality Disorder in school, but seeing it in action is a whole different thing." Then, looking up too innocently and teen-like, she added "Ya know?"

Kathryn worked hard to act as if she were brushing the whole business off, and smiling said, "I know."

A little too hastily, Kirsten added with a vacuous smile, "Well, I'll see you after lunch. Oh, kay?"

Exhausted now, Kathryn replied cheerfully back mimicking Kirsten's sudden Valley Girl demeanor with an ironic singsongy, "Oh-kay."

But as Kathryn began heading back to her office, she couldn't shake off the feeling that she had somehow just been tested by this "intern." As if something very important depended on it. And as ridiculous as it seemed, the idea of being tested by a college student after what had happened to her last night, felt quite unnerving.

The walls seemed to Kathryn like they were beginning to close in on her. Walking out of the treatment room, she hadn't gotten further than a few steps down the hall before involuntarily shuddering again, quickly putting her hand out against the wall to steady herself.

She almost hoped that it was a sign of the flu coming on, but with it coming so soon after Kirsten's—

"Get to my desk," she told herself.

But as Kathryn began heading back to her office, she couldn't shake off the feeling that she had somehow just been tested by this 'intern.' As if something very important depended on it. And as ridiculous as it seemed, the idea of being tested by a college student after what had happened to her last night, felt quite unnerving.

The walls seemed to Kathryn like they were beginning to close in on her. Walking out of the treatment room, she hadn't gotten further than a few steps down the hall before involuntarily shuddering again, quickly putting her hand out against the wall to steady herself.

She almost hoped that it was a sign of the flu coming on, but with it coming so soon after Kirsten...

"Get to my desk," she told herself.

When she was finally sitting in her office with the door closed, she closed her eyes to collect herself for what she felt was only a second. Luckily, enough time had passed since last night so as to not have the nightmarish images pop to the surface when she did. All that she saw there, even with the fluorescents crackling above her, was a calming grey featureless blur.

Startled by an insistent knock at her door, she rubbed her eyes, realizing as she did that she had drifted off for longer than she had intended.

Sighing, Kathryn asked, "Yes. What is it?"

Kay opened the door and looking intently at her as she said, "Sorry to disturb you Doctor, but Sgt. Wolfe is on the line.

"You could have buzzed me, Kay."

Smiling that strange look again, her secretary said, "I did. And when you didn't answer—"

"Oh, I'm sorry," Kat said, once again not responding.

"Do you want me to take a message from Tom so you can call him later?" Kay asked.

"No," Kat squeaked, becoming more fully awake at the sound of his first name. Kathryn lunged for the phone, the desperation in her voice rising as she picked it up. Not even looking in Kay's direction now, she sighed his name "Tom," into the receiver.

Waving her hand in Kay's direction, she melted into the phone as soon as she heard the door click shut. Letting her voice crack with emotion now, she added a girlish, "Hi, Tommy."

Her boyfriend's rough voice crackled through the static at the other end. "Hey babe. Rough day?" he said and she immediately began to relax.

His voice somehow always seemed to have this effect on her. Even though she was sitting in her own office, in a respected institution, as a respected authority in her field with several degrees from prestigious colleges on her walls...

Whenever Sgt. Thomas Dietrick Wolfe called her, she immediately became a sixteen year old girl again. Sometimes it rankled her when she thought about it during her extended crisis periods and he wasn't available. But then he would call and all would somehow magically be forgiven, doubts floating away like clouds scuttling away at sunrise.

"Oh, the usual," she told him casually, even though she was feeling anything but casual.

And then, a flash of red blurred her vision for a moment, and her feelings changed. Somehow, somewhere deep inside of her, another part of her rose up to protect her.

Changing the sound of her voice suddenly, she remembered back to how desperate and terrified she had been, prompting a response that surprised even her. "Tom, I really needed to talk to you last night. Where were you?" she said with an edge she rarely used with him.

"Hey, hold on there, Kat," he said, sounding like he was trying to laugh this sudden comeuppance away. But he couldn't disguise the hint of anger that was not too far below the surface. "I got a late night call on one of the cases I've been working on, and had to go to the station house.

"Besides, if you needed to talk so much, you could've just paged me. Did you try to page me, Kathryn?" he said, suddenly sounding accusing.

This stopped her cold. She flinched at the sound of the accusation in his voice.

And then she thought, *Why didn't I tried to page him? Or for that matter, why didn't I try paging Ellen, either*? She had tried calling each of them, but never once thought of paging either.

"I... I don't know why," she said, truly at a loss. "I just... I guess I didn't think of it."

"Must not have been that important then," he said with a hint of malice. "You know I'll call you if I'm not in the middle of a case."

She blanched at this, feeling her grip on the phone loosen to the point of dropping it. His words didn't seem too harsh, but the feeling they left her with was as if he had just smacked her across the face. Hard.

Biting her lip and choosing her words carefully again, she finally told him, "I had another one of those nightmares, Tom. I was just — just really shaken up, I guess. I'm sorry for accusing you. I..."

The stinging quality in his voice suddenly changed back to that smooth, soothing one. As if he had just flipped a switch. "Well, that's all right I guess. Just don't let it happen again," he said, half-jokingly, but still with that underlying edge she could even feel.

She could feel there was some real anger lying underneath his reply, and Kathryn was a little taken aback again at the severity of it. There was something in his voice that she didn't like at all, but couldn't pinpoint.

As if sensing her reaction, he softened his voice and lowered it further into "the growl" that she liked to hear so much. "Sorry babe. Had a rough day myself today."

As her reaction softened, she wondered how he could make her feel the way he did by just lowering his voice like that. As soon as he did it though, she just couldn't stay mad at him any more.

One part of her not that far deep down, resented the hell out of the fact that she could be so easily manipulated like this. And yet there was another part of her that really liked that she could be.

He almost wouldn't have to make love to her, or even say something obviously seductive when he used That Voice with her. She would still be carried away by it. Carried... Somewhere Else.

"So, can you still come over tonight?" she said seductively back, purring into the phone. "Or will you have a case that'll take you away again tonight?"

"I'll... Arrange to leave my pager at the office. Ok, babe?" He could be so smooth when he wanted to, she thought.

And she liked it. Oh, how she liked it.

"Six o'clock then?" she said, putting a pouting sound of pleading into the request.

"How about six thirty?" came his level response, bordering on emotionless.

She knew that was about as good as she was going to get, so she asked him, "You promise?" in as little girlish a voice as she could.

"Cross my heart," came his pat answer.

Tom was always getting paged and pulled away, to investigate some crime scene or some other excuse he wouldn't tell her the reason for. And then he would say it was something that he couldn't talk about. "Official Police Business," was the "official" response.

As soon as she was off the phone, she realized she hadn't eaten yet, and realizing that, also suddenly realized she was starving.

Passing through Kay's office, she saw that her secretary was mysteriously on the phone, so she flashed the fingers of both of her hands at her letting her know she'd be back in ten minutes.

Kay merely nodded abstractly, and Kathryn continued out the door and down the hall.

Nodding absentmindedly in the direction of a pair of her colleagues as she passed them, she made her way to the elevator.

The luncheonette was in the basement, and she'd go down quickly and grab a sandwich to take with her back to her desk. She hated to eat in her office, but it was better than not eating anything at all. And she still had clients to see this afternoon.

Her notebook perpetually in her hand, Kat was becoming so engrossed in thought as she walked. Not looking at the writing on the page, her mind was racing now.

Her powers of observation have been pricked wide open and hints of something she didn't understand had begun filtering in.

Motes of Darkness seemed to be floating in front of her, falling like malevolent snow or ash in the garishly lit institutional halls in which she walked.

When the bell for the elevator sounded its arrival, she jumped slightly, catching herself with an internal, *Now, Kat*. The door opened and several other Doctors and their Residents began walking out.

She was feeling her comfort level getting scrapped raw and eying several of the well known faces exiting the elevator in passing, half-consciously nodded to each of them. She let them pass and stepped inside.

As the doors slid closed, she had a funny feeling of falling as she was pushing the "B" button for the basement level.

As the doors slid closed, Kathryn mentally brushed this off with a frown. *Haven't had that happen before*, she thought.

The elevator was almost as old as the building itself, having been installed back in the fifties and been fully refurbished just before Kat had arrived in the seventies. It had always struck her as (once again) feeling quite appropriate for the nature of the facility. Normally though, she took it for granted and had long ago accepted its decrepitude as just being part of this building's "charm," as it were.

The trim was painted with the same nasty institutional green that everything else around here was painted with, but with what had become sickly yellowish-looking highlights. It also came with perpetually flickering fluorescents, that, no matter how often the bulbs and ballasts were changed, maintained their eery dance.

Today though, and especially after the previous night and most of her earlier queasiness, this elevator no longer had any charm attached to it. Looking up from her pad finally, she noticed how darkly ominous this whole interior seemed.

On all three sides of her, there was atrociously simulated linoleum wood panelling from the fifties still in place. Looking at this previously seen as innocuous patterning, it now seemed to her that it was somehow full of eyes. And all of them felt as if they were staring at her.

Laughing uneasily at this ridiculous thought, she chided herself with, "Oh, God. Maybe I have been at this for far too long." The seeing of patterns where there was only randomness was one of those pesky signs of mental instability, she reminded herself, with Paranoia and all of its many cousins.

Turning her back on this panelling and focusing on the overly burnished copper of the door, she failed to notice as the patterns of the "wood" began to subtly move and shift, rearranging themselves behind her back.

What had been "indistinct" had suddenly become very distinct during her choice to ignore them. Weaving themselves into new patterns where images of faces now began appearing and resolving themselves into malicious demonic specters, these faces were all now leering directly at her.

Sighing heavily and feeling something suddenly amiss, she stood there for another few seconds waiting for this beast to move. Her mood spiking as she began getting worried when the elevator simply sat there instead of starting its descent, she began pushing the already glowing basement button a few more times.

Beginning to panic, she hit — and then began hitting furiously — the "Open Door" button as well.

70

She suddenly noticed a small placard on the wall over the button panel that she hadn't noticed before now. It read something to the effect that— "This elevator will not fail. Be calm if the doors fail to open, as there is plenty of air to breathe.'"

"Right," she told herself. "No need to worry at all."

Being on the fifth floor had never bothered her, but with there being no reaction from the elevator, her panic began to rise out of control. She started banging on the door frantically, her breath starting to come in spurts.

The longer the elevator stood still and showed no signs of moving, the more agitated she became. She started to look around at the walls, feeling that they were closing in on her.

Closing her eyes and beginning deep breathing exercises to calm herself, she felt her sense of calm returning. She was about to punch the button for her floor once again when there was a sudden jolt. Letting out a sharp scream, she began shouting, "Help! Someone. Help!"

Reacting instinctively, she grabbed for the railing, trying to go back to breathing deeply to calm herself again. "Someone will have heard me by now. They'll come to rescue me," she told herself. "Breathe in, breathe out. Breathe in—"

Just as her nerves had begun once again reaching a state of calm however, the elevator jolted again, only this time with a scraping noise. "No," she shrieked, as the lights began flickering wildly.

Suddenly, it felt to her as if the bottom was dropping out from underneath her.

Shrieking once more as she felt the elevator begin dropping, Kat struggled to reach for the control panel as the elevator floor number indicators began pounding down through the numbers — FIVE... FOUR... Then— THREE...

As a wild-eyed Kat found herself sliding down the wall, a change began coming over her. Her eyes began taking on a steely cast much like Kirsten's had earlier. TWO...

And the floor indicator finally slowed to a stop, leaving her at the 'B2' level — the lowest floor level to be found on the board.

As the doors opened on the dark cinder block-walled hallway, a now obviously shell shocked Kat began exiting the elevator to finally find staff people running in her direction.

Hitting the wall and sliding down, she was reaching the solid floor when she began sobbing, her hands reaching for her face, her body melting there. The suppressed waterfall of conflicting emotions and fears of her flight down let loose as she began choking back the screaming fright, and her mind once again fled to that blank inner safety.

Not hearing the sound of the voices surrounding her now except as a blur, Kat's sobbing was quickly turning into hyperventilation. Her body barely registering the many hands helping it to rise and lead it back up the five floors to her office.

But Kat was *elsewhere.*

Once in her office and sitting down, Kathryn Runyon was now steeped in a dissociative calm. Kat was staring vacantly in the direction of the door as Kirsten burst into the room, exaggerated teenage emotion falsely bubbling up all over. "Oh, my God! Oh my God! Are you ok? Oh, my God!"

Still in shock as the younger woman came in, Kat was finding herself standing and suddenly smothered by Kirsten in full flustered frenzy. With an electrical charge running inside her from head to toe, Kathryn was finding herself fully back in her body, tensing at something only the deepest part of her recognized.

Kirsten's face though as soon as it was safely over the older woman's shoulder, was quickly showing anything but concern. As all of the previous feigned emotion drained away, her concerned look was again quickly replaced by that steely look from before, her eyes now clouding completely to Black.

Not seeing but sensing a change, Kat disengaged a little too quickly and Kirsten's eyes still had a hint of the black now quickly disappearing.

But in a second the mask had snapped back, and Kirsten's face returned to the "concerned friend" look, her eyes fully back to normal. Kirsten asked all a-flutter, "You'd tell me if you weren't ok. Wouldn't you? Right?"

Nodding shakily, Kat began descending back into her chair. *Say nothing*, some Part of her said to her.

"I'm ok," she told Kirsten. "Just still in a little shock. That's all."

Looking up at the now obviously dangerous "young woman" in front of her, Kat said, "I'll be all right. I'll send Kay down for something before my afternoon sessions."

A little too coldly, Kirsten added, "I don't know whatever could have happened to have caused that. I mean, that sort of thing just doesn't happen. Does it?"

What is really happening to me? Kat thought. Looking up however, she only saw the "concerned" mask on Kirsten now, pulled once again more tightly over the "young-seeming" face.

Suddenly she heard herself telling Kirsten, "Maybe I just need some time off," hoping that was the answer that Kirsten was really looking for.

"Could you please ask Kay to reschedule the rest of my afternoon clients till tomorrow?"

"Are you going to be ok driving home?" this time Kirsten asked, with a hint of real concern in her voice.

"I'll rest here for a little before I try," Kat told her.

SEVEN

Kat had gotten into her car an hour later or so later and driven home. At least, she *knew* she had driven home, because that was where she had found herself sitting when she *woke up*.

In her car... Outside her apartment building in Amherst. Twelve miles after she had gotten herself into her car outside of Hawthorne. And apparently not having been conscious for the entire drive in between.

It was still early in the afternoon, and she would have laid herself down to rest, between what happened today and last night.

But not wanting to possibly fall back into the dark nightmares once again, she had instead used the opportunity of being home early to begin setting the table.

Even though Tom wasn't going to be there for hours, she set about cooking the food in the oven on low. Any excuse to steady herself.

The table was laid with her favorite white lace and linen table cloth, which coordinated with her favorite simple white spaghetti strapped evening dress she'd chosen to wear.

If this doesn't please him, she thought, *nothing will.*

She only wore this dress on "special occasions," (although she couldn't remember any of what those "occasions" were right now). It was low cut, and she hoped it would drive her boyfriend, Det. Wolfe into a wolf-like frenzy after dinner.

She needed to be held. Needed to be reassured — desperately needed to be reassured. After the events of the last several days...

She had been applying makeup in her mirror earlier to complete the seduction, but she'd barely noticed the hint of dark circles under, and widening fright stalking her eyes. Still shaken from the "accident," she was suppressing the urge to scream now as she waited for Tom to finally appear.

With the candles on the table lit now and the sunlight slanting low through the windows, Kat was pacing her living room nervously.

She'd made his favorite meal leaving the steak as rare as he liked it, but that was almost an hour ago. When he finally did manage to show up, she was going to have to reheat it and risk cooking it too much.

Although he had promised to be here by 6:30, it was now approaching quarter of eight, with still no call and no knock at her door.

76

Why was she still waiting on him to show her some real affection, she wondered. They had been like this for countless years — living in a kind of suspended animation of a relationship.

He had never once suggested that they live together, like the boyfriends of other women she had known usually had. He had never even come close to proposing to her. And sometimes, they didn't even see each other much less sleep together, often for weeks at a time.

When she had questioned him on the occasional fit of self confidence, it was always the same old tired excuses — that he was either working on an in-depth case that he was in the middle of and couldn't be disturbed while he was conducting it; or that she didn't really want to get any further involved with a cop who might at any minute get killed in the line of duty. Etc., etc., etc.

Even though she had never questioned why an officer in the relatively quiet college town of Amherst would ever have anything happen to him, much less being killed. Or indeed, have so many "cases" that would require so much of his time.

A long time ago she had just taken it for granted that this was the way it was going to be with Det. Wolfe. But that had been over a decade ago.

And for some reason that she couldn't fathom, she still stayed with this particular man instead of seeking out other men to see. Other women no doubt (she told herself when she allowed herself to think about it), would be questioning their men quite fervently if they did the same sort of often disappearing act.

Were they seeing other women? Did they have some secret family hidden in some other part of the country? But Kathryn didn't question. And she hadn't for the most part, even questioned why she didn't question.

She was still an attractive woman, on the younger looking side and quite slender for her age. She was approaching thirty- five, and if she was going to have children, that time would soon be gone.

She found herself continually making up excuses for why he acted like this, and why she in turn accepted this kind of treatment from him. All she could think to explain it was that she had grown comfortable with being uncomfortable — a place she had once said that she was not going to allow herself to find herself having settled into (or gotten stuck in).

But here she was.

Something had kept her with Tom throughout the years, but she didn't know what. It wasn't because he was that great of a lover (that is, when they actually did make love these days). And it wasn't because he was just so ruggedly handsome that she couldn't live without him (although he was still very easy on the eyes). And he also hadn't seemed to age much beyond the 27 years old he was when she first met him.

And now the whole unfulfilling aspect of her life that was her relationship with Tom was the least of her worries, she told herself.

The dreams she had begun having for the last several months now, (dreams, nightmares — whatever they were). Although she was also having her doubts about that being the case now. *Dreams don't haunt you*, she thought.

Could it really just be that her daytime work was bleeding off into the rest of her life? Maybe that was what was causing the horrific scenes she lived through at night.

And yet, they felt far too real to her, and increasingly were growing in both regularity and intensity. She was now feeling that the "nightmares" were bleeding off into her daytime reality, to the point where she was starting to feel that everything about her life was a dream becoming a nightmare.

As her grandfather clock on the fireplace mantle piece began striking eight, she startled once more out of her dissociation.

She found that she was sitting on the couch staring at the fireplace, as the flames were now gone. What had been a big pile of logs in preparation for her boyfriend showing up, was now only sullen remains of that fire, now banking down into coals.

An occasional POP! sound of a log catching its last bit of moisture, would then abruptly bring her back again to the present.

On the verge of falling back into that dreaded form of sleep once more, she was startled fully awake this time by the loud knock she had been waiting for (finally!) at the front door.

Kat almost jumped out of her skin, her heart suddenly racing to catch up with her mind, as her body was springing off the couch and heading for the door.

She'd suddenly forgotten her worries, all her ruminations of the nightmare her life had become. She didn't know why, but her heart leapt alive at the thought of *He's here*!

Spinning like a fairy tale princess once before getting to the door, she began composing herself as she reigned in her sudden giddiness and began striding purposefully towards the door.

But instead of opening it, she stopped. Putting her ear to the metal door, she called out through it in a sing-songingly little girl voice, "Who is it?" asking playfully.

From the other side of the door, the gruff, exasperated sounding voice said in response, "It's the big, bad Wolfe. Let me in little girl," he said, adding way too forcefully, "Now."

Reacting in a mock startled little girl voice again and obviously relishing her little game, (especially after the days earlier events), she told him (even though he had a key), "Oh, I don't know if I can do that, Mr. Wolfe."

"If you don't," he said in a more anger tinged voice, "I'll huff and I'll puff, and I'll blow your door wide fucking open."

"Hey, wait a second, buddy. Aren't you supposed to be saying that to the pigs? What kind of Wolfe are you?"

"A big, bad undercover police wolf. Now open your door little girl, or I'll arrest you, too."

80

"Is that a promise, Mr. Detective Wolfe?"

Sighing almost loud enough to actually blow the door down, he began using his key to open it — up until he found the chain in place snapping tight.

"Do we really have to go through this tonight, Kat? Been a long day," he said through the cracked door.

Taking the chain away from the door and opening it, she found Sgt. Thomas Wolfe, lounging seductively against the door jamb, looking like he really was about to eat her.

Ruggedly dressed in casual wear but topped with a leather jacket, *He really is any woman's dream*, Kat thought. Although tonight he had a rather distant, with a distracted look on his face and wasn't looking particularly inviting.

"I swear, Kat," he said, as he pushed through and past her. "This little game of yours goes on a little too long sometimes."

Changing his attitude as he begins sniffing the air, the smell of dinner (like a real wolf), he asks her with a ravenous and sly dangerous look, "What's for dinner, Wench? I'm starving! So it better be good, or *I will eat you.*"

"Is *that* a promise?" she asked, throwing herself at him, the long wait before his arrival disappearing into a haze. Kat wasn't in the clear minded mood to be able to notice though, that Wolfe was only coldly accepting her embrace.

"I heard about your accident today," he said, without much

compassion in it. "I'm sorry you had a rough day, too."

Suddenly sensing the distance but not knowing (or wanting to know) what was causing it, Kat felt her mood plummeting. Reacting strangely cold at this and not knowing why, she replied icily and perfunctorily, "Thank you. Dinners ready, by the way."

Clutching his bigger hand in hers, his remained limp as she began almost dragging him to the table. "So... How was *your* day?" Kat asked forced cheerfully, hoping that some warmth would return to their conversation.

Sitting down across the table from her, his face remained impassive. "Oh, the usual suspects," he told, her without any trace of emotion.

"Oh," she said on the outside. Inside however, she was screaming once again.

This was obviously not going to be the comforting night with her boyfriend that she had hoped earlier it was going to be. A part of her started retreating, going deep and preparing for the worst.

Getting up from the table with their plates and heading towards the kitchen, she asked as she was beginning to reheat their meal, "Is this a really long case you're working?" Asking, even though she knew she wasn't going to get a response from him.

He pretended not to hear her question, as she half expected he would.

Bringing the plates back into the dining room in a few minutes, they began eating in chilly silence. Looking up at him every once in a while, he would occasionally give her a phony feeling smile back in between bites.

At other times though, she felt she was being paranoid as she saw his expression grow suddenly cold, sometimes chillingly cold. *Calculatingly Cold.*

Once she looked up and she swore she saw a hint of inky blackness creeping into his eyes.

Eating the rest of their dinner in awkward silence, Kat kept glancing at this man across from her, trying to figure out what was different tonight.

Something was off about him and unpleasant in the extreme. Something that seemed to be behind both his looks and his mannerisms. Something that chilled Kathryn to the bones.

After they had finished their awkward eating, she pretty much had to drag him to the couch as well.

While kneeling in front of the fireplace, she started putting additional logs onto the fire to bring it back to roaring life. Somehow when it did however, she was still feeling cold.

She was also feeling the hair on the back of her neck rising, as if something malevolent were watching her from the couch.

Turning and putting her best seductive look on despite not feeling it, she rose and joined him sitting down hoping to get a conversation started to match the now roaring fire.

Her hopes were quickly dashed though as not only did they continue sitting in the silence that had begun at dinner, but Tom had made sure to create a physical distance to match the emotional distance that was growing like a gaping chasm between them.

Without any conversation to dull the knife edge hovering over her from the day, she found herself staring dreamily into the flames. With the intense red of the fire drawing her in, Kat found herself blinking, every now and then, as if something had just flashed at her. Something bright Red, stabbing at the back of her mind.

Looking over at Tom suddenly, she caught him looking at her in one of those calculated moments she had begun noticing tonight, turning eerily into a leer that seemed to bore deep inside of her.

Perhaps it was a trick of the flames off to her right, but she thought for a flashing instant, that there were real flames from a much bigger fire reflected in his eyes. And he wasn't looking in the direction of the fireplace, either.

Shaking her head as if to clear it, she tried to smile but couldn't. She felt her face beginning to match his in its lack of emotion.

"You know, Kat... It's a good thing I know you're only joking with me about this little "big, bad wolf" game," he said, trying to toss it off lightly and not succeeding. "But sometimes it seems that you take it just a little too seriously."

"This from Mr. Serious himself?" she said rhetorically, trying her best to be replying jokingly as well. Growing serious again though, she added, "And I thought you liked it just as much as I did."

With the lids of his eyes closing more and more into a growing dangerous look, he leans towards her and says with an intensity that had no playfulness in it whatsoever, "You know, sometimes Kat," and leaning in even more intensely, "I think that some of your crazy patient's nuttiness is rubbing off on you."

His eyes belied the lightness of his vocal tone though now, growing darker in the waning firelight. She almost thought she saw them turning into black pools, but convinced herself otherwise.

"I wish sometimes," he continued, his voice growing darker by the minute, "that you'd let me in on all of these "secrets" that some of these crazy people tell you. I'm sure that some of them are a real hoot," he finished, without any levity whatsoever.

A part of *her* was now on the defensive, as Kat told him angrily, "You know I can't do that. Any more than you can discuss any of your cases with me." Her feeling of being attacked was growing now by the second.

With this exchange, another long period of silence began, with Kat returning to staring back into the fire again. Suddenly, a series of red flashes seared her eyes. Scenes of other Flames and other Fires – the Pyre of her nightmares — seemed to be reaching in, trying to burn her from the inside out.

Starting, she looked back over at this person she felt she was beginning to see truthfully for the first time. He was now eyeing her with the look of a dragon about ready to strike.

"Are you ok, Kat," he asked, chillingly earnest. "Maybe if you told me some of those stories of your clients—"

Turning very adult-like with a knife-wrenching feeling in the pit of her stomach, she lowered her voice closer to his, saying, "Oh, come on Det. Wolfe. Don't tell me I need to give you one of Dr. Runyon's famous patented confidentiality talks, do I?"

"You never really tell me much of anything about your work," he continued quite forcefully.

This is beginning to feel like a duel, she thought, her fear (and surprisingly, her anger) growing by the second. "And you know why. I can't reveal anything more about what they tell me than you can about a case that you're investigating. I can't divulge anything—"

"You don't have to name names, Kat," he said, with an echo sounding in his voice that she felt suddenly as if she was being commanded (coerced) to speak.

"That's not the issue, and you know it. You know I can't. I can't discuss anything about my clients. It's the nature—"

"Jesus Christ, Kat! I'm your fucking boyfriend, as well as a cop on top of that. Don't you think—"

Reaching a hard line inside her, she lowered her voice again, with a sound that she hadn't heard before creeping into her tone this time. "No," was all that *Part* of her said, emphatically.

86

Pausing for a second and deciding on a new tack, "Do you know what I think?" she began innocently enough.

But he interrupted her forcefully, "No, Doctor," and pausing to give it the proper venom. "Tell me what you think."

Taken aback with an almost visceral shock even with her defenses at full strength, Kat tried to regain some sense of the playful, knowing inside, that "playful" was not anywhere on this evenings agenda.

"I think that you like your job just a little too much," she said, with a tone surprising her. "I don't think that you're ever going to give it up and retire. There's something—"

With a cold fire replacing his previous anger and leaning in to physically intimidate her, he said in a deep Voice, "So. Is that what the good Dr. Runyon has decided?"

Folding her arms protectively across her chest, her reaction chilled as she moved to block the fire she now saw licking at his comments, saying roughly, "Yes, I have."

About to reply, his pager suddenly went off. Taking it off his belt and looking at it, he pushed himself away from the cushion and began walking forcefully over to the phone on the end table.

Without thinking, she waived him off a sullen, "Ok," as he began dialing. With the intensity of the last few minutes released like a rubber band, she felt exhausted and almost glad he was going to be leaving soon. *This happens a lot*, she also suddenly realizes.

Answering it with a brusque, "Wolfe," he continued on with his usual conversation of this sort in her presence; guarded responses intermixed with a lot of "Yeah"s, and "Uh, huh"s, ending with the (also) usual, "Be right there."

These last words when Tom uttered them usually meant, "See you in a few days," to Kat.

Lately, this is how her evenings with her "boyfriend" would end, with his walking out just after he'd finished his meal, leaving Kat unlikely to have anything to show for her efforts at attempting to dress to seduce.

Usually it was like clock work. As if someone had been watching them and waiting for the right moment to page him. Just after he'd finished eating, but before anything more "personal" could interrupt his availability for "police business." He would get paged, answer the "call," and then be gone.

Finishing his call even further out of her hearing range than he normally did, this time he looked back at her with a sharp look before ending it with an ominous, "Right, of course."

Dropping the phone hard into the cradle, he gave her a searing look.

Visibly shaken this time, she felt another of those now-becoming-regular chills run up her spine.

He turned towards her, unsympathetic and cold once more, tossing off a— "They just turned up some new evidence," at her. And in the blink of an eye, he was at the door and it was open.

Her mental state now careening towards the point of hysteria again, Kat asked him in an almost pathetically little girl voice, "Can't it wait? You really just got here."

"Sorry," was his only verbal response. His eyes though became small and intense.

"Tom... Tommy," Kat began to plead. "Couldn't you leave that thing at the office for once, like you promised? My God, Tom—"

"Oh, grow up Kathryn," he tells her, almost out the door. Blanching at the sound of her formal name, she felt knocked back physically again, as if his words had a force of their own. "You know I can't—"

"What? Leave your goddamned job at work for once? Just for one night? Come on, I—"

Turning quite acidly on her suddenly, "I've got a murder scene to go to."

"You know," she continued, her anger replacing her fear, "For a sleepy little New England town, this place sure has an awful lot of murders to solve."

Cutting her off with, "I'll call you when I'm done," he tossed a nasty look at her as the door slammed.

Shell shocked in the wake of all of this, Kat continued sitting silently on the couch long after the door was slammed shut. With the possibility of crying and shrieking threatening to erupt from her, she sat and rocked to force it away.

But with the pull of the tide of the negative power struggle having left with Det. Wolfe, she rose from the couch, now in full dissociation. Her body continued on into the bedroom on autopilot, leaving behind everything on the table (including the still barely lit candles).

She crawled back under the covers, with eyes still wide and unseeing. Until she drifted off into a (for once) dream-less sleep.

EIGHT

In the treatment room the next morning, a once again calm and collected (and professional) Dr. Runyon was working with another very large woman lying on the treatment couch this time.

In the midst of asking her Patient flatly, "What was the bunny really, Kimmie?" she found her eyes were not seeing much of anything in the room, however.

Neither her close to three hundred pound patient, much less the greenish glow even now beginning to become visible through the silver of the mirrored plate glass to her right. Kat was half here and half *elsewhere*, a tinge of the color Red seeping into everything and everywhere she looked now.

This patient's birth name was Andrea, but this Alter that was now out, called herself "Kimmie," representing a "little girl" of around four or five. "I can't... You don't... They won't... Let me," Kimmie answered, staccato in her little girl sounding voice.

"Who won't let you?" Kat sighed. *Yes, this is getting very old*, she suddenly thought, *and I am very tired.*

"Them," the Alter said emphatically.

"And who is this Them?" Kat asked by rote.

"**Them**," the Alter replied again cryptically.

Then the voice deepened, dropping through at least five octaves that this woman had only exhibited twice in their sessions together, ominously repeating— "**THEM**."

Kathryn's face changing and showing recognition at this, she asked her patient, "Scorcher?" sure that it was one of this patients "demon" Alters coming to the surface that she had dealt with only recently. Asking for verification, "Is this really Scorcher I'm dealing with?" she only got a sullen silence in response.

She asked this with deepening suspicion — and for some reason this time, more than a little fear.

These women often exhibited alternate personalities that were male as well as female, with ages ranging from infants barely able to speak, to those who represented themselves to be older than the patient was, sometimes even elderly.

There was no explanation for this phenomena, except that they were just some psychosis from the patients past trauma creating these *fictions.*

And many times these Alters told stories of lives that should have been outside of the life experience that the patient had lived. The Alter that called itself "Scorcher" in this particular patient, was one of these.

"Scorcher" was an *older male* Alter that had described *himself* (itself?), as being in his sixties, (even though the patient was only forty-two).

Sometimes *he* cooperated, delighting in telling Kat things that *he* would then physically cringe about after recounting and reverting to the patient on the table, as if afraid of the consequences of the telling. But *he* always told these *secrets* with a boyish smile belying *his* years, as if *he* were being both naughty and relishing in it at the same time. As well as the patient fearing the consequences.

"**Them**," *he* repeated ominously. "You know Who."

Pausing for a moment before continuing, Kat was about to ask *him* again about the *Who he* was speaking of... when the lights flashed off.

Wanting to stand and head for the light switch, she suddenly realized that she was already standing: Outside. In the woods. In the Dark. With something very powerful and dangerous lurking in the darkness there.

And then in another flash—

The lights were back on, and she was sitting down once more, back inside the building. And looking up to see Andrea's face twisted into a Scorcher wickedly lascivious grin. "See," *he* told her gleefully. "You know Who."

Her head reeling from the sudden shock of the vision, her grip on the steno pad in her lap loosened and it slid onto the floor, opening up to another page of another client there.

Closing her eyes to collect herself, she was once more seeing internal flashes of Red. Trying to *open* her eyes again, she felt that they are already open.

Looking around the room that had the illusion of being outside, her eyes were adjusting to the *darkness* that surrounded her.

Forms and faces began floating out of the darkness and into her awareness. Some of these faces formed into recognizable persons, not only of politicians (some of whom had been holding High Office), but also actors and other *famous individuals* she felt as if she had once known.

She also began to see recognizable faces of heads of state and others that she felt she *knew personally*. Or rather, that some part of her was unaware of before now, she knew personally. That were part of this Darkness.

The sound of chanting was beginning around her as she looked around, and she was suddenly—

Back in the treatment room at Hawthorne, with the wickedly grinning Scorcher beaming back at her like the Cheshire Cat out of the face of her "patient."

"Them," *he* repeated this time lowering his voice even further and drawing the word out. With a very satisfied sound denoting pleasure that *he* had the "power" to reach inside of her and pull these — memories? — out. *He* said again, "You know **Them**. Don't you." *His* voice dropping into an even more deepening octave, saying, "Doctor," Its Voice dripping with demonic irony.

Twisting and turning again, her patients face without warning began contorting into another form.

The large body of this patient now began rising off the couch as if on invisible strings, and it was loosing its flabby quality, changing and taking on a form that was now not only definitely masculine, but also horrific in nature.

"You will stop," the Voice coming out of the body now boomed into the room, with a distinct echo as it turned in her direction. "**Now**."

Sitting up straighter in her chair, she prepared for the worst. "Who are you?" she began. "What—"

"You know *what* I am," *He* said menacingly. And with a strange smile crossing her/*IT*s face, "Does that frighten you?"

Pausing just a little too long, she responded with, "I see no reason to fear." But now she was shaking from the inside out.

"You should," this *Other* said coldly, yet darkly.

She had dealt with two Others of these deep level demons before, and had bested them. But this was different. Very different. This "patient" had begun transforming before her very eyes. That along with these Visions stabbing at her from within, was elevating her sense of both danger, and twisting her sense of reality.

Leaning in towards the couch, she asked in a whisper, "Why?"

"Because I am more powerful than you can know," *It* said, and without moving in her direction, Kat felt herself being pushed physically back into her chair by this.

Yes, this one was different. "Then— What are you?"

And with a very strange look, it lowered its' face and eyes towards her. Looking down at her with chilling intent, like a beast about to spring, the Voice changed to an even lower octave then Kathryn felt possible. "Call us Legion, for *We* are many."

Feeling herself calming and another part of her taking over, she asked with knowing entering her voice, "What are you really?"

With the Voice booming out with the strength to now shake the room, her chair, and the mirrored glass, "**I am your worst nightmare**," It said. Kat was now smelling a sense of burning fire and ash rising off of this *person*.

"I'm sorry, but that phrase has already been used," she tried saying with some humor. But inside, she knew that this was unlike any other Alter that she had ever dealt with before. This was more powerful, more *real* than anything she *ever* wanted to deal with.

And there was nothing humorous about this *It*.

Reaching down to the floor to pick up her steno pad, she made sure that her eyes didn't move from the "woman" now appearing to float over the couch for even a moment. On the page that was facing up in her peripheral vision, was the word bolded and underlined several times, "**IT**."

"You know what I am. I am the purest form of *He* which you would

96

go up against. Unlike these other *shadows* you play with."

Her mind racing to figure a way out of this maze, she asked again, "So, what are you really?"

"Allow me to give you a taste of what you can expect if you continue to evade my commands." Lifting fully off the table now, this body began turning in the air to face her. Raising *It*'s hands, an energy began pulsing out of this now transforming body, radiating more demon than human.

Her notebook began sliding from her lap to the floor again, as Kathryn's hands began lifting up in response, beginning to glow with a faint, pale, bluish light as if from the inside of her, as if to counter this threat.

Her expression was changing now as well, moving from the previous look of fear and abject terror, into one of concentration and power. Even the air around Kat was beginning to take on a sparking bluish glow. Her eyes reflected in the one way mirror opposite her, began glowing all white as well.

The floating Figure was reacting to her new stance, twisting and turning away from the Light now distinctly emanating from the transformed Kathryn's hands, a look of pain on *Its*' face. The look on her face had now become cold and without emotion as the roles reversed.

Slumping to the table again, the patients face and form began melting, returning to that of the overweight middle aged woman again, and not the demon that had been rising up from it moments earlier.

Exhaling from the effort, Kathryn slumped back wearily into her seat, exhausted, her sense of her own self returning once more.

But with only a moments rest, the door to the Observation Room burst open, and a still exhausted Kathryn began turning towards it. That part of her that went beyond "Kathryn Runyon" was knowing instinctively that it was Kirsten who was entering. And that she was no longer either innocent or pretending to be. Her eyes were now Black and her face contorting, she began walking menacingly towards Kat.

Rising with a face of growing calm, Kat began transforming again, too. Turning towards and stopping Kirsten/The Other with a mere glance and driving her/*It* back against the wall, a trance-like Kathryn reaching her white hot glowing hands up in the air, began pinning the body of Kirsten up against the wall. As *Kathryn* was raising her hands, the body of Kristen climbed up the wall and onto — hanging — from the ceiling.

Waking with a start while walking, Kat suddenly found herself in the hallway, very confused and already on her way out to her car. Taking the stairs this time, she was exiting the building before she was aware of it.

As she reached the parking lot, clouds were gathering above the buildings, turning the daylight towards dusk. The lights of the parking lot began flickering on and off again, and then started sparking, like the elevator fluorescents.

With a feeling that the worst wasn't over yet, Kat turned back towards the building. Where several of her *fellow staff members* were now walking towards her, all with the same completely black eyes that she had finally witnessed in Kirsten, who wasn't far behind them.

Kirsten. What had happened back there in the clinic? With the events leading up to what she had done flooding back into her consciousness, she also knew that she was in grave immediate danger.

And that the Part of her that had risen to confront the Others inside, knew exactly what to do now.

The Others came to a stop just outside the front doors, and were just standing there. Physically, they were no different than they were during any other ordinary day. Except that this was no ordinary day.

She began purposefully striding towards her car, when suddenly another car began drifting out of its parking space and began hurtling towards her, picking up speed as it came silently in her direction.

Turning to look at it, Kat blanched as she suddenly noticed that there was no Driver in it. The steering wheel was turning, directing it towards her, but no visible hands appeared to be turning it.

Now coming directly at her at an increasingly higher speed, her hands began lifting once more towards it, the car reacting by swerving out of its path towards her and crashing against other cars now starting to pull out of *their* respective spaces with rending sounds.

These other cars were now changing direction once more to match her location and veering towards her again with gathering speed, Kat finally turned to face it head on.

With a shield of energy forming in front of her body once again, the car began spinning wildly out of control, careening into the line of other cars between them in the parking lot, with loud shearing and grinding sounds.

With a wave of her hand, this car flipped over onto the direction of the other cars starting to pull out of their spaces.

A number of other people were coming out of several of the other buildings and were now running towards her. With most of the group raising their hands glowing sickly green as well now, Kat waved both of her hands, and other cars began pulling out, piling up into a larger and larger barricade between Kat and The Others.

With a final blast of energy from her hands, the cars began fusing one into the other, solidifying into a barrier of molten glass and steel.

Once again in her own car and coming back to her sense of being "Kathryn Runyon"again, she turned the car on and threw it into reverse, the tires spinning up a cloud of rubber and quickly driving away.

Her breathing ragged and her newly found Other Self sense of resolve melting away inside, she began sobbing as she drove, placing her head dangerously close to the steering wheel. She drove like this for a mile or so before hearing a police siren off in the distance.

Her head lifting away from the steering wheel and her eyes changing once more to white, she was heading towards home on auto pilot yet again.

shadows and **LIGHT**

NINE

Back in the seeming safety of her apartment, her front door double bolted with a chair locked under its knob, the now thoroughly exhausted Kat had barely made it inside before turning and melting onto the couch. Her eyes wide and looking more than a little insane, she felt herself folding up into a fetal position and burrowing into the couch, alternating between crying and sobbing hysterically.

What felt like decades later, Kat found herself sitting at her dining room table. Looking over at the clock on the wall, shaking her head realizing it was glowing 7:36. She had just lost five hours.

Calmer now and sitting in the dark after what she had been through earlier, the makeup she had insisted on putting on this morning was now smeared into track lines from where the tears that had been shed in the last few hours had been running black and red down her face.

Standing slowly and walking into the kitchen, she began the act of preparing dinner, still in a trance, as if Tom would be here any minute now with open, loving arms.

Another hundred or so hours later, the table was set, and Kat was rearranging the food on it for the third time. Now dressed in a slinky black evening dress, her eyes continued shooting once more to the wall clock that was reading 8:45.

Jumping once more at the sound of knocking trying to break down the front door, she squeaked out of her reverie. Composing herself and striding purposefully towards the door, she paused before taking the chair away and opening it.

Standing outside was a nowhere close to loving Thomas Wolfe, with a look that was almost murderous in intent.

"So... How was your day—" she began, as if the rest of her day hadn't happened. "—Tommy?" she started saying, abruptly changing emotional course with, "Leave. Now."

"Or you'll do what?" he said icily. "Kill me?"

Shocked beyond where she thought she could still be shocked, she found she couldn't say anything.

Not even bothering to hide his true nature now, his eyes were clouding black with the threat from earlier manifesting.

Blanching at this, she backs off. "So. This is it?" she asked, as she felt herself growing colder and the Other part of her self rising up. That part of her that she felt was coming to her defense at Hawthorne earlier during the *accidents* and her encounters with both the *Demon* and the real *Kirsten*, were now rising in defense against this Threat that she could no longer deny was coming from Tom.

104

Or *Whatever* the individual was, who called himself Tom Wolfe was quickly revealing himself to be.

The last thing that she remembered before blanking out this time, was Tom's eyes. They were both glowing with a raw hatred in them that she had never seen before, and they were manifesting the pure evil that she somehow knew were there all along, but she had tried so hard to deny. Now they were pure Black with Red glowing from them, like a physical manifestation of pure evil.

Had her eyes been playing tricks on her?

And then she woke up again, an hour later, in bed and with the sheets up around her shoulders, the straps of her evening dress still showing above the sheets.

She was feeling calmer now, staring up at the ceiling with the lights from the parking lot outside the only illumination through the trees outside her windows. She felt herself on the verge of erupting at any moment with sobbing out of nowhere.

And Tom was... Where was Tom? What was it about Tom that was trying to grab for her attention like some lost child?

She remembered... What was it she was trying to remember? About... Whose eyes?

"Tom?" she cried fitfully. "Tommy?" the lost child inside began wailing.

Suddenly sitting and reaching desperately for her phone, she was again dialing furiously in the night, trying to find some comfort and solace in the veils shifting this way and that. With the click on the line, the other phone was finally ringing.

But instead of another human voice, it was the answering machine again. "Hello, you've reached the phone of Dr. Ellen Rodgers. I'm not available right now—"

Holding the receiver away from her face with a look cascading into madness, she was frozen by the sound of the long beep that finally came.

Suddenly shouting, "Ellen! This is Kathryn Runyon. Please call me! Soon. Now. Please?!" and throwing the handset back onto the receiver, she returned to the safety of the covers once again, pulled them up to her eyes.

Quickly crossing the line into full blown hysteria (but also starting to quickly forget why she was feeling this way), Kat drew her legs up into a fetal position once more and began rocking back and forth, shaking violently under the sheets.

At any other time she might have been rocking herself back to sleep...

With the passage of another (seeming) hundred hours, the living room clock was only showing 10:15, as Kat was pacing back and forth in front of the still set table. The food cold and the candles now burned down to only pools of wax, there were no signs of struggle, but still just a feeling.

Tom was gone, and Kat was—

TEN

Now dressed in a sweat suit and with a vacant look creeping back into her eyes, she came to a dead stop.

A decision made somewhere deep inside her, she was crossing over to the front door and without hesitating, opening and walking through it.

Leaving the door wide open behind her.

Aimlessly walking in another zombie-like trance state, Kat was barely sticking to the sidewalk, occasionally weaving out into the street.

Lost and without any sense of even being outside, she was wandering aimlessly with no where to go, her whole life now proven to be a lie and lying shattered in her still fracturing mind.

Crossing over into the grassy area of a nearby park with swing sets, she wandered into a poorly lit area of large trees with imposing shadows. About to sit herself down in the wet grass, a deeper Shadow emerged from behind one of the pine trees close by and began silently approaching Kat from behind.

With The Figure grabbing her and wrapping a hand tightly over her mouth, she returned to full consciousness and began thrashing, fighting in an attempt to break free of this grip enough to scream.

Merely holding her in place with one hand firmly placed over her mouth in a grip that allowed no movement, Kat began feeling a warm blanket falling gently over her mind.

Her struggling began subsiding, calming down, and in whispered tones the Voice told her, "Don't worry. I'm not here to hurt you."

Fighting the grip this man had on her for a few more seconds longer, Kat finally stopped her struggling, going limp in his arms.

Loosening his grip slowly and taking his hand away from her mouth, he told her in a very soothing voice, "Please don't scream or make any loud noise."

"What do you want with me?" she asked, once the grip on her mouth was releasing. As she felt the hysteria from earlier returning, she as on the verge of sobbing. "If you want money..." she began to say, but then another realization came into her, "Or... Is it something else?" she asked, fearing the worst.

"I need to talk to you," the Voice said calmly, and pausing for dramatic effect, continued with, "Dr. Runyon."

Turning abruptly at the sound of her name, Kat began the steady descent back into shock, whispering, "How do you know my name?"

The voice was now attached to a shadowy face, "Because we've met before," was all he said. Walking away from her, he stopped after a short distance asking her without turning back to look at her, "Don't you want to know where?"

Why couldn't she manage to focus on him? It's dark out here, yes, she thought. But it's not *that* dark.

Following him but feeling too exhausted to play games with a stranger, she asked him without hesitation, "What *do* you want from me?"

Once they were in a more lighted area, the Figure finally stopped, turning slightly in her direction, "To save you," he whispered, with a grim laugh. "Interested?"

He's almost ten feet away from me, Kat thinks, *But he sounds like he's standing right behind me, whispering in my ear.* Walking warily over towards him, his features began to become clearer, as if he'd just stepped out of a fog.

"What do you want from me?" she asked again more forcefully.

Catching up to him, his features began to loose their focus again. "Walk with me," that Voice told her. "But this time keep to the lesser lighted areas. We don't want to be seen tonight."

As she followed, still warily a few steps behind him, she noticed that the Figure in front of her had long hair and a beard, and was dressed in a full ankle length coat. (Even though the weather was on the warm side at this time, even for New England.)

But when he finally turned around, what struck her the most were his eyes. Stopping, she pleaded, "Won't you at least tell me your name?"

Walking back to her, his features began coming more fully into focus, his expression calming and sympathetic. "I'm Devon Woolsley," he said. Cocking his head curiously, "Remember me now?"

Her mind was racing but his face was still not touching any chord of recognition. "From the conference on Dissociative Disorders back in 91," he prompted.

Suddenly remembering now, Kat grew defensive again, also remembering how he had pressed her hard on... Something. Something that she couldn't quite put awareness on right this minute.

What had it been? she asked herself, as she racked her brain to remember.

"What do you want from me? Why are you here? Now, of all days" she asked again, this time coldly.

"Like I said. To save you.

"Although from how you handled those accidents I witness earlier today and yesterday—"

Going from angry to shell shocked in a second, "How do you... What do you..." And finally, "Were you there?" And then back to angry with, "Are you the one that caused them?"

Laughing strangely at her, "Caused them? Not quite," he said, pausing, to let her next question hang in the air. "Witness them?" he

112

finally said, more of a statement than question, and he answered ominously with, "In a way."

Her mind already reeling from the day, she still found the energy to get upset. "Do you mind telling me what this is about?"

His face growing suddenly clearer in her mind, then flashing with an image of the very serious and clean shaven psychiatrist from the conference, he bowed his head. "You already know, Doctor."

"I do?"

"Yes. You'd been suspecting that your nightmares were real for some time, but didn't want to face what you were thinking."

Stopping in her tracks, "How do— Do you—" she started to ask, but let it go. "Why don't you stop playing games with me and just tell me?"

His eyes now in razor sharp focus, "Because I need for you to figure this out for yourself. That's why."

"But... Why?"

Hesitating, as if he were unsure he wanted to tell her, his whole demeanor changed once again as he turns back towards her, sighing, "Because I have to be sure."

She didn't like where this was going. "Be sure of what?" she asked coldly.

With some hints of a ghost light mysteriously flickering across his face, "That you aren't one of **Them**. That you weren't part of setting a trap for me."

The full force of what he was saying began slamming fully into her mind. Sitting down abruptly on the wet grass, Kat became silent.

"You've attracted the wrong kind of attention recently," and with a deep emphasis added darkly, "Doctor."

Dazed even more, she asks, "What do you mean?"

Kneeling down on the grass in front of her, "You've begun believing your patients stories. You've begun to suspect that they are not just psychotic delusions. That they may in fact, be quite real."

Waving his hand in front of her like a hypnotist waking a patient, "And you've begun remembering things yourself. Things that you shouldn't."

Kat's mind was suddenly plunged back into the "nightmare," with the image of the Hand raising the jeweled knife. The Blood Red Knife, ferocious in the firelight.

And the shriek when it fell.

Slamming her back to her present, Kat's mind was reeling as if from a non-physical blow to her head. "Oh, my God."

This man — Devon — whispered into her ear from where he was still kneeling four feet away, "God had nothing to do with it."

Beginning to sob now, Kat was not only finally accepting what was happening to her, but she was also unable to block out what she could only accept now that she *knew*. "But I thought—"

"That they were just 'nightmares,' he suggested, filling in her thought.

114

"Yes," she barely whispered.

Standing now, he began walking away. Even as he did, she could still clearly hear him say, "But you knew that they weren't."

Realization dawning on her face, she asked, "What a second. How do you know all of this?"

Turning towards her, so she could see his face now, "I've been following your progress for a while now," he told her.

"My...?" Her mind now shifting back and forth between angry and appalled, her face tightened again. "How do I know that *you're* not one of— "

"Because if I were," he interrupted, "You'd have been dead by now. I would have killed you—" and pointing back to where she had entered the park — "Back there."

Sobering up, Kat felt her stomach sinking as she suddenly knew that he was telling her the truth. Unsteadily trying to stand, she is about to fall again when Devon — returning to her side in an instant — catches her, steadying her with a firm hand at her elbow. And with his other one around her waist.

"Then... Why are you here?" she asked. "Besides..."

Beginning to walk her back into the darker areas again, "We have much to discuss," he said, sounding ominous without sounding ominous. "But not here. Not out in the open," and even more ominously, "And most certainly not at night."

"But where are we going to?"

Sighing, "Somewhere where I can better shield us."

Too exhausted to protest, and somehow trusting this stranger that she had not known more than a seeming ten minutes before, she allowed herself to be physically helped to a nearby car. He opened the passenger side and placed her, gently but firmly in the seat.

Her mind barely registered what it was that she was being helped into. After he had crossed over to the other side, he said, "I know it's not the newest and cleanest," getting into the drivers seat. "But it blends in the way I need it to."

At this point, Kat all of a sudden just wanted to sleep, knowing somehow that the demons in her dreams would finally be kept at bay.

For now.

ELEVEN

After a short ride where Kat could only remember street lights gliding by as if in a dream, they pulled into the parking lot of a less than reputable looking motel off Highway 91.

Pulling into a spot there, Devon got out and walked over to the passenger door and gentlemanly opened Kat's door and extended his hand kindly to help her out. Shaking her head from out of her dangerous exhaustion, she managed to get herself upright without nausea interrupting.

Once he knew she was stable enough, Devon left her leaning against the car door and walked over to the nearby door, and quietly inserted a key.

But instead of just moving directly into the room, he opened it slowly. As if there might be a rattle snake just inside lying in wait He stopped and put his hand in carefully, waving it around on the inside from side to side while putting his other hand up, his fingers wide with a warning for her to stop.

As exhausted as she was, she was ready to laugh at this seemingly ridiculous gesture, but felt herself compelled to stop anyway. "What are—" Kat tried asking, but suddenly felt her throat tighten, with it clamping down without her doing it.

Feeling the hysteria ready to mount another attack, she relaxed and went to breathing deep breaths to calm herself. It worked this time.

After a few more seconds of this antic that began amusing her, he opened the door fully and walked in. Waving her in silently behind him as well, he turned and nodded.

Once they were both inside, he began relaxing a little, offering, "I had to do a check."

Still finding herself amused after everything else that had happened in the last several days, she asked frivolously, "For what? Fairies? Witches? Dragons?"

"Closer to that than you know," he said, in a way that sent a shiver back down her already exhausted back.

She was about to flick the light switch on at the door, when his hand was suddenly on hers, "More things in this world than even you're aware of just yet, Doctor. Consciously, at least."

He moved past her to shut the door quietly, saying, "But you're beginning to be."

"What are you—"

Drawing the curtains completely closed and pointing to a chair next to the TV, he told her authoritatively, "Sit," and she felt the compunction to comply.

Crossing over to the bed and sitting on it, Devon closed his eyes and remained silent for a few seconds. He seemed to be going inward and she felt a calming presence begin to wash over her.

Meditating? she thought, as she sat in the chair waiting patiently for him to say something. Even with the feeling of peace that had begun to calm her, she was finding that she was still on edge.

At the point of saying something, she was interrupted again. As if coming to a decision, he said without opening his eyes, "You've been getting into deep territory with your clients lately. Hearing about too much, starting to believe too much, and now... experiencing too much."

"What are you talking about?" she asked innocently.

As if he hadn't heard her, he continued, "There are forces in motion in this world at this time which very few on the planet are aware of. Dark forces."

Blanching suddenly, Kat found herself back in the forest. Except this time instead of being on the outside of the circle of chanting figures looking in, she felt she was on the inside — chanting and swaying — looking out.

Illuminated in stark red in the center of the circle was — an Altar. And on that altar was a child. Screaming its lungs out. And suddenly, the Hand raising the blade high over the child's form was—

Suddenly back in the motel room, Kat shuddered violently as she felt herself slam back into her body.

As she was opening up her eyes (not having been aware that she had closed them), she looked up to see a very intense Devon staring deep inside of her. "Now you're starting to understand," he said ominously.

"What just happened?" she asked him in a daze.

"The same thing that happened to me."

"What are you talking about?" she asked, her mind still reeling from the force of the vision.

"You see, I was just like you. Up until a few years ago that is."

"How—"

Standing and pacing as he speaks now, "I was a practicing psychiatrist too, as you well know, dealing with my dissociative patients. And I also thought that they were just crazy as well."

"But—"

"But I began having the same dreams as you. And then, I knew that they weren't dreams any more."

"So what did you do?"

Cocking his head to one side as if listening to a far off sound that she couldn't hear, he turned to her abruptly, sighing, "We have to leave. Now."

"What are you talking about?"

"They're on the move. Things are beginning."

Grabbing her hand and leading her towards the door, "It's not safe

120

for you here anymore."

"What makes you think—"

A grim look on his face, he turned towards her getting very up close in her face, "Are you prepared to die here tonight?"

Blanching again, she croaked, "No."

"Good. Because there are things in this world that are far worse than death," he said, with a deeply chilling tone.

Turning again and heading towards the door, he stopped with his hand resting on the handle. Without turning back in her direction, he said, "But I can't make you go with me." Turning to face her, he said, "You have free will. You need to agree to go with me.

"Or you can stay here—"

"But, that's not—"

"In your best interest? No."

"Where are we going to?"

Grabbing at her hand and pulling her painfully in to within inches of him. "I can't tell you that," he whispered. "You have to trust me," and suddenly realizing what he had done, let her hand go.

Although she felt she knew the answer, she asked him, "Why should I do that? Tell me."

As he turned away and began slowly opening the door slightly and peering out first in each direction, he said without looking back, "Look inside your self. You'll know the answer."

"I need to at least go back to my—"

Emphatically turning with anger now in his voice, "Your apartment is not safe. Your *boyfriend* will have made sure of that."

"How do you know—"

"Because as you know even now — if you would let yourself to — that he's one of Them. He's what's called a "Sentinel" and his sole purpose was set up to be with you to keep tabs on you."

"But—"

"In your heart you know what I'm saying is true. Godness knows, you've seen enough today to not have to keep playing this Doubting Thomas routine with me."

Godness? she thought, and then let it go. *For another time I guess.* Sighing and shivering involuntarily, she asked (with just a little too much of a whining sound in the question), "But what *am* I going to wear for clothes?"

"You have clothes on," he told her matter of factly, pointing and indicating her sweats. "And we can get you other clothes to wear later."

"But—" she tried to object again.

Turning to her and grabbing her by the shoulders, this time much more gently, he asked her exasperatedly looking her full in the face, "What's more important to you now? Your appearance? Or your life?"

122

"But..." she tried again.

"I can only protect you so far," he said, shaking his head wearily.

Turning and popping his head out the door, in a moment he was once again fully inside. "Although," he said, giving her an approving look, "You've done a pretty good job of protecting yourself so far, I do have to say."

Blanching again, "What do you mean," she asked quietly, that sinking feeling returning again.

"They should have been able to kill you today. After all, they sent some very powerful wielders of power against you, both demon and human."

Pausing a moment for effect, he continued with, "But they didn't. Apparently they couldn't."

Laughing grimly, he smiled for the first time. "Probably surprised the hell out of them, too."

Stunned once again, "Were you watching there, too?" she asked. What had this man's part been in all of it, she thought. "Were you—"

"Didn't need to be."

"Uh, huh. But you "saw it." Right?"

"I see a great many things, Kathryn" he said matter of factly without any ego in his voice. And looking her dead in the eyes he added, "And so do you. When you want to recognize them for what they truly are, that is."

"Such as?"

"What you saw in the Sentinel called Kirsten earlier."

"Sentinel," she repeated again.

Waving his hand in front of her eyes once more...

She saw the face of Kirsten, eyes black and with her hands up—

And then, switching to the sight of the demonic alter rising out of the form of her patient Andrea, telling her in that inhumanly low voice, "Call Us Legion."

Returning to her current surroundings with a jolt again, Devon said, (staring into her soul), "Your abilities with that elevator. And then, all of those cars."

"Accidents," Kathryn insisted, shaking her head from side to side desperately trying to clear her head which was now swimming in a growing confusion.

"You're proving far too powerful for those they've sent against you so far. And they've—"

"What do you mean," Kat asked with another chill.

"Sooner or later," he told her. "They would bring an entire army of powerful Adepts against you."

"Adepts? What are adepts?" she said, putting her hands to her head as it suddenly began hurting. This was all coming too fast and furious for her.

"You would call them *magic users*, or even *wizards*," he said in all seriousness.

Laughing hard at this, she shook her head in disbelief. "Oh, come on. There's no such thing as magic."

"Then what do you call moving cars around a parking lot with just your mind?" he countered, looking tired.

Grasping at straws, she said, "Chance," a little too quickly. "It must have hit a rock in the middle of—".

"All of them? There were half a dozen—"

"All accidents," she said, hysteria now rising fully in her voice.

"We don't think so," Devon said quietly.

Stopped in mid-reaction, Kat asked with a heavy reluctance and suspicion, "We?" Was this man a multiple himself? Or was he just some sort of psychotic nut case after all?

As if he could read her mind, "I'll explain later," was all he would give her. "But right now, we need to go."

It was Kathryn's turn now to become the petulant child, as if that could be a defense against her condition. "Why?" she whined.

"That army of adepts I was just telling you about?"

"Yes," she said cautiously.

Another swipe of his hand over her eyes and she saw...

An image so grotesque, she couldn't even believe it was human. Or had ever once been. Except that in her mind she knew that had been

125

the case. Once upon a time...

Staggering in her step and gasping at the pain, anguish and stark terror emanating from the— "What was—" she began to ask, but part of her knew perfectly well what it was. She had seen it — known It — before. Even that brief touch of knowledge, left her reeling inside from the unspeakably stark and utterly screaming Pain and Anguish of— **That**. Whatever **That** was.

"You really don't want to know the answer to that one," he told her grimly, and proceeded out the door leaving it standing open. And not looking back to see if she followed.

Only nodding in exhausted shock and on the verge of crying furiously and madly, she silently began following him, trying to catch her breath again as she did.

Oh, God. The pain! she whispered inside. *Oh, my God.*

"Trust me. God had nothing to do with *That*," he whispered to her unspoken anguish.

A feeling of mourning unlike any she had ever experienced in her life, was now rising up for that life which she thought that she had led, and it was threatening to drown her. The veil now being ripped away, it had left her feeling both haunted and vacant at the same time.

Everything about the person she had thought of as Kathryn Runyon was apparently a lie. From her earliest memories, to the moment that she had had her first confrontation with the Evil that had risen from the table earlier today in the treatment room. And that was now seeming

126

so long, long ago, even though it had only been that morning.

Stepping outside, Devon walked up to a car that she hadn't seen fully before. It was a beat up old Dodge Dart, the likes of which she hadn't seen recently, with a dull, peeling gun metal gray paint job complete with a pitted windshield. She wasn't sure it was going to serve to get them out of the parking lot, much less wherever he thought that they were going to.

She shivered, looking in the window before opening the door. Not exactly one with modern conveniences, she thought as she slid into it. With things like a comfortable seat.

This is going to be a very long trip indeed, Kat thought. However far — wherever it was — they were going to.

And what exactly was waiting for her on the other side?

shadows and **LIGHT**

TWELVE

They had been driving for several hours in silence before Kat had ventured to ask a question of him. "Where are we—" she began to ask, but felt again that glancing, unspoken command for *Silence*.

She went back into her brooding, both wanting and not wanting to think about the last few days. With the droning of the engine of this ancient car that Devon drove, Kat had fallen asleep in spite of herself.

Waking with a start, she realized that she had actually managed to get some dream, vision-less sleep. She felt refreshed in a way that she hadn't for a very long, long time.

There were dark shapes resembling houses passing them by on both sides as they drove on into the deepening night. With the occasional appearance of lights popping out of these darker shapes indicating the occupants were still awake, these ghost lights were whispering Home to her.

And now Home (with all of its various shadings and meanings), was a foreign concept to her and not at all what she could still call reality.

Devon was driving now as if he were in a trance. Shooting him the occasional worried and puzzled look, Kat was unsure whether she should ask him more questions or just let him drive. He seemed to her as if he were concentrating intensely on something other than his driving.

For the time being it seemed, Kat was left to brood on her situation. Not that brooding was likely to be of any help.

Without warning and apparently not coming out of his trance, Devon careened onto an exit ramp that Kat had missed noticing the signs for, and they were now on a smaller highway heading west into the hills.

Suddenly coming out of his trance, he startled her with asking, "You think an awful lot. You know that?"

Caught off guard once more, she gulped suddenly. "What?" And after a few seconds of recovery asked, "Don't you?"

"No, that's what meditation is for. What you're perceiving as a trance state.

"Look. I know you have many questions. But you also know that all you have to do is go within for those answers." And looking at her with a dismissive look, "Most of what you want to know... You don't."

They drove further on in silence for what seemed to Kat like hours that were quickly turning into days. The houses they passed were starkly illuminated, vanishing like ghosts coming and then gone before you blinked.

The street lights that they had passed with regularity before, now thinned out to become only occasional pools of light off in the darkness, giving way to trees she could barely make out the outlines of. Everything became a dark blur of unreality.

Soon they were far enough out in the Berkshire Mountains that, with the exception of the occasional sparsely populated town, there was nothing but darkness. Not even stars helped to lighten this landscape.

There was only the beams of the headlights lighting the road in front of them, and if she looked in the right side rear view mirror, a hint of the red coming from the rear lights vaguely illuminating occasional points in the darkness there. White light ahead, and the red hints of the danger and greater darkness that she was hopefully now leaving far behind.

She was beginning to think that they were going to drive like this for the remainder of their trip. That she would be watching the miles go by in darkness, with this strange man beside her sightlessly staring silently ahead as he drove. The look of concentration in his features were barely lit by the weak dashboard lights.

She looked at Devon for a long time wondering who this man

really was. What it was like to be him, and what was going through his head that cause this trance. Was he somehow sleeping as he drove? Was this somehow how he slept while he drove? And... Was it safe?

He startled her by suddenly coming out of his trance and turning to ask her, "Do you understand what's happening to you?"

Part of her did, knowing now that both the nightmares and the client sessions at Hawthorne were altogether too real.

But wanting to play dumb to find out what else this Devon knew, she asked him, "Does this mean you're going to explain it to me now?"

Without looking at her, he said, "Not completely. Not until daylight."

Her curiosity piqued, she asked in earnest, "Why?"

"Because most of what I would tell you, would only serve to bring their attention to bear on us. And I need to use most of my attention to keep us as invisible as I can while we're driving at night."

"So, why don't we find somewhere to stop?"

With a sigh coming up from surprising depths, he said quietly, "Nowhere safe. Not yet."

"Oh," she said, wondering if she even wanted to know why.

Pausing now as if searching in his mind for how to phrase it properly, he began saying softly, "When I first began awakening to what it was I was dealing with, I was a little more prepared than you were."

This isn't helping, she thought. "Ok. How so?"

"I was already steeped in the deeper knowledge of the esoteric side of life — magic, the occult and the like. When I was brought up against the wall separating what I thought my life was and what it had really been, I thought to myself at the time, "So this is why I'm drawn to all of this dark material."

"I had been trying to find some way of understanding, on a subconscious level, this life that I'd been living without knowing I was even living it for most of my life.

"But it was more than that; much more than that. As I came to realize the extent of my travels on the Dark Side, I found myself getting into places even I wasn't prepared for."

"Oh," was all she could think to say, wincing inwardly. "You're making it sound like Star Wars," she added, trying to leaven it into the less dark. "*Use the Force, Luke,*" she intoned, in what was, even to herself, a poor sounding imitation of Obi Won Kenobi.

Ignoring her jibe, he turned to give her a serious look, "But you," he continued turning to face her full on and not acknowledging her attempt at levity, "You've always been the rationalist. That was your way of dealing with the Darkness that part of you knew was inside of you. Ignore it, you seemed to think, seeming to say to yourself, as in *If it can't be proven rationally, maybe it'll go away. It can't exist, therefore it doesn't.*

"Besides, you no doubt said to yourself, it's only psychosis."

This was conjecture on his part, she thought. It might be how she would have thought, if she'd even thought about it at all. But what she said was, "Yes. I've always been a firm believer in proof."

"And yet, how did you end up getting involved with treating multiple personalities? Not exactly what you'd call a rationalist course of action. Is it?"

No, it wasn't. She hadn't thought about it in quite that way before. With a sinking feeling that startled her, she blanched as she realized how driven by other circumstances (and others choices) her whole life's worth of choices had been. "I don't know. It just... I don't know... It— Just happened."

Turning suddenly, shock overcoming her uncertainty, "Why are you asking me this?" Her shield of denying her condition seemed quite strong, even now.

"You just fell into it," Devon continued, his voice dripping with sarcasm. "Treating people with multiple personalities. A strange, highly esoteric fringe practice of psychology, and you just—. "managed to fall into it"."

Turning towards her and giving her a look that chilled her to the bone, he said darkly, "Nothing is ever as it seems, Doctor Runyon."

"What do you mean?" she said apprehensively, shoveling on the deep denial, even though it was crumbling inside of her now.

Letting his right hand stray from the steering wheel without looking at her, he pinched her on her left leg. "Ow," she cried out, not so much hurt as shocked by his action

134

"What we see and feel as the physical form," he said, tapping her where he had pinched her — and suddenly, the sharp pain of the pinch disappeared as quickly as it had come. "Is only a very infinitesimal fraction of who — and what — we really are."

"Ok," was once again all she could find to say. And then, hurt with the realization she said, "You still really don't trust me completely. Do you?"

She asked this with a sudden sinking feeling. She thought somehow that he had begun relaxing and letting his guard down with her, but obviously that wasn't the case.

"I can't," was all he said, returning his gaze protectively to the road ahead.

"Why not?" she asked, although she felt she knew the answer.

"Let's just say... I've been caught like this before," he said simply, with only a hint of emotion bleeding through. But that hint was enough.

Shivering unexpectedly, she just repeated, "Caught," as if that explained it all. *Just what exactly has he been through*, she thought with another shiver.

"I've had traps laid for me. Subtle traps that even I didn't see coming."

"That what? Almost got you killed or something?"

Looking at her now with a chilling glance, "Kathryn," he paused, "Once again, there are fates far worse than death." And then, lowering his voice three octaves suddenly, his voice boomed out in the car reminiscent of some of her patients in the treatment room, "*You ought to know that.*"

Starting at this, she found herself trying to mold her body to the form of the door at her side, as if in an attempt to escape. "You mean..." she asked, "Like being a multiple?"

"As in, having your soul sheared from your physical form by—" he started to say, and then stopped.

Turning and looking at her now with deadly earnest, "But you wouldn't know about that though... Because you've never had a patient describe how it felt to you. Have you?"

Shivering again, this time violently, all she could say once again was her stock answer, hard felt this time, "Oh."

"Yes. Oh, indeed," he said, and left it for her imagination to fill in the terror and horror that his short explanation had started to imply.

Now it was Kat's turn to grow quiet, willingly, for the next few hours. *Better to not even think about it*, she thought, as she tried to fight off sleep.

Somewhere in the middle of the Pennsylvania night of rolling dark hills, Kat woke with a start.

Looking around and coming to terms with the passing telephone poles blurring along the highways edge and mountains in the not too far distance, caused her to sit up. She quickly started coming to grips with where she remembered she was.

Right, she thought. *I'm in a car with a strange man I don't know, on the run for my life. Going from supposed safety and daily routine, into a dark future without anything I had once thought I could take for granted anymore.*

The full force of exactly what she was leaving behind was only now managing to scratch away at the years of denial she had managed to forge around the illusion. The devastation that she felt was yet to come, was only a dark horizon for her now. But the weight of the memories that she now knew were only shadows, were quickly turning into wisps of smoke disappearing behind her.

Her new life's landscape hadn't solidified into anything tangible yet. Other than the hard, barely cushioned side panel she had managed to sleep against without nightmares. And the seat that she had managed to sleep on, wasn't in much different (or any more comfortable) shape.

The waxing moon gave the landscape around them a strange, almost comforting glow to her. It almost negated her situation.

Then there was the strange man sitting next to her. Driving apparently without seeing the road in front of him, he was apparently escorting her into an unknown future that she wasn't sure was going to be any more comforting or safe than the one she had apparently just left.

This "Devon" was sitting there, his hands on the steering wheel but with his mind somewhere else.

As she had the opportunity to observe him now without his obscuring her vision for a while now, she saw a hippie-ish looking man with a long beard, disheveled and dirty looking. As if he hadn't had a shower in days.

Nondescript, she thought, *as in a homeless looking kind of way. Someone that most people in this society wouldn't look at twice, except to make sure that he wasn't following them or otherwise paying attention to them.*

Every once in a while when Kat would glance in his direction, she would have flashes of Devon in his lab coat, clean shaven and doctor-like.

This would soon be followed other flashes of his being in a strange Valhalla-like aerie of a mountain top retreat center. In these, he was surrounded by other people with long, flowing bright white or other colored robes.

In one of these flashes, she saw they were all sitting in a big round building, without any lights she could see. But the whole room seemed somehow to be glowing.

All of these people were sitting on the bare ground in various yoga positions in a great circle, sort of like an anti-version of the Red Circle Pyre gatherings. This whitish Glow was somehow counteracting a hint of red flames that seemed to be there just outside the hint of high topped windows.

Was this last some kind of past life in some monastery, she

wondered? No. In some scenes she could see cars and trucks clearly parked off in the occasional distance between this and other more modern looking buildings. But was the glow she saw around these people some sort of an illusion?

Was he feeding mental images to her while in his trance, that were designed to give her something to think about? Images to hint at other aspects of himself to comfort her? Her feelings of raw edge and misgivings were bordering on raving madness, and these images did seem to be calming her down adequately over time.

Or was he doing this to lull her into a false sense of trust in him? He could be just as much the Deceiver as the Cult was. He could also be the trap — for her, and she was just sleeping her way through to her demise.

No, that Other (Deeper) part of herself said. *Relax. Sleep.*

Once when she looked, there seemed to be a faint ghost light she saw occasionally around his face, as if he were radiating a peaceful presence while he drove.

She couldn't figure out whether this was another one of his machinations to calm her into acceptance? Or a byproduct of something Else that he was experiencing.

Or? Perhaps both.

shadows and **LIGHT**

THIRTEEN

Driving for about another hour or so, there was a hint of light beginning to creep over the mountains that were still surrounding them. Once again unexpectedly, Devon began banking suddenly off the main highway, taking another barely announced exit she had also almost missed seeing.

On a side Service road now, Kat saw that they were heading into what should have been one of the last remaining dingy motels on the East Coast. Except they had driven a sufficient distance during the night that they had to be somewhere in Ohio by now, (or so she thought). Except that there were still mountains.

Or is this still Pennsylvania? she thought. She couldn't know for sure because of her sleeping for most of it. And also because the other road trips she had made with Tom, may have been largely illusion as well for all she knew. They hadn't stopped (that she knew of), so they had only driven through the night.

Had they driven a thousand miles already? Was that even possible?

I'm not that tired, she thought. And then she realized that, although she had slept, she had not dreamed. No nightmares had brought her violently awake.

Then she realized that he hadn't slept either. He had driven throughout the night. *Doesn't he need to sleep?* she wondered. *Or is this trance state all that he needs?*

"Yes, I do sleep," he said suddenly, as if in answer to her unvoiced question. Pulling into a space in front of an open door that appeared to be the Office, he glanced at her and may have said to her, *Wait here.* Or maybe not.

It would almost be comical, this seeming reading of her mind by this strange man, she thought. If it weren't for the absolute madness that she was currently running from, that is. Not to mention her falsely lived life of desperate deception behind her. Too weary to say anything, she let it pass and watched silently as he went in.

This was the sort of motel that harbored the kind of low life riffraff she's always seen in movies, that couldn't afford a more modern motel or hotel to "stay in." They often lived in these "motel'" rooms for years on end, these movies implied, as they drank themselves to death. *So what are We doing here?* she asked herself.

After returning to the car from visiting the office, Devon was still stone faced, betraying no emotions she could see, much less the growing sense of terror that Kat was feeling, rising up in her when she least expected it.

Silently and still in a half trance, he drove them up to the front door of a room. After turning off the engine, he once again got out cautiously.

Snapping back to being fully in the present now, he began looking first one way and then another. Almost as if he expected some phantom to jump out at them from any one of the nearby shadows or bushes the moment he let his guard down. His held his hand up suddenly as she opened the door to get out, and put it up to silence her as she did.

At this point she was feeling too groggy from being on the road to really object to this. She'd have to ask him when they got to this "safe place" what it was that he thought he might find doing this. But once again, she was not sure she wanted to know what the answer would be.

Having apparently scanned the area to his satisfaction though, he began gesturing cautiously to Kat to get fully out. As she did, an owl or some other bird called mournfully off in the distance, echoing her sense of loneliness and isolation.

Walking up to the door, Devon cautiously slipped the key silently into the lock and began opening the door again ever so slightly. He did this only enough for him to stick his right hand in once again, to do this strange scanning thing before entering.

As she reached the door and was about ready to step in, his left hand shot up yet again, signaling for her to stop and she froze.

Satisfied finally that all was clear, he visibly relaxed and pushed the door in, gesturing silently for Kat to follow.

Devon entered with Kat closing the gap between them quickly. He crossed over to where the proverbial motel lamp sat on the nightstand, pulling the chain. And just as suddenly, he was then standing next to where Kat was just inside the door and about to flip the switch for the overhead.

Pointing to the light of the dim lamp already lit, he said quietly, "That's enough light for our purpose. For now."

"What do you mean," Kat asked with trepidation. "Do you mean we're still—"

Closing the door she had left ajar with a subtle click, "We need to attract as little attention as we can," he said, sighing. "That means we only use enough light to barely see by, and no sudden movements. Only careful and considered actions. Do you Understand?"

"Even though it's daytime?" *We can't still be in that much danger, can we?* Kat thought incredulously. *Surely there's enough miles in between Us and — Them — he can relax?*

Walking back to the far side of the bed, he passed his hand over the phone, sensing that it was safe and that the final sort of trap had been avoided. Now more fully satisfied, he visibly relaxed to a point that she hadn't thought his body could up until now. *Although only by a little.*

"It's not that easy," he told her wearily, as if he had heard her last

144

mental comment. Devon smoothly moved past her, grabbing one of the two chairs in the room and placing it under the door lock to block the door.

Turning in her direction but not moving to get any closer to her physically, he continued emphatically, "And, yes. We are still in very great danger. And we will be until—" he said, and left it at that.

"Oh," she said, sitting down in the remaining chair by the TV. And then not being able to help herself, she asked, "Why?"

Tilting his head from side to side, this direction and that, he sighed finally looking directly at her. "Because there are Many out there who would very much like to find us."

Sensing her unease is once again with him, "I don't intend to harm you, Kathryn. Or do anything else to you, for that matter. I was sent to protect you, not molest you. Any further than you already have been, that is. And besides—"

Not having been aware of how much she still didn't trust him, she began to object, "But—"

"You'll sleep in the bed," he said, pointing to the cheap none-too-firm motel mattress. "And unfortunately, I'm not going to be sleeping much at all again, either today or tonight."

She just had to ask him. "You do need to sleep, don't you?"

Sighing and deflating onto the other side of the bed, the constant driving and being on guard was now obviously showing signs of having taken its toll on him. He sighed a deep wracking sigh and told her, "Now more than ever," looking as if he were going to drift off where he was.

"But I can't afford to. And I'm not that advanced yet to do without rest completely."

Advanced, she thought, still having a hard time believing in the dire nature of her/their situation. No matter what had already happened to her.

Chalk that up to denial I guess, she thought. "We're still in that much danger?" she asked him again, this time more fiercely.

"More than you can realize. They're—" he began to say and then thought better of it.

Growing calmer and softer, he rose from where he very much seemed to want to remain, and gestured for her to take the bed.

"So, please. Sleep. I need you to be as alert as you can be by tomorrow morning. We still have a very long ways to go, and still a very dangerous drive ahead of us. I will need you to drive for a good deal of it, once we've gotten further along the road."

"Will they try and attack us during the day?" she asked.

"I don't think so," he told her, now looking very tired and old. "And I'm going to need to sleep some in the car while you drive during the day."

"But—" she tried to object.

"Not now. Please," he said, cutting her off. "I still need to maintain a watch. While we're not... Where we need to be... Just yet. And as

146

long as you sleep, I can't afford to not be vigilant."

Kat began moving towards the bed as Devon traded places with her. Drawing the curtains to maximize the darkness in the room with the rising sun outside turning to full day, he turned his back on her, emphasizing his comfort in her presence.

Settling into the chair once he was fully satisfied the room was safe and closing his eyes, she got the impression that he wasn't really falling asleep, however much he might want to. He was just concentrating, cutting off the outside world and extending his senses in other directions.

She in turn, turned her back on him warily and began slowly drawing the covers of the bed back. Wishing among other things that she could fully trust him and he her, she began crawling cautiously into bed with her clothes still on. She pulled the covers up to her chin and trying not to make it obvious that she was keeping her eyes on him as she thought, *Who can I really trust?* as she drifted quickly off to sleep without thinking, exhausted.

With her eyes closing and knowing that she was exhausted and would sleep deeply, Devon cleared his mind and prepared for being with Those Who would know better what to do with This One.

Relaxing himself into the deepest state that he could go to without falling asleep, he closed the miles between himself and the Council of Elders that he was doing the bidding of.

The Darkness and Quiet of Peace began slowly revealing subtle colors in a mist that resolved as if into a glowing cloud being lit from behind. Coming out of the *night* that was the featureless Void, Forms began materializing out of the formless, gaining solidity and resolving into the representation of various Bodies.

The Council of Elders was his metaphysical order, led by a woman who was known as Angelus. She was also called "The Ancient" by many of the Order out of a sign of respect, as she was both very old but also appeared to be ageless at the same time. This agelessness was secretly inspiring to most of those who lived around her. She seemed to float wherever she went, as if defying gravity.

No one really knew for sure just how old The Ancient was though. She never referenced anything but the Present, and if any new ones coming in had the temerity to ask, she would just ignore their questions. Devon once asked her if she was hearing their questions, but Angelus had simply responded, "Yes, but it is not necessary to know."

The form of Angelus fully materialized, and as usual, got to the point. *Are we losing her*? she asked without feeling the need for words here; without any pretext of greeting.

Devon floated within the circle of figures. "They are working on gaining power over her, but not yet. She is very strong."

Angelus looked at him with a somewhat disapproving eye, as she could clearly see in his aura, another influence that was having its way

148

over Devon.

Without speaking to what she saw, she asked dispassionately, *Are you still willing to do what is necessary, should our worst fears materialize?*

"Godness forbid it should be necessary."

I asked if you are still willing, Young One.

Another figure in the Circle nodded to speak, and after Angelus nodded faintly, he turned to say, "After all, Devon. We almost lost you once as well."

Anguished at the insinuation, he replied curtly, "Yes. I know, Brian. I'm well aware of the dangers."

She is a very powerful being, this Kathryn, Angelus *said. They will not loose so powerful a being that they have worked to create for so long, so willingly.*

"If she is not successfully brought to us," another other Elder said, "She must be destroyed. Utterly. We cannot allow for the possibility of —"

"I know," Devon interrupted forcefully. "And I am willing. That is all that I can say to all of you.

Angelus continued as if everything was normal, *She is one of the most powerful beings I have seen for many, many centuries, if not for a very long time. You must not fail at your task. If she is not what she appears to be, We would lose—*

Sensing where this was going, Devon replied grimly but

respectfully, "I will do what is necessary, Ancient."

We understand your attachment to this one, Angelus continued, as if she hadn't heard. *But you must not let it—*

Very weary now, Devon nodded, "Yes. I know."

Angelus continued, *We will help you as much as we can. Our very lives are bent to this purpose until she is safe.*

"I understand, Ancient."

If she falls, or should be bent or willingly turns to their Dark Intent, our time here may be at an end. You know what we must do then.

"Godness wills it," Devon ended with a mental bow.

Angelus merely nodded silently and began fading along with the other members of the Council, back into the purple-ish darkness once again resolving into the illusion of distant clouds.

FOURTEEN

The next morning Kat woke with a start once again, sitting up in bed and remembering where she was. Not in her own bed, but in a strange motel room with a strange Man, sitting in a trance at the door.

She relaxed back into the lumpy mattress she was surprised had let her sleep, and began first taking in the tattered ceiling paint, and then the curtains barely covering the windows now blaring daylight. She also realized that she had slept once again, throughout the night. *Without nightmares*, she thought.

The smell of the room was not to her liking either. It seemed musty and ancient, as if this motel had been here for hundreds of years.

Looking around this strange shoddy motel room, her eyes finally came to rest once again on Devon, who was still sitting in the same chair he was in when she went to sleep the morning before. As if he had not moved at all.

Except that this time his eyes were open and his hands were steepled in front of his face, and he was staring intently at her. *Have you slept at all*? she wondered.

"I trust you had a good nights sleep? No nightmares?" he asked her, just a little bit too dispassionately.

"Um, yes," she said tentatively, searching her mind to make sure she hadn't. (And that there weren't any remnants there waiting to jump out at her.)

"Thank you," she replied a little less tentatively, but still wondering why he was asking. Brushing back the covers slowly, unsure of what she would find there, she found she was still dressed in her what was now quickly turning grubby sweats.

Searching her mind once again, she felt that she had indeed had had a good nights sleep. And probably for the first time in a very long time. She felt both gratitude and surprise, telling him "Thank you," once again, and this time truly meaning it.

"How long..."

"That day and the next night," he answered.

"Oh."

Rising from his seat and pushing it out of the way, he told her with a little more compassion this time, "Good, because we need to leave now. And we have a very long ride ahead of us today."

Opening the door to the day slowly and carefully, the strong light from outside struck him full in the face, showing her it was sometime in the early morning.

Still with an edge of sleepiness she thought, (surprising herself), *He*

152

is kind of handsome after all.

"By the way," she said with a hint of her growing comfort coming through, "My friends call me Kat."

Was that a smile she thought she saw on his face for a second?

He turned and without further ado, walked out to and climbed back into the car. And she, wiping the sleep out of her eyes, followed him groggily into the blaring light of day, shaking her head to clear the sleepiness of the night.

Out to the car and off into another day of danger, she thought wearily.

It was cruising into late afternoon, and Kat was driving while Devon slept in the passengers seat beside her. She had had an entire morning of silence to think about her situation.

They were almost crossing over into Ohio at this point, having spent the night apparently somewhere in the eastern part of Pennsylvania. They had now gone into the tip of West Virginia, and of course, taken the hilly roads to get to this point.

When they had crossed over into this state, the signs had said, "Almost Heaven..." and for an instant Kat laughed at this, saying to herself, "I'm far from heaven at this point."

Self-conscious suddenly that she might have woken Devon up, she glanced over and saw that he hadn't moved a centimeter, so she returned her attention to the scenery in front of her and kept driving.

Cresting the ridge into Wheeling, West Virginia that the Old National Highway Route 40 took, she could see the state of Ohio from this high vantage point, leveling out flat in the hazy distance.

Devon had insisted on taking the back roads and staying off the main Interstates, so their progress was apparently much slower than it could have been. (Or she felt it should have been.)

"I'd do loops far north and south if it would help us to stay out of their line of sight," he had told her earlier.

"How are they supposed to see—" she had started to ask, and at the look that he gave her, had thought better of asking further.

She was in over her head here, and was catching the drift that she wasn't going to get any real answers until they got to wherever it was that they were going to.

Devon must have driven for a very long time before they had stopped at that motel for the day and the night they'd spent there. He had insisted though that they drive on back country roads only, as best as they could. "Driving on back country roads will allow us to stay as "off the radar" as much as we can," he had told her earlier.

"They'll expect us to flee as quickly as possible in as straight a line as possible," he'd said. "They'll be looking to the main interstates. And I don't want them to have a clear path to follow."

As she drove, she had been stealing occasional glances at him all morning long. Although his eyes seemed to be open at various times,

154

they had a vacant kind of stare, as if he were still in some sort of trance. She decided to let him be and just continue driving for as long as she could, doing her best to not linger on the seeming hopelessness of her situation.

The miles were removing her from the dreaming nightmare of her previous "life," and led on into the living nightmare her current reality had become, adding up as she drove (which was fine by her). The more miles she put between herself and That Place, she thought, she had hoped would bring her some kind of rest, if not peace.

There were many strange things about this man in the seat beside her. Looking back she figured, she must have stumbled out to meet him some time about ten o'clock that night. Since that night — the one in which what she considered her former "life" had "died" — she had not gotten any more assured that this man was what he was saying he was.

First there was his behavior at the motel he'd obviously been staying at. (Although it still seemed very strange, she was getting used to the strangeness of it.) And then there was this *trance* of his.

He was still as much of a mystery as a person though, more than just his name and that he said that he had been like her. Had he really been doing work somewhat similar to what she had been doing? *Perhaps*, she thought, *you're not that much more of a self-realized person outside of what you've told me that you've done than I was.*

155

It was hard to think that, considering her life had been an illusion, she still had to think in terms of having actually lived a life. Whatever that was.

She was going to have to find out all over again what this thing called "living" was supposed to be about. That was perhaps one of the most pressing (and depressing) questions that she was beginning to think that she should ask him.

Was this what his life had been like? *What kind of life was this for anyone?* she thought.

Returning to thinking about her present situation, she began piecing together the reality of her life now. *I've got to move forward,* she thought. *I can't keep on revisiting my former life, or otherwise I'd go stark raving mad.*

They had pulled into the motel from last night (yesterday?) sometime around six yesterday morning, she recounted. Even though she had slept through the first nights worth of driving, Devon must have driven almost six hundred miles since he had "rescued" her. Or had they?

Her sense of time was obviously as distorted as was the illusion of her former life. Could she really have slept through that first night and then through another day and night?

No, it didn't seem possible. When she and Tom had driven across country, it had taken most of a full day to cover that distance.

Devon must have driven back roads, twisting and turning for most of it, but they had still been in Pennsylvania when she woke up. She felt she remembered that much.

But being in a strange car with a strange man, she wouldn't normally have been able to sleep. And adding what had happened to her before...

She just couldn't have slept all that time, she decided. Could he have actually driven that whole time? She'd have to ask him when he "woke up." It just didn't quite make any sense.

"As if anything in my life does anymore," she said gruffly to the air.

shadows and **LIGHT**

FIFTEEN

The afternoon was quickly fading, bending it's way towards evening when Devon finally opened his eyes, suddenly seeming very wide awake.

"Are you doing ok?" he asked her, seemingly out of nowhere.

The sudden question hit her like a rifle shot after the hours of long silence and the rhythm of the road with its endless passing cars. She almost jumped through the roof of his rust bucket, as she suddenly found herself back in her body, after driving without being there.

Her rapidly beating heart and mind were trying hard to catch up, but all she managed to say was a weak "Yes" that sounded more like a mouse squeak.

"Maybe I should take—" he started to suggest.

Now back in the present, she wasn't sure she wanted to let him drive just yet. "Start by telling me more," Kat said, hungry for the knowledge that he obviously had. "It's still daylight, and surely we're far enough away that we should be safe enough to talk about it."

He was looking at her with more compassion than he had shown before; even more emotion — period. He sighed, and she felt that he was looking deep inside of her.

"Not really," he finally said.

Softening some more, his hand even began straying in her direction, he asked cautiously, "Are you sure you're ready—"

"Well, let's see. I've just left the only life I've ever known behind me," she interrupted, and it quickly turned it into a crazed breathless litany. "After finding out that that life wasn't what I thought it was; that the life I thought I'd led was all or mostly a lie.

"I've gone off in the middle of the night with a strange man that I don't know, who for all I know is a truly psychotic individual playing all sorts of mind games with my head. Who also — for all I know — had hypnotized me into believing that what I thought had happened actually happened when it didn't.

"And, I've done it all based on what most professionals would no doubt tell me would make me certifiable," she said as she finally stopped to catch her breath, loosening the iron grip she realized she had had on the wheel during this. "How much more ready do I need to be?"

He smiled grimly and said, "Fair enough," and shaking his head, thought to himself, *Maybe this was worth while after all.*

"What has my life—" she began to ask again.

"Not what you think," he said, stopping her before she started again with a gesture.

"Perhaps it's time for me to be driving again. That is, if we're going to be getting into this kind of discussion."

She was about to object, when she suddenly realized that she wasn't going to be able to keep driving much longer anyway, no matter how much she wanted to do her share.

"Ok," she sighed, and began pulling over.

As she did, she saw that they were slowing near a sign that said "Zanesville, 10 miles" on it. Zanesville, Ohio, that is. They were only in the middle of Ohio, after what she had felt was like driving all the way cross country to her. *Are we really going that slow?* she thought. *It feels like we should be in Missouri already. Or even...*

Then she remembered that she had just driven through West Virginia and into Ohio. *What's wrong with me?*

She felt woozy when she had opened the door and tried to stand. Before she knew it, Devon was at her side, with her elbow steady in his hand. She hadn't felt this way before as she had tried to get out.

Had she really been so affected by what happened back in... She tried to think of the name of the institution where she had been working at just a few days ago, but the name escaped her now.

"Why am I..." she tried to say, but thought better of asking.

"They're searching for you. While you were driving, you were calm. Once you started to move, They—"

"Know where I am?"

"Not exactly. But now you're feeling their attempts to find out where you are."

"Are they going to—"

"Find you? Not if I can help it," he said, with more emotion than she thought he could muster.

She found her strength returning as she felt her anger rising. "You know, I really wish you wouldn't finish my sentences for me. It's really annoying."

Gently letting go of her elbow, he surprised her by blushing. She felt her heart begin to melt at this simple emotional gesture; that he seemed to be genuinely sorry at this intrusion.

"I'm sorry," he said sighing quietly after a moment. "I know you're still just getting used to all of this. I apologize for—"

"Don't worry about it," she said, interrupting him this time. She felt her right hand wanting to rise up and touch this strange man. *He's been a gentleman ever since I met him*, she thought, and then blushed herself, realizing he could probably *hear* what she was thinking.

He continued walking towards the drivers seat and she towards the passengers. Once they'd changed places, each sat back in their own seat and paused.

After a long moment, Devon closed his door and turned the key. Before driving off, he turned in her direction to smile, but found that she had drifted off to sleep.

"Time enough for trauma later," he said to himself, glad that she had at least fastened her seat belt before she had fallen asleep. "I hope you're stronger than you seem even now."

She had cinched the seat belt and had adjusted herself to the bucket she was in, and felt as she let a breath out that she was suddenly sinking into — and through — the seat.

The car shimmered around her as if it were speeding up and she was staying behind, and then just as suddenly the car and Devon beside her disappeared in the distance, as if she had fallen through the seat and was standing on the now deserted highway.

She looked up at this and saw that the sky around her looked strange. It seemed as if it were daytime, but she could see stars above her now. The sky looked as if it had a shroud stretched across it and the stars shone now through the shroud.

Kat turned in the direction in which they came. As she did, it seemed to her that the sky darkened into deepest night, and the stars began going out in that Darkness. Even Darker *clouds* seemed to begin writhing up from the horizon, turning into numerous Dark *finger-like* *"clouds"* that floated this way and that, on an ill wind.

One such Finger began floating up in her direction. And as it did, the other fingers of Darkness began coalescing and then following It, growing as They/It did.

Kat turned around once again slowly, ready to panic and wanting to run, but saw that the car was there once again, as if it had never left.

163

A bright white Light was now surrounding it, pulsing and growing, as if some powerful night light had suddenly been lit in the growing darkness, and was growing stronger the more she focused on it, pressing back against the Darkness behind her.

Looking over her shoulder one last time, she saw now huge dark tentacles of a Black "cloud" trying desperately to close the distance between her and — Them, she knew now for certain — but couldn't quite decide in what specific direction she was standing.

These *fingers* now danced this way and then that, and then retreated and scattered themselves, venturing off in other directions.

And suddenly she felt herself slam back into her body, opening her eyes and sharply gulping air, as if she had been holding her breath for minutes. The car wasn't stationary but was cruising along at close to fifty, and the jolt left her feeling nauseous.

Turning towards Devon now, he had a strange look in his eyes. Not trance and not suspicion per se, but not a look she had seen before now.

"Now you know what it feels like. Yes?" he asked her darkly.

But "What was—" was all she got out, working hard to put words and sanity to the experience she had just found herself in.

She tried to find the words to describe what she was looking for — What was looking for her — and couldn't. Shaking her head to clear it, Devon's expression softened.

"As you rightly said a while ago, you only remember a small

amount of what you're used to calling "your life." What you just saw was—"

"Is that what you meant when you said that you *saw* what I did the other day?"

"Yes... And no. What you just saw now however was a glimpse. You still don't rely on your other senses yet, so you can't see visions clearly, but only as dream-like hints.

"Your life has not been your own up until now. You've lived and breathed for Something that you didn't even know you served. You now know that."

Stunned at this blunt acknowledgement, she just managed to let out a pitiful, "Ok." She hadn't expected for him to agree with her assessment so quickly and readily.

Not that he hadn't basically told her as much before, but it was just the sound of the finality to it that left her speechless and hurting. She wasn't at all sure now that she wanted to know any more of the answers.

With a sigh turning into a shiver, she did her best to keep her eyes on the road in front of her. At least that hopefully was solid and unwavering, she told herself.

He almost told her, *No, not really*, but stopped himself.

Sizing her up and probing deeply once more, he lowered his voice. Whether it was for her sake or not, she didn't know, he said, "You are now becoming altogether more aware of what your previous life held you hostage with."

Hostage. "Were the patients really hearing the voices that they were listening to?" she asked quietly, already knowing the answer.

He sighed and shook his head. "No. You know the difference between the two. The experiences your "clients" recounted to you are what they experienced; what they are now and have been through — not a "who" they were listening to.

"There's a very big difference between a dissociative's personalities and those that a schizo-effective person is hearing. In the case of a schizophrenic, they're listening to humans who have have left their bodies when they died, but have not fully crossed over yet into the full Totality field of Spirit.

"Because of the schizophrenic's genetic makeup, or misuse of drugs which triggered that potential, they're listening to "voices" that, even though they no longer have bodies and wouldn't be considered "real" by most, are still very much real."

Pausing to let this sink in, Devon thought Kat would have an avalanche of questions. Instead, she took this in waiting on him to fill in the blanks.

"Those Voices that the schizophrenic hears, are of those that have chosen to stay behind when their bodies die."

"You mean, Ghosts?" she asked, not sure of whether to believe any of this either.

"Yes. The Ones that have been around a long time after death.

They still manage to have some semblance of corporeal form, but without a body to inhabit. Like that which we are fighting, They develop the ability to *influence* the *physical* realm, and feel that they have power over it. That they remain close to the physical, even if They're not still in it."

Her eyes wide again, she whispered, "But Multiples—"

"The "Voices" you've heard coming out of Multiples however... Those are the formerly "real" beings who though they no longer have a body of their own, were killed specifically to "share" that body for further Ritual purposes.

"Your *patients* were reliving what they had lived through — and with many of them, also how they died — when you got them to that point."

She knew that what Devon was telling her was true, but she was still having a hard time grappling with the reality of what she'd been a part of.

She thought of asking him more questions, but found she couldn't gather her thoughts. Everything was still very much hazy, as if she were being protected from the full knowledge.

"Up until now, you've only dealt with the petty little demons that some of your "clients" represented," Devon began again, now very much in earnest.

"Petty little—" she repeated, the shock deepening.

"Negative souls who had been grafted energetically onto the bodies

167

of the "clients" you had been dealing with," Devon continued, pausing to let this last one sink in.

And the souls of the tortured dead, he also wanted to tell her, again stopping himself.

"But then, you started to get too close to the territory of truth. You began bringing up "conversations" with the Not So Petty, but altogether too real Demons."

Knowing how, but still wanting it explained, she asked with great trepidation, "So..." she started. Even though she had been guided through the process by her patients memories many times over, she still wanted him to verify it as truth.

"Through the Rituals. Designed to metaphysically sheer the soul from the body of the sacrificial victim, which then gets grafted onto one of the energetic bodies of another participating — although we use that term quite loosely — victim. They do this in order to use the spiritual essence—"

"Satanic..." she began to say, feeling as if her insides were being flayed all over again, along with those of the remembered victims.

"Yes. Only the Being that you're thinking of that's central to all of this, what you would call Satan... is not what you're thinking It is. Not what—"

"Not what I'm thinking," she repeated, this time dully. "So... What exactly is—" she said, and then paused before repeating the usual title that she had heard numerous times. But this time she was both feeling

168

and reeling from the reality of — "It?"

There is a reality to all of it, but not in the so-called Biblical Sense. That's just a myth to hide the real Truth.

"Millennia ago, the Being that is now referred to along with many other names as "The Father of All Lies," created the central Lie around Itself — that It was a... Fallen Angel. That It had been at the *right hand of God.*"

"Ok," she said quietly.

"Then it created the similar mythology that, in another guise, it was also that very same God that it supposedly sat at the right hand of."

"Well, that's quite a feat," she said, trying hard not to laugh at this. "And just how did the—"

"Christianity has basically been a process of co-option of all the multiple gods that the pagan traditions that It wanted to supersede had worshipped.

"It," he hesitated to say That Name with the approaching night, "took all of the primitive religions — including the whole 'vengeful god' thing that was at the core of the primitives way of explaining what we now call *Acts of God.*"

"So you're telling me that Christianity is all the work of the Devil?"

Sighing and giving her a look, Devon paused. "That's not what the man behind the religion wanted."

She paused and turned towards him full on. "So, you're telling me that — It — took what Jesus said and twisted it?"

"They've done their best to pervert whatever they could. Emperor Constantine put it most bluntly when he said, "If you can not win over a people by dint of war, move in and take over their religion, and win them thusly"."

"Constantine?"

"The Emperor of Byzantium? The Byzantine Empire that took over after the Roman Empire fell? He took the opportunity of this new religion and used it to conquer both the Jews and the new Christians."

"So you're telling me that all of Christianity is a lie?" she asked him, flabbergasted.

"No. That's not what I'm telling you. I'm saying that the Forces of Darkness always try to pervert everything to their own advantage. That doesn't mean that they succeed.

"The Truth is still there, no matter how many lies they try to heap on top of it."

She slowly began turning back around and started slumping into the seat. Letting go a great big sigh, she said (without hope), "So there's still hope. Even though is seems like there is no hope."

"Yes, Virginia," he said with his first hint of humor, "There is still a hope clause in our contract. Otherwise, do you think I would have come to your rescue?"

She couldn't help it, but a smirk began growing. "You're my knight in shining armor?"

Growing more playful himself (even though he wasn't feeling as

170

positive as he was trying to convey to her), he said, "Let's just say that — I felt you were worth saving. We all did."

This last comment struck her sour once again. "We. You keep on referring to a We."

"We — are the group of that which You are going towards." Unable to keep his fears from completely showing, Devon grew pensive. "And I wish I could tell you more about this mysterious "We," but I can't tell you until I get you there. We just can't risk it."

Her mental state plunged once again as she realized (not without reason) that she was still considered a wild card at best. Since she had not known of her real life before (was it really only four days ago?), she also realized that she could not know whether she wasn't indeed a trap laid to kill this mysterious *We* that Devon had referred to or not.

She could be a dark double agent, trained to look like something *worth* saving, and then turn against these surmised soldiers of Good once she was in their den.

"Am I ever going to know if I'm dangerous or not?" she asked, with a little too much of a little girl-sounding whine creeping into her voice. She was suddenly feeling both tremendously sad, as well as dangerously anxious.

Keeping his eyes straight on the road ahead, Devon said both quietly and carefully, "I think that you are what you seem. That whatever Their plans for you had been, you are still represent The Truth behind their Lies."

Pausing for a moment, Devon began saying almost as if to himself again, "I wouldn't have risked my life, if I didn't think you were worth it."

Instead of hearing the passion in his voice, she only felt crushed by this. The weight of not knowing was leaning down on her heavily and was breathing a foul breath that was making her begin to feel nauseous.

"I want to know," she said. And then said, "I need to know."

His voice softening, he turned to her with a very compassionate look on his face. "We would also like to know, Dr. Runyon."

Please! Call me Kat, she started to say again, but stopped. She didn't want to feel anything at this point. But didn't know if she felt that the bond of trust that was growing between them was a lie or not.

She so wanted someone — this man, perhaps? To actually know her and love her for who she really was.

But she couldn't trust herself to know *who* she was, even to herself. *How can I ask him to be familiar with me if I'm not even sure I'm familiar with myself?*

As if picking up on this, he said, "Trust your Inner Self. Trust That which came out of you and helped you to get away from them.

"You've shown up to this point that you're not one of Them. You can't let doubts poison your beliefs to the point where you allow yourself to become one of Them.

"I know it sounds corny, but you have to have faith in yourself

172

first. And then perhaps you'll know the Truth inside. Know whether you're of The Light or one of the shadows of the Darkness."

"I wish I could just be sure. I'd want to kill myself if I turned out to be a mole bringing Them to destroy you."

Reaching his hand out, this time in a gesture of physical comfort and not psychic manipulation, he started to say, "Once more, Kathryn —"

But she reached out her hand to meet his, and said, "Call me Kat. Please?"

Their fingers touched, energetically if not physically, and a slight charge passed between them.

After a long silence with Devon driving and Kat relaxing, she turned towards him, wanting to ask him more.

She had spent the last few hours with her eyes closed, trying to piece her life together, shifting through the memories to feel out what was real and what only seemed like it was real. She wanted to ask him more questions that might help her in ferreting out those seeming secrets.

But looking in his direction, she could tell that he was once again in a trance state, going wherever he went when he did. She supposed that he was only meditating, but hadn't worked up the courage to ask.

He seemed to sense her looking at him after a while, but kept his eyes focused on the road in front of them. A moment or two more, and he turned to look directly at her.

She hadn't told him, but it still freaked her out even after all his driving, that he didn't appear to be watching the road while he drove.

"I'm not entirely absent," he said, upsetting her once again by reading her mind. "I'm sorry, but if you don't ask I can't address your concerns any other way," he said, this time smiling.

His smile was starting to work its magic on her, much in the same way that Tom's voice could.

Except that she didn't feel that Devon was manipulating her with that his smile. She felt it was genuine, helped by the frequency with which it was now appearing on his face.

"Don't you get tired of driving without looking?" she asked playfully.

"It helps in circumstances like these, when I can't get a lot of sleep," he replied.

Encouraged by his transparency, she said (equally playfully), "So, where exactly do you go when you do this trance thing?"

"A great many places. But mostly, just inside."

"Inside. And what happens if something suddenly jumps out in front of you while you're driving and you're — inside?"

"Then I quickly come *outside* to deal with it."

She was skeptical, but she had to admit that he did manage to know when she was looking at him, or was thinking of talking to him. "That easily," she said, her playful skepticism dripping with sarcasm now.

174

Smiling that smile, he turned around to face her once more with, "Yes. It's that easy."

His expression changing from playful to serious unexpectedly, he continued. "You see, even when it seems that I'm not here, I am. On some level. And—"

"On some level," she repeated, curious but unsure if he was telling her the truth now.

"It's hard to explain if you don't know how to do it," he said slowly. Taking a deep breath in, he continued carefully. "It's like dissociation, except it's a kind of willful dissociation.

"And unlike with dissociation, I'm still aware of what's going on around me."

"How can you be aware if your eyes are closed?" Was this his way of not wanting to tell her what was happening?

"Well, as you've probably noticed," he said, growing back in the direction of playful, "My eyes stay open. Just in case I need them to be more open quickly."

"Oh, come on. You're pulling my leg now."

She looked over at him and was surprised to see a mischievous expression on his face. Wishing that she could read his mind as readily as he could hers, she said warily, "Ok, I'll take the bait. Explain it, mister magician."

After a silence that started veering into brooding, Devon continued. "When my eyes seem closed and blank, I'm not seeing the outside world as you and others see it, so much as I'm seeing it as fields of energy. And other levels of reality."

Her mood began plummeting. She had managed to engage him in a less burdened conversation for a little while, but it hadn't — unfortunately for her taste — lasted for very long.

She had found herself starting to wish that she and Devon had met under much less dire circumstances. If they had, perhaps they could have looked forward to a fun road trip together. But that wasn't the case now.

"Other levels of reality?" she asked, unsure she wanted to pursue it.

"Did you ever read the Don Juan books by Carlos Castaneda?"

"Yes. Once upon a time," she said.

"Well, although most of the books were a mixture of fairy tales and summations of real truth, the basic tenets of the books were based on reality. If you can call what they talked about as reality," he added.

"Reality is *real*? Isn't it?" she asked tentatively.

His smirk returning, he said ironically, "Not really."

Closing her eyes now, she asked with great trepidation, "So what is it, this thing called *Reality*?"

"You obviously haven't read much Buddhist thought, either. Have you?"

"So you're saying that "reality" is an illusion," she stated, although she didn't really believe that.

"Well up until a few days ago, your whole life's reality, forgive me

176

for saying it, was an illusion. What's so hard to accept that reality in general is an illusion?"

"I guess because I need to think of something around me as being real.

"Even if it isn't," she said, deflating into her seat.

"Well, since you read Castaneda, you know that we are all energetic beings."

"That part is true?" she asked.

"Yes," he said, with a simple answer that answered nothing.

"And this is supposed to make sense to me," she said quietly.

"What I'm seeing when I'm in trance, is the energy flux or signature of everything that is around us. I can see lines of energy that tell me when something is coming in our direction. Something that I need to pay attention to."

"Lines of energy." Kat was once again beginning to feel sorry that she had asked. It was almost too much for her to take in.

"This can wait for later discussion, if you're feeling overwhelmed," he said, his look of compassion returning to his formerly blank state.

Kat was feeling unsure of what, if anything, she was prepared to hear at this point; much less to try and take in. She was feeling as if she really needed to be asleep right now, but was also feeling that she needed to stay awake.

Even if she didn't dream, Devon was — in her mind — still running on empty. She had to be ready to take over if he needed her to.

177

"What I'm trying to explain to you," he continued more softly, "Is that I *am* paying attention to my driving. Just not in the normal way. And my meditation also helps me to take care of my lack of sleep."

"Meditation does that?"

Reaching to find an adequate way to express it, she saw his eyes searching.

"We're calling it meditation for ease in translation," he said.

She wanted to say to him, That doesn't really explain anything.

"When I go inside," he continued, in answer to her unasked quandary, "I am going beyond space and time. Where I go, I'm able to tap into energy in a way that our bodies are not able to get from food."

"So you're saying that this trance state is actually better than sleep?" she asked.

"Different," he said. "I will still need to get sleep soon, though. I still need to rest on both the body and mind level."

"You mean, you won't dream?"

"Can't say. I might. Then again, I might not."

"This isn't making any sense," she said, exasperation threatening to take over. *Maybe some things are better not to know,* she thought.

Tired of dealing with all this philosophy, she asked another question she hadn't felt comfortable asking. "And what is our part in all of this supposed to be?" she asked. "What is my life leading up to? Do you know? Can you see that?"

Shifting direction, he returned to watching the road and not talking

178

for a long time.

His silence began growing so long that she started to suspect that he had gone into another trance. Except that his eyes didn't have that faraway look to them. He seemed to be searching once again for what to say.

Finally he began, "We're entering what the Fundamentalists call the "End Times," and what we call *The Shift*."

Laughing lightly, she echoed, "The Shift. What the hell is that? You make it sound like—"

"Shift in consciousness. As in, the whole planet if we're lucky."

Stumped by this, "So... What do you mean by lucky?"

"Because it comes down to choice... And Free Will."

Shifting uneasily, she finally turns toward him fully. "But what if —"

"The deepest darkness is in the mind."

"But what about—"

"The Red Circle is merely perverting the powers that all of us already have. Using those powers to prolong their physical life, and to gain Power over others.

Turning towards her and appearing to become... A glowing Being of Light. "You see, we are all powerful beings. We choose to forget that power when we come into this life."

Just when Kat thought that her eyes would never be able to get any wider than they had in the last few days... She fought going into her dissociative self at this — illusion? — that he was showing her.

Snapping back to his regular appearance suddenly, "The Red Circle is using that power for Its own purpose and not that of God's."

She wanted to look away from this man. She wanted to get out of the car the next opportunity she could and run away.

But she also knew that that would be the death of her.

After a while, all she could think about (softly) asking was, "Then there is a God?"

"Of course there is. Just not what you think of as God."

"You mean just like the Devil too, I suppose?"

"No. The *Devil* is a physical entity. But That Which Is — what most of humanity calls God — is not. The Other It... is beyond most humans capability of even imagining, much less understanding.

"That's why even naming It is considered blasphemy."

"It. Then... How? What Is... It?"

"That, my dear, is a discussion for much later," he said, and left it at that, realizing that Kat was at the end of her being able to process any more.

"Why don't you try to get some sleep. I'll wake you in about another hour or so, so I can rest."

Kat reluctantly sighed, and laid her head against the glass of the window. The subtle vibrations of the road and the rocking motion of the car, soon put her once again back into her dream-less sleep.

SIXTEEN

Kat woke up again suddenly, finding that it was full night. The cars that were passing them on either side were blurs of white, and then red lights.

Playfully she asked him, "Are we there yet?"

Having gotten more out of Devon than she had thought she would earlier, she was reluctant to ask him about the even darker areas of her life, especially now that the night was deep. She knew she couldn't risk waking anything she didn't need to.

"Why don't you tell me about you?" she asked suddenly. "What was your life like before all of this?"

"Largely a lie, like yours. I was a workaholic of course, even though I didn't know why. I had had a succession of girlfriends, but never felt that I could really take enough time away from "my work" to get married or "settle down".

"I found out though that, much like you, that wasn't really my choice in the matter. It was all merely part of their plan."

"So you were just like me?"

"Yes. I was a Sentinel as well. Just like you were," he said, with a weight to his words that she had not expected.

"A Sentinel. You keep using that word."

He paused, looking as if he were doing his best to break it down simply and succinctly. "Sentinels are those of us in the mental health field who are placed there by... The Cult. Set in place to watch over multiples; to make sure that they stay in their place, and that their *stories* don't get *validated*. Especially by any Press. That they and their stories are kept in the arena of *crazy people talk*."

"We were there to put them in their place if need be, and to keep them silent," she said, and out of nowhere, "And docile."

"Yes, quite frankly. And most of us did our jobs as we were directed and influenced to."

"But you and I—"

"You and I are the ones that They can't control. When we go rogue as it were, most of us are influenced back into the mental underground of the Cult. Or killed, as they tried to do to you."

"But why aren't there more reports of missing children and all of these strange activities? Surely it's not just the multiples who are a danger with keeping this secrecy?"

"They have their own People in places both high and low. Like your boyfriend, Detective Wolfe."

"*High* and low?"

"Police. Judges. Reporters to Corporate Magnates. They make sure that any news of — those kinds of activities — are minimized, and if they do pop up, are readily and easily discredited.

"And yes, that's also where Sentinels come in," Devon said, pausing for a moment and going inward. "The whole "false memory syndrome" industry is there to counteract the revelations of therapists uncovering repressed memories. To either turn them into laughing stock quackery, or *scientifically prove* that they don't exist."

"But why don't they just influence those therapists like they influenced us?" Kat asked.

Coming back to the present, he turned to her and said, "They can't influence everything. That's why UFO's continue to stay in the news."

Laughing outright at this one, Kat said, "And now you're going to tell me that the whole UFO thing is real, too? Right? Let's take the girl for a ride?"

"What did you think I was telling you about... That Otherworldly Being? If It's not a fallen angel, then what is it supposed to be?"

"You're saying that *It* is some kind of an alien."

"Yes. That's what I've been telling you. I didn't think that I had to fill in between the lines."

"But you're talking about..."

He hesitated for a long time before finally saying, "It has been alive for an extremely long time. The lifetime of one of Its kind can normally be thousands of years."

Still incredulous, she hesitated to ask but did anyway. "And It is... how many years old?"

"By the accounts of those who should know, It is close to seventy thousand years old. When they call It *Old Scratch*, they aren't kidding."

Her mouth was now almost hanging open again. She closed it and began asking in a horse whisper, "How—"

"That, my dear Kat, is what — what happens in your Nightmares — are for. Prolonging *Its* life. Far beyond that of even Its own kind."

Kat wanted to laugh at all of this, but closing her eyes she knew that what Devon was telling her was Truth. No matter how crazy it seemed.

"It has used the psychic energy stored in us, to live the life that It has."

Feeling quite exhausted now, Kat wanted to close her eyes again, and tell Devon that she wanted to go to sleep.

Except that she was afraid now to go to sleep, fearful of what dreams would be breaking in to interrupt.

After a good long while of thinking, she asked him quietly, "Are we ever going to win this war?"

"That's not up for us to decide," he said quite grimly, facing forward.

"It's not?" she asked, feeling herself sinking into a black pit inside.

"No," he said, with exhaustion beginning to really show.

"Are we at the next There yet," she asked in an exhaustedly playful way. Inside, she knew that they both needed to sleep. If they could.

"Not yet. There's just a little way more to go, and we can stop for the night."

Reaching his right hand out in her direction, she suddenly felt her mind calming, as if he were reaching out towards her in some sort of metaphysical way to calm her.

She felt the tension that had begun at the beginning of this necessary discussion to begin releasing from her body, and she felt her head sinking towards her chest. With a lot of effort (and no doubt Devon helping her in this), she began pulling it back up.

She was about to suggest that she drive for a little while, but sleep was still a closing of her eyes for a mere few seconds away. No sense in their driving off the road and crashing, she thought.

"So, if... It—" she began to ask.

Looking at her and somehow judging her credibility level wasn't up to the explanation, he said, "What It really is, is probably something we shouldn't be discussing, even here and now. Even with the sun at noon, but much less now."

As he told her this, she realized that while he had been focusing on both driving and the discussion, she was surprised that he had talked about what he did.

"Come to think of it," he said, "Now isn't really the time to be discussing any of this."

"When is going to be the time?" she asked, both wanting to

continue the conversation and also wanting to put it off as long as she could.

"During the day. And preferably in the safe location."

"Is there any such place as a safe location?" she asked, not believing there was such a place.

"This isn't much of a vacation, is it?" he asked, more of his darker sense of humor popping through again.

"Oh," she said, and let it go at that.

After a while, she drifted back off to sleep.

She was brought back to wakefulness by Devon very gently tapping on her shoulder some time later. Even through the touch she felt the gentleness as much as the physical pressure. And as soon as he could see that she was awake, he asked her suddenly, "Would you mind taking over the driving? At least for a while?" He had begun to start feeling quite exhausted.

"Of course," she replied, stretching. She had been getting some good, dream-less sleep while Devon drove, but her body was also starting to feel it. Even with the cushions under and behind her that he had finally retrieved from the trunk earlier.

His kind look reinforced the feeling that was coming off of him. "That is, if you're up to it," he added.

She didn't *really* feel up to it, but she was becoming concerned that he was doing all of the driving, and that sooner or later, he was not going to be able to keep it up. "Of course," she said. "I probably have a couple of hours in me at least."

"That'd be good," he said, smiling sleepily. "That'll be all we need, actually."

Concerned that he was going to try and drive almost the whole way, she was almost to the point of suggesting they spend another night at a motel.

She wasn't sure of what his finances were in all of this, and since he wouldn't let her get any money out of her bank account, he was paying for all of it.

Or perhaps the mysterious Others that he was working with supplied him with whatever he would need to do his work rescuing people like her.

"That'd probably be a good idea," he said, kindness resonating in his voice. "Actually, we'll be stopping soon anyway. We're far enough away to have another nights rest in a motel." And turning to her, he added with his head turned to the side as if assessing her, "Don't you think?"

"Oh," she said once again, beginning to feel redundant.

As he was pulling over to the shoulder, she started to ask him where, but once again as if he were answering her unasked question, "There's a safe house another few hours' drive away from here, where we can spend the night and there'll be someone to help in keeping watch."

"A safe house," she repeated, unsure completely of what that meant for them. *Like we're spies in some Eastern Europe country*, she thought. "Does that mean you'll actually be able to get some sleep?" she asked, starting to think of other things besides sleep.

Not catching the last part of her intended meaning, he answered with a weary, "Yes," and left it at that.

"If you sleep for several hours, will that be enough time for you to drive the rest of the way to this "safe house"?"

"It'll have to be. Just let me know if you start feeling sleepy. Ok?"

She nodded her head. She hoped that this trip would be over soon. She wasn't sure of how much longer either she or Devon would be able to drive like this.

Switching seats, Kat eased herself across to sit behind the wheel, as he got out and walked around to the passengers side door.

SEVENTEEN

As a sort of a benediction to their long days travel and having finally reached somewhere where they could relax, the sun had given off a last glancing glow to the rooftops of the cars and trucks that were in the distance in front of them. The rear view mirror showed a patch of the last sun glinting off the old asphalt highway stretching back off into the East where they'd come from.

She had been at the wheel when they had crossed the Ohio/Illinois State line. *It seems like we've been driving for weeks, she thought. Where are we going to?*

"Pull over here," Devon said suddenly. She hadn't even realized he was awake again, (if he'd even really been asleep, that is).

Sitting behind the wheel for as long as she had this time, she realized that not only was the drivers seat a little more cushioned, but that even with the seat under her as lumpy as it was, it was good to get out of her constant sleeping. She hadn't driven quite that far and without breaks for quite some time. (Or so she remembered.)

They were at another one of those run-down motels out in the middle of nowhere. He got out of the car and heading towards the dingy looking office, left her sitting there.

She suddenly realized how much trust he was placing in her. *I could just drive the car away at any moment*, she thought. Except of course, she didn't.

As he got back in, she caught the look of absolute exhaustion in his eyes he'd been careful to conceal before. Even with that short sleep, he must be getting very tired, she suddenly realized as well.

Kat began to ask, "Why can't we—".

"I think you know the answer to that one," he told her with a smirk.

"But wouldn't one of these old run down flea bags be more likely to be run by—"

"Maybe. Except I chose this one specifically because it's safe. I know they're not the most appealing of places to think of staying in, but the corporate motels are the ones that They actually watch most particularly."

"And wouldn't they also know that?"

Turning towards her and faintly smiling — *Why have I yet to see him really smile*? she thought to herself.

"They know a great many things. But they still have to find us." And now definitely smiling, he added, "Mrs. Woolsley."

Stunned, she said to the air, "He's just made a joke." At least, she

190

thought it was a joke. Maybe here in the midwest it was a good idea for them fit in as a married couple.

But she was still a little stunned. "Does that mean we'll actually be able to take a shower?" she asked hopefully.

"Not only that, they even have some clean clothes for us."

Suddenly realizing just how much she had not been aware of her other senses besides sight and hearing, she leaned down to smell her sweatshirt and was appalled at what she found herself smelling. "That'll be good. Unless they also have a washer and dryer as well."

Growing grim once more, Devon looked at her solemnly and said, "That's not a good use of our time at this point."

Brought back to the perilousness of their situation, she sighed. "No, I guess not," she said deflating.

"And they're not exactly going to have the latest fashions, but they'll help us fit in a little more for the times and places we'll be around for a while."

"Ok," she said without any emphasis, her hands loosening their grip on the steering wheel. She also felt her head leaning towards the window a little too quickly. Her mind was already leaning towards sleep.

With the last light of dusk having faded outside, not much of it was pushing its way through the curtains. The old neon motel sign with half of it's letters barely lit, cast a strange, eery and garish glow through the top and bottom of the severely ratty curtains that gave them negligible privacy.

Kat had taken a shower and washed her hair, but hesitated at some of the towels. They were a dingy yellow, as if used too many times. She picked the least yellowed one, and after smelling it, decided to used it. It didn't smell as old and bad as it looked.

She wrapped herself up in it afterwards, feeling once again that she was human. *What I wouldn't give for just a little bit of perfume and makeup*, she thought.

Handing her the clothes before her shower that he had been given by his "friends" here, she had taken them reluctantly. No, she was not going to be winning any fashion shows in these. They were plain — serviceable, and clean — but that's all she could say for them.

Without having taken them into the bathroom with her (it was highly questionable anyway with the shower and it's dirty tile and not exactly sweet smelling water), she was coming out of the bathroom dressed in only a towel.

The thought crossed her mind suddenly that, *although I've only known this man for five days, I already trust him enough to walk out of the bathroom in just a towel. And still feel safe.*

Finding him where she left him, sitting in the chair propped by the door in meditation, she continued drying her hair.

Trying to decide whether she should leave him to this rest or not, she asked, "Don't you ever get tired of being on the run like this? I

192

mean, this is your life, isn't it."

Opening his eyes slightly at this, "Yes," he whispered loudly. "But it's necessary."

"And don't you get any rest? Isn't there somewhere where you can just relax and be yourself? Without always needing to shield yourself, that is?"

Sighing and sitting up fully in the chair, "That's why we're doing this; taking you to that someplace safe. Somewhere where I *can* relax again as well."

Perking up at this, "You keep telling me this, but are we going to get there soon? We don't have to drive all the way to the West Coast, do we?"

Sobering suddenly, his face closing up, "I can't tell you just yet," he told her sighing. "I wish I could, but we'll be there soon enough."

Deflating, Kat returned to vigorously drying her hair. "What I wouldn't give for a good hair dryer at this point," she said, half to him and more to herself.

"At least you were able to take a shower," he smirked. It didn't hurt her feelings that she had caught his eyes wandering down her towel-wrapped body discretely.

Throwing her hair towel at him, "You know, it wouldn't hurt for you to take a shower every once in a while. I'm sure they wouldn't find us if you relaxed your guard for just ten minutes."

Devon rose with a smirk again and began walking towards the

bath. "Yes, dear," he said jokingly. And passed within several inches of her.

Feeling an emotional charge as he passed her, she was flinching as he closed the door behind her. Kat sighed and then shivered.

Looking away and catching a glimpse of herself in the dingy mirror over the desk, she was shocked to see a look of intense, deep longing creeping over her face. She once again found her gaze being drawn in the direction of the bathroom door.

Throwing herself on the bed, she pinched the clothes she had worn for days now, and really wished she could get a quick washing for them too.

They'd have to go in the trash though, she thought. God knows she'd gotten — what? Three, four good days out of them?

She walked over to the bed, hesitating to pull the shabby covers down suspecting the worst, but found that the sheets and covers at least looked clean. This wasn't so hard to let herself do, she thought.

Laying down on the newly turned bed and looking up at the ceiling, she reached up and pulled the towel free, laying it neatly on either side of her like wings. She lay there naked wondering what this man was going to do coming out of the bathroom and finding his "wife" lying naked, waiting for his presence to descend on her.

She had been with Tom exclusively for almost her entire adult life, but looking back on those years now, she hardly felt at any time that she had been in a real relationship.

194

And apparently, she hadn't been. Part of her had felt that all those years, quietly acquiescing to the will of the very Cult that she hadn't believed existed, were devastatingly wasted.

But here she was, in a strange (and not very inviting) dingy no-star motel. With a man she had barely met before just days ago, who had jokingly (not more than an hour ago) called her his "wife," (merely for all she knew, for the sake of their "safety" and "cover"). And here she was leaving her still moist towel wide open, offering her body for his taking.

She hadn't been a hippie. Indeed she had spent most of the late sixties in school for her various degrees, more concerned with studying than having random sex. She had only had one relationship with a man (a boy?), before Tom had entered her life (which was apparently planned). Perhaps her previous boyfriend had been a plant as well?

Fingering the ends of the towel, she let them lay where they were. Then, she rose off the bed suddenly, whipping the towel off the bed and lay back down pulling the ragged covers back over her. She had felt altogether too naked in the last few days for her to stay lying still and uncovered in this cold and grimy room.

She heard the water of the shower squeaking to a stop now. Imagining this man who she wouldn't have looked at twice before now, much less consider being in the company of, she was now *seeing* him in the shower. The world being very different, she imagined him shaved and smelling nice. And she imagined him desiring her in a way that Tom never had.

She looked at the ceiling, now blurred by a pool of tears, and wanted comfort. She wanted to be loved. And she didn't even know if, having what she wanted, she would even be able to feel anything, much less love.

Her life had not been her own — none of it apparently. Of that she was now becoming quite painfully aware of and certain. She had done what was expected of her, both at the hospital and in the occasionally accepting arms of Tom. But the growing ache was quickly approaching becoming an avalanche of pain.

If Devon were as lonely as she was (and she suspected he was), she would take whatever comfort he would — perhaps could — give her.

Not hearing the water anymore, she began composing herself in what she thought was a seductive pose, hoping that he wouldn't come out and laugh at her. Or at the worst that she could imagine, rebuff her for laying a trap for him.

She was feeling a rising excitement in her heart as well as her body, when the door to the bathroom opened slowly.

A refreshed and surprisingly relaxed Devon was coming out, sighing and shivering, not from cold but from the exhaustion that had been washed away.

Wrapped unselfconsciously in his own towel tied at his waist, he was coming out almost unseeing in his own world, that had nothing whatsoever with when he went in. He wasn't in a trance; only a state of exhaustion.

That is, until his gaze fell on the naked Kat lying in bed with the covers pulled down invitingly.

"My friends and family call me Kat, Mr. Woolsley. I figure if we're married, you might as well call me Kat, too," she said, pulling her legs open and stretching seductively. "Ready to come to bed, honey?"

Standing there dripping and in shock himself for the first time, the only thing he could manage to get out was a feeble, "Yes, dear" sort of automatic response. His eyes though told a much different story. There was a hunger there she had not seen before.

His hair and his beard now clean and combed, he was not only looking "presentable" to Kat's eyes, but she realized that his featureless "dress to disappear" clothes had hidden a lean muscled (though not sculpted — he was no Adonis) body that was most likely the result of his being on the run. *Not exactly body building material,* she thought, *but real easy on the eyes.*

Seeing him now almost as if for the first time, she found she was admiring this man as a man, not fearing him as some mysterious and dangerous stranger.

For his part, once he began recovering from the unexpected presence of the body that was lying there invitingly open, he began seeing her almost for the first time as well.

He saw her desperate vulnerability. How much she had been

aching for some true contact which she had so obviously never really had. And he saw a mirror of his own wants and desires.

As he began moving slowly towards the bed in anticipation as well the hunger of his own, he untied the towel as he walked, letting it fall as enticingly to the floor as she lay there in all her naked glory.

He smiled warmly and fully at her for the first time since they had met, now feeling sure in his heart as well as his mind that this was no trap.

A satisfied smile came creeping over her face as she watched him move towards her. She sighed eagerly, witnessing his growing interest rise as he came closer.

She opened her arms up to him, feeling as if her heart were going to explode before they touched. As he first touched and then began kneeling on the bed, he slowing and gently lowered himself down to land (also ever so gently) on top of her.

She opened her legs even wider to accept him, folding him into her arms, letting the warmth of his lean body press down comfortingly on top of her.

This wasn't going to be like one of the rushed, perfunctory moments of animal sex she had all too infrequently been *allowed* to have by Tom, she realized. Not like the usual *granted* imitation of *intimacy* that she always felt, *as if Tom were just doing his duty*. She always somehow felt that he didn't even find her attractive.

This felt real to her. As if she were a virgin, and just having sex for

198

the first time in her life.

Kissing her tenderly, she wrapped her legs around him as she felt him entering her.

"My God, what I've missed," she cried to the ceiling, as she moaned and felt herself whimpering as he began slowly — and lovingly — thrusting into her.

Several hours later, Devon was still lying gently on top of Kat, in her arms with no hurry to get up and flee. Occasionally kissing her on the lips, on the forehead, and on the cheeks; he wanted to eat this woman up.

But especially, he wanted to be with this woman for the rest of his and her life. Knowing that this was never going to be able to happen, he said nothing of what he was feeling inside and longing to say.

"So... How long has it been?" she asked him, after a few moments of caressing and staring into his eyes.

"Too long," he said, shuddering involuntarily, remembering the last time he had let his guard down to find comfort. That time it was a mistake. "It's hard to be able to find someone I can trust."

"You mean, it can be—"

"Dangerous. One of those traps I was telling you about."

Pulling him closer still and kissing and caressing his forehead, "Well, I guess I can understand. My life hasn't exactly been what it was supposed to be. Or even what I thought it was, for that matter.

"I guess I've never known a time where I was having someone in it that I thought I could trust. I always knew on some level, that the person I had been with—"

"Tom Wolfe," he said gruffly. "Now that's a name," smiling grimly at his assessment.

"I guess we don't really know anyone. Do we?" she asked.

"That's what this is for," he said, hugging her, "Getting to know someone who really opens up to you."

"Hmmm," she said, smiling deliciously. "Are we safe enough to fall asleep like this?" she asked, hopeful.

"The people who run this motel are part of our network. They're doing what I would normally be doing—"

"Being on guard."

"Yes. They're here specifically to provide a safe haven for those of us who are on the road."

"Can I ask how many people in this mysterious Us there are?"

"Of course you can ask," he said mischievously. "I just can't tell you."

"Oh."

Kissing her to take away the sense of pain he is again seeing in her eyes, he leaned in to whisper in her, "Sometime soon, you'll know a lot of the answers to your questions.

"Unfortunately... just not yet."

"How will you know when I'm worthy of trust?"

200

"When we get where we're going. There are Elders there that you'll be brought before, to find out once and for all who — and what — you are."

"What," she repeated with dread.

"Whether you are indeed what you seem."

"Or whether I'm merely a clever trap."

"I don't think that's the case. Otherwise, we wouldn't... be here, now. The way we are," he said, dipping down to kiss her shoulder.

Moving her legs up his side and angling herself to create more here, now, she laughed playfully.

Laughing with her, he said, "If you are a trap, you're a very, very pleasant one."

"Am I pleasing to you?" she asked, fearing the answer.

Looking deep into her eyes, he said, "Of course. Why did you think you wouldn't be?" If she were a trap, she was a very convincing one as well.

Locking her legs around him, "Oh, I don't know. I'm not all that experienced." Grimacing at the pain threatening to drown her, she added, "And I can't be sure that Tom wasn't turned off by me."

Becoming serious and disengaging from her, he sat up on the edge of the bed, turning away from her. Making a decision and turning back around towards her, he leaned in and started kissing her at her heart, moving up kiss by kiss, kissing every inch or so until he reached her lips. Then he sat back up, and looked at her without any mask

201

whatsoever.

Sighing, he hesitated before saying, "There's something else you need to know about this Tom."

"Ok," she said, not sure that there was anything that Devon could tell her now that would be a surprise.

"Everything about your "relationship" with him was essentially a lie."

Even having figured this out on the drive since that life died to her, his saying this truth still hurt her deep inside. Not because he'd said it, but because it was too true.

"He was in your life to keep an eye on you," he said quietly.

"But why me? What am I that I needed to be kept *an eye on*?"

"Don't you think that how you handled those three attempts on your life showed you why?"

She was confused even more now. "Three," she said, stunned once more. "What three?" she asked, her arms going limp at the prospect.

Caressing her face, "The first attempt was the elevator. That one could have crushed you with the force of the magic brought to bear on it, powering it down.

"The second was in the parking lot after you proved too powerful for the Sentinel who was acting as your "resident"—"

"I'm sorry," she said, even more confused than she was before. "You keep using this word sentinel."

"That's something that I'll need to explain to you more fully during

202

daytime."

"Kirsten. That was my residents—"

"No, unfortunately. It probably wasn't."

"Ok," she answered, looking at him obliquely now. "Isn't there anything—"

"Your name is real. Outside of that, I can't be sure what is and what isn't." Lying back down beside her and taking her face in both of his hands now, "I know how hard this is for you. I only wish—"

Tears began coming to her eyes, as she closed the distance between them and kissed him passionately, cutting off any further discussion. Drawing him down towards her, she wanted to feel pleasure for another couple of hours to start erasing the pain.

Before they needed to be back to running for their lives again.

"Isn't it safe enough for us to stay here a few days?" she asked hopefully, a soothing while later.

He was resting beside her, both of them now exhausted from their several hours of their "decompression. "

"No, I only wish it were, but we can't rest that long. Not yet."

And rolling back over her to give a last, languorous kiss, he rolled over away again and began getting out of the bed, moving in the direction of the shower.

Reaching the bathroom door, he turned again, "But you don't need to stay up with me. Why don't you get some sleep?" he said, smiling as he closed the door behind him.

Turning over and away from him, she began contemplating the chair notched up against the door handle across from her.

Sighing deeply, she closed her eyes allowing sleep to take her. "For a moment," she told herself before drifting off into what was going to be a deep, unbroken sleep.

In her dreams, she once again confronted Kirsten in the treatment room. The details that were blurry before, became blindingly and frighteningly clear to her now.

The terrible *Hatred* that she saw, first in the thing that her patient had transformed into, and then the pure evil that the at times oh, so innocently-seeming Kirsten became, shocked her almost awake.

Then, the entire room began glowing a soft iridescent yellowish white, as if the sun were shining full force through the dingy peeling ancient wallpaper ceiling.

The twin figures of the bodies of Kimmie and Kirsten began shrinking and melting into the floor from where they both respectively floated and stood. Then the whole room began to have this glow, as the walls melted away into a featureless haze.

She lifted her dream hands up towards her face and they began melting and dissolving into this Light as well.

Waking with a start in the middle of the night, it took her a moment to realize where she is.

Still on the dark side outside, she could see the faint light from a nearby streetlight filtering in from the bathroom window with the curtains fluttering there from a light breeze. It seemed so peaceful and quiet for the moment, that the dream she had just had was far from her mind now.

Turning over, she found a wide awake and now fully dressed Devon, sitting in the chair at the door, smiling back at her.

"Good morning, beautiful," he said, with a much lighter tone she could hear than that from the strained, concentrating Devon of the previous several days.

"Ready to make the last leg of our perilous journey?" he said, standing and coming over to where she lay in the bed.

"No. But I guess the sooner we get there..."

"More than you'd probably care to know," he said, a hint of pain crossing over his eyes. "And there's still a lot of miles in between now and there."

"Sure you can't come back to—" she started to say to him lasciviously, knowing that the answer would be a "No."

Laughing at this and grabbing her hands held out to draw him back in, he instead used her gesture to pull her upright, grabbing her by the waist and heaving her into his arms.

"Are you normally this romantic first thing in the morning?" she asked, giving him a playfully dirty look.

"Not for a very long time," he said, his enthusiasm dimming.

"I'm sorry," she said, burying her head in his hair.

"It's ok," he whispered back softly.

Carrying her like this to the bathroom door, he gently set her down once more on her own two feet. "I hate to rush you, but we have a long day ahead of us. And I'd like to get us there safely before dark."

"I'll just take a quick shower then," she said, with her elation at last night's activities dimming with reality dawning.

It was still dark outside as Kat crept silently to the car. After dropping the key in the office slot, Devon got into the drivers seat, looking refreshed.

"Off we go," he told her with a smile in her direction. Turning to look out the rear view mirror though, his smile faded quickly into an unhappy expression.

It had begun to get cloudy in the last hundred miles or so, leaving Kat to drift off into a restless sleep.

As the miles stretched on, Devon once again went inside, putting the driving on "auto pilot," but keeping a portion of his mind vigilant to any possible attacks from "Outside." This allowed him to both see the physical road *in front of him* and The Darkness of the meditative state clearing and shifting.

Coming out of trance and back to the physical present, he sighed.

Our little liaison last night was a bad move, he thought to himself. But God help me, it felt right then and feels right now.

Looking lovingly at this woman who had been a stranger just a few days before, he began to reach out in her direction, wanting ever so much to gently run his hand down her arm and touch her hand.

But he stopped himself, some sense of control reasserting itself over him. He was sure that she was in no danger of falling into the Dark Ways. If she was going to do it, he told himself, it would have happened before now.

And he was hoping that this was not just another part of the Dark Plan, another way of infiltrating their stronghold. The other time had been when he was just beginning this conscious way of living. He had let a woman in who he almost knew was not to be trusted, but he'd lived at that point for almost two years without feminine contact, either on the road or at The Community.

Angelus had told him at the time that it would be hard, that insanely knowing smile of hers gently mocking him, but he dismissed the threat — to his almost demise. Even though she was obviously much older than any of The Community of Light could imagine, she had become the mother figure denied to him for most of his life.

Kat was sleeping in the seat next to him, totally unaware of how her fate, her very life, hung in the balance. And how he agonized over all of it. She was sleeping fitfully however, so maybe a part of her did indeed understand the danger she was in.

"Sleep, sweet princess. Sleep and gather strength for the trials to come," he said softly in her direction.

At this, she calmed once more, as if taking his words in in, in the midst of her sleep.

EIGHTEEN

They'd driven in silence for close to two and half hours, and the sun was now well over the horizon behind them.

Against his better judgment, Devon had gotten on Interstate 70 a little while before. "There are only so many ways to cross the Mississippi River," he said. "From here on out, we're going to need some speed."

Kat had welcomed the light after their early morning start. She'd felt the tension lessening in Devon as soon as the day had officially started, although he was still tense and stayed on full alert, even during the day time.

He made a point of turning and smiling at her every once in a while, and she returned the gesture thankfully. But she could also sense the underlying tension he was feeling, and had started worrying about it. This kind of baseline stress was probably wracking his body, and sooner or later it was going to take its toll. Whether his going into his Trance state was helping him or not.

They had only stopped momentarily along the way so far to get food to go before hitting the road again. Kat had been previously surprised (although she knew she shouldn't have been), that Devon already had had a store of food in the trunk for eating between any regular meals. But whether there was any danger or not, she was hoping that they could stop and get some real food at some point.

As if he were sensing this, he asked her, "Are you getting hungry?"

Playfully she said, "I really wish you couldn't read my mind so easily." But inside it really bothered her that it was so easy for him to do. She didn't like not having any privacy, especially after the previous weeks revelations.

"I'm sorry," he said, and she could hear that he really meant it. "But I think that your mind wasn't the thing I was probably reading."

She became aware at this mention that her stomach was making its emptiness known, even though it had just begun making noise a minute ago. "Sorry," she said, sheepishly in return. "I guess I am getting hungry."

And I'm getting tired of fast and finger food, she thought.

"I have just the place to go to in mind, little lady," he said, switching to a country accent. "And," he said, turning off at the next exit and gesturing at a massive truck stop off the interstate, "Here we be."

"This isn't too dangerous?" she asked, with both her anxiety rising as well as her anticipation.

210

"Safety in numbers," he said, but adding, "We also need to get gas anyway." Rolling up to a pump, he turned as she was about to get out. "But you should stay in the car until we're ready to go in," he said, tension rising once more in his voice.

Tempted to laugh at his sudden seriousness, she caught herself sobering suddenly, and agreed. "Ok," she said, and sat back where she was, no matter how tempted she was to walk inside and use the rest room.

Devon got back into the car after fueling it, but instead of driving over immediately to the entrance, she didn't question when he went into trance first.

After a few moments, he returned to the present and said, "There aren't any of the really big, bad guys here. Only just your garden variety sort of bad."

Puzzled at this, she gave him the noncommittal "Ok," once more. *You'll tell me when you can*, she thought.

"Hungry?" he asked again suddenly with a glint in his eyes. She just looked at him and gave him a *you better believe it, buster* look. "Ok," he said. "I know I'm pressing it."

"Can we go in now?" she asked, in a plaintive little girls voice. "And can I pleaseeee go to the little girls room?"

"Sure thing, hon," he said, and turned the car over.

Constraining her tendency to bounce out of the car after last night, she removed herself slowly when they came to a stop. *The better to*

211

not attract attention, she said to herself inside.

But for her, they couldn't get inside quick enough.

Devon put his arm out invitingly old fashioned style towards Kat, who had quickly but lovingly intertwined her arm into his as they went inside.

Leaning in closely to whisper, he said (as they were waiting to be sat after the restroom break), "Now you understand that this represents great danger? I may not be all that much company while we're inside, working on keeping us safe."

Being brought back clearly to their situation, she merely nodded a Yes in his direction.

The restaurant at this truck stop was one of the old style, non-corporate ones. With it's Old West decor and funky 50's style linoleum, cracked leather and yellowing formica, it seemed a throwback to more innocent seeming times.

Of course, Kat thought to herself, *That was probably the best time for them to hide their activities. Fighting Commies while worshiping Satan. Duck and cover, indeed.*

The waitress showed them to their table, acting deferentially and moving slowly with them. Devon by her side, was matching the slow stride and patting her arm as they went.

The smell of the food had nearly knocked her over when they'd come in. Kat hadn't been aware of just how hungry she had been

212

becoming before now.

Between the shock of the events in Massachusetts and the night before with Devon, she had been preoccupied. She had been filled alternately with more pleasure than she had ever felt in her life... And was also more highly charged with more terror than she had ever allowed herself to consciously feel before now. Hunger hadn't really been a pressing issue.

Watching the happy talking and eating crowd around them, she could almost fool herself into thinking that the last (four?) days hadn't happened. Except that she was feeling woozy with the undercurrents that she could now feel swirling around them.

Now that their food had arrived, she was hard pressed to not begin wolfing it down in record time. Except that that would no doubt cause attention as well.

She restrained herself, doing what she had heard mothers saying to their children on those trips that she and Tom had actually gone on. "Don't be such a pig," she had heard them say, secretly jealous that these children still had mothers to restrict their urges. The children of these mothers obviously didn't hold their mothers teachings in high regard.

"This food is only passable," she told Devon. "But right now it feels like four star restaurant food."

Smiling lovingly at her, he said, "Just don't eat it too quickly."

"I'm ok," she said. Subdued now, they both finished eating in silence.

As she was finishing the last remains on her plate, Kat had begun looking warily around at the other diners, barely hearing the clatter and clank of the service and cooking going on not more than a few feet away. Try as she might to forget their flight, she was feeling that there was something not quite right here.

Looking up from finishing his meal and scanning the room, Devon brought her back to the present she hadn't been aware of having been gone from, by whispering, "Tell me what you're seeing."

Kat looked over at him for no more than a second and began looking around the room again. Suddenly she saw swirling grey-greenish mists around a good half of the patrons, some of which (women mostly) had sickly dark green specs in these *mists*.

And as if she hadn't noticed it before now, she now saw that the eyes of almost all of the diners and quite a few of the staff who had this mist surrounding them, were all black.

"Their eyes," she said, gasping quietly.

"What about them?" he asked rhetorically.

Now feeling as is she had had the wind knocked out of her, she said, "It's... Like looking into something like black holes," she said, a feeling of vertigo creeping up on her. She returned to looking at him for stability, as if he were the only source of gravity in the room. "Like I could fall in and keep falling."

With a sad look on his face now, she could see that even though he clearly didn't like what was around them — what was now evident to even her — there was compassion there as well as anger and fear.

"Yes," he said after a long moment. "After generations of being in — those activities — there's an emptiness to them. All of the Light that children come into this world with, in most cases, gets sucked in and devoured. Like you said, like black holes."

"Why don't they see us? I mean, you and me, for what we are," she asked him, the emotion welling up.

"It's not that they don't see us, my dear. Rather, it's the us that they do see."

Shaking her head and missing the point again, she asked him at a loss, "What do you mean?"

"Look outside for a second, and then look at me again," he told her.

Unsure of what he was up to now, she allowed another, "Ok," and looked out the plate glass window beside them to the trucks pulling in, and the families getting into and out of cars at the gas pumps.

Looking back in Devon's direction however, she felt the shock of seeing an old man sitting across the table from her now. Although she knew that it was Devon, she felt the same kind of disconnect in seeing him like this that she had felt looking around the room earlier.

Devon was now looking as if he were in his late eighties, severely balding with a wisp of hair still barely holding on in the back. And other hairs in places where she wasn't sure she'd like to find them. *Is this the man that I would be with in forty years?* she wondered.

Shaking her head sadly, she was about to speak as Devon slowly morphed back into his thirty-something self that she had begun growing quite fond of.

"You'll get used to it," he sighed. "Seeing the illusion that is. What it needs to be at times."

Turning quite serious again and looking around the room with only his eyes, "I only hope that you never get used to seeing what's behind that illusion though. It's not a comfortable sight. Nor is it a happy one."

With tears forming in her eyes and blurring thankfully the vision she couldn't shake around her, Kat quietly returned to finishing drinking the last of her coffee to allow herself some time to contemplate. Devon was silent for a long time as well.

The check paid, they made to get up and head out.

At her side quickly to help her up (like the elderly gentleman he appeared to be), he placed his arm around her waist to complete the illusion and they walked slowly out.

He turned them towards the plate glass, and Kat could see the *Old Couple* now that the Others around them were seeing. She gasped at her own image next to his aged one. She was bent over, and her hair, now all grey, was barely a thin cloud around her head as well.

Gasping, he asked her, "Do you really want to grow old together?"

In spite of herself, she gave a soft, "Yes," to him, feeling yet another intense longing that some part of her knew was never going to happen.

216

As he was "helping" her gingerly back into the passengers seat, she asked him, "Don't you ever get afraid; seeing what you obviously see, I mean?"

"Afraid? No," he answered, sighing. "Sad? Yes. Tired and lonely? Most definitely yes."

Pulling back out onto the Interstate, Kat was not sure now whether she should cry out of fear, or out of sheer sadness.

Merging into the fast moving traffic, she sat silent for a very long time afterwards, letting the farmlands roll monotonously by outside masking her pain.

shadows and LIGHT

NINETEEN

Much later and after hours on the road, Kat and Devon had switched taking turns driving a couple of times each. The length and the miles were both taking their toll on both of them.

They were in Kansas City, Kansas, having just crossed the Kansas line now, with Devon as the current occupant of the drivers position. As he drove, Devon had carefully steered the conversation away from anything serious and deadly a number of times; even though Kat still had many unanswered questions burning holes in her mind.

"Why am I still having a hard time remembering and knowing what you said I needed to know?" she had asked at one point.

"My dear, you have just in the last few days found out that your whole life has been—"

"Well, not my whole life," she objected.

"A good deal of it then, shall we say."

The weight of what he was saying began dragging her emotions down, as she slumped against the half open window. "Ok. I give up."

"You don't need to give up," he said softly. "But give it time. And give it till we're in a safe enough place to fully dredge up the Darkness inside. Once we get to where we're going to, you'll have more than enough time, as well cause enough, to dredge and ask to your hearts content."

"Or perhaps, discontent?" she asked plaintively.

"And at that time, you'll probably know more and find out more than you ever really wanted to know."

She felt like going to sleep again, her head hurt so much from the pain of her situation and her need to know. She wished that she could just go to sleep until they got to wherever they were going to, but knew inside that Devon needed her to both drive as well as be conscious.

"You can sleep for an hour or so, if you need to," he said, once again reading her mind. "I can keep what I need to say at bay for a while. And Kansas is a very long State to travel through."

Her tired head needing to do just that, she decided to stay awake anyway though. "No. I don't want the whole burden to be just on you," she told him, reaching over to stroke his arm where it lay on the seat.

Taking her hand in his, he held it up to his mouth and kissed it. And still holding on to her, he let their hands drift down to the broken leather of the seat between them. He then went back to looking forward, the glaze of trance state taking over once again. After a while his grip loosened, and she let his hand go entirely.

Kat was driving again, while Devon appeared to be sleeping. However, after a long brooding silence, Devon returned to the present and continued answering her unasked question. "We're entering what the Fundamentalists call the "End Times" and what we call *The Shift*."

Laughing lightly, she repeated, "The Shift. What the hell is that? You make it sound like--"

"Shift in consciousness. The whole planet, if we're lucky."

Stumped by this, she started to laugh it off. Except that he was being too serious. "So... What do you mean by "if we're lucky"?"

"Because it comes down to choice. Free will. And you know how most humans handle that."

Shifting uneasily, she finally turns toward him fully. "But what if--"

"The deepest darkness is in the mind."

"But what about this--"

"The Red Circle is merely perverting the powers that all of us already have. Using those powers to prolong their physical life, gain powers over others.

Turning towards her, Devon began appearing to become a glowing Being of Light. "You see, we are all powerful beings," this *ball of Light* spoke. We choose to forget that power when we come into this life."

Returning slowly to his *regular* appearance— "The Red Circle is using that power for Its own purpose, not that of God's."

"Then there is a God?" she asked.

"Of course there is. Just not what you think of as "God"."

"And a Devil, too? I suppose."

"Yes. But once again, not in the way that most of humanity thinks of It."

"Then... How? What is... It?"

"That, my dear, is a long discussion for a later time," he said sighing, and left it at that.

Devon was once again driving. Looking at him with worry, she could see that the weariness of the last few days was weighing more and more heavily on him.

Talking quietly while he drove, "The irony is... White/Black, Jew/Arab — If they hate and kill in the name of Hate, instead of serving in the name of Love... They're both on the same side anyway. Serving the Beast."

"I don't understand."

"You've had this whole other separate life."

"Such as?"

Turning to look at her with a grim look, "Such as being married."

Stopped short at this, she laughs suddenly, as if she'd just heard a truly absurd joke. "Umm. But I've never been married." When this doesn't get the fooled you reaction she had hoped for, she adds, "And besides—"

Cutting her off, "Yes. Unfortunately you have," he told her definitively.

Laughing nervously and then cringing, feeling inside that he's telling a truth she wasn't aware of before, she challenged him with "Ok," waiting for the absurd answer. "Who then?"

"Your former *boyfriend*, Tom. That's who."

Stuck between laughing hysterically and wanting to lash out at Devon for this, "Tom. Married to me," she laughed nervously. "He's never even proposed. I've wanted him to, but—"

Choking with tears, she didn't know what to think, or who to blame.

Growing tender for a moment and rubbing her arm lovingly, he continued with, "It was a Cult marriage, not intended for either your pleasure or satisfaction. When you're *married* in the Cult, it's not for wedded bliss. It's done strictly for ritual purposes. It's a bonding on a metaphysical level, called the "Marriage of the Beast"."

Suddenly in a state of shock, she repeated, "Marriage of..."

"Yes. For Ritual purposes only."

"I think I would have known— About something like that."

"Like you knew before that you were involved in the ritual sacrificing of children?"

Stunned into silence with this, her face goes through a full range of emotions before returning to shock.

Finally, "How could he— Why would I—" And then soberly came

to, "What else don't I remember?"

Suddenly aware of what else, her face registering the additional shock. "Children. My God. Have I had—"

"Probably," he said, but his face told her a different tale. "Only you would know that for certain."

"How?"

"You'll learn a great many things that you don't remember that you know. Once we're somewhere where it's safe for you to know them, that is."

Then, looking down at her midsection, she laughs again, a little less this time than she had before. Saying defiantly, "I'd think I'd know. You know? Stretch marks? I think I'd have stretch marks. And my—" hesitant to say anything close to anything at all clinical, "Lady parts. I wouldn't be as—"

"When was the last time you had sex? I mean, before you and me. With—" and here he hesitated to even say the Name, much less Title. But he did. "Detective Wolfe," he said, spitting out the name in disgust.

It was a good thing that she wasn't driving. Her whole body began to clench at this, and she felt herself dissociating yet again.

Making a conscious decision this time, she brought herself back sharply from that edge. *Do I really not have any control over my body and mind?* she asked herself.

"You just did," he answered, looking at her with a look of loving compassion that melted her heart.

"Am I ever going to know everything I've done and has happened to me?" she asked in a trembling voice.

After a long moment of silence while he contemplated how to tell her, he eventually looked at her again and said reluctantly, "Unfortunately... yes. And you'll find out more than you ever wanted to know."

She was about to ask him if this had happened to him, but thought differently when she looked at his face and saw the anguish there. She felt like crying. I don't want to know, she thought, and in the next second, knew that she would find out enough to break her heart. And possibly also her mind.

"Evil is like an act of a child," Devon continued in the awkward silence. "No matter what the scale."

This snapped her out of her internal wailing and she spat out incredulously "Like a child? What the hell are you talking about? The Circle is Evil. How can you compare the evil it's done to the act of a small child?"

"Because when it comes down to it, evil is all about acts of childish control..."

"Yeah. World control."

"I know it's hard for you to believe, but The Circle can no more control the Universe than a child can control themselves — much less the world."

"But—" Kat began to object.

"Yes. They twist and reshape this reality, true enough. But in the large scheme of things—

"But Evil is monstrous. Look at all of the things that evil has done in even just the last century."

"Yes, and no."

Sighing in frustration, Kat shook her head. "I guess I'm supposed to look at the big picture? Right? Whatever the hell that means."

"Yes. You're thinking in terms of a lifetime or years. But before we're done, you'll be thinking about whole worlds. And time in terms of millennia."

"Millennia? You mean... Like thousands of years?" Turning to look out the window, Kat began crying in her frustration. "This whole thing seems hopeless."

"When you look at in terms of this life, here and now... Yes. It may be."

"My whole world has fallen apart, and you're trying to get me to see some sort of mythical big picture."

"I know it's hard for you," he told her, reaching out with his hand to lightly caress hers. "It was hard for me too. I went through the same thing you're going through now. We all have."

Not even looking at the road, "Do you want me to tell you about real magic?"

"You mean, like the kind that the Red Circle performs?"

"No, I mean real magic. What the Circle does is stage magic compared to real power. It's only a shadow of the true reality."

"Shadow," she repeated. "And that's why they're going to loose?"

"Well, yes. Otherwise they would've already—" and removing his hands from the steering wheel in a way that frightened her, used his fingers to make air quotes while he said, "—won."

She watched his hands drift back down to grip the wheel that hadn't moved while he was not touching it. *Can he control physical objects, too?* she thought, as her mind showed her herself in the parking lot mere days earlier, moving cars around like chess pieces on a board game.

"But they haven't. Have they?" he asked, with a surety in his voice. "If they only sought to work with, instead of against, the Greater That Which Is."

"—and ever Shall Be?" she finished off with a laugh.

"Amen," he said with a small cynical laugh. "That's where they have it both very right... as well as terribly wrong."

"What do you mean?"

"There is no end, you know? World without End, Amen?"

shadows and **LIGHT**

TWENTY

They had been traveling a long time since leaving the motel, without much rest except for the breakfast at the truck stop.

The day was turning into late afternoon and they were somewhere in western Kansas. The Rockies had yet to make a full appearance, but Kat felt she could see a hint of them on the horizon. For all she knew, they could still be days away.

"Hungry?" he asked her once more. "We need to get out and stretch our legs."

The skies had cleared a short while before, opening up to that high brilliance that he had always loved about the flat Kansas plains, with tall clouds stacking to heaven and marching eastward.

They were both starving. He had stopped at some little Mom and Pop that he felt was safe in the lasts little pit stop town they had crossed out here to get supplies. This was the last leg of their journey, and they couldn't afford to stop till they reached their destination.

"There doesn't look to be too many people here."

"Why," she asked again, feeling a hint of nausea. "Is there still really that much danger ahead?"

"There's danger all around us, all the time," he told her soberly. "And yes," he said, "We will still be in great danger. Until we reach the Safe Place I've been telling you about, that is."

Pulling into a parking space that was close to the end of the area, she noticed that he pulled a little beyond the end of the space. And before turning the engine off, went into trance and scanned the area.

Coming out of trance and pointing to a family happily at play several picnic areas over. "That seemingly innocent family over there, for instance. Could be a trap," he said, matter of factly.

"How do you know?" she asked.

He continued to drive the car into a small ravine and over to another hill just beyond, stopping when he had the car over a slight depression.

"Watch out when you step out. It's a little bit of a drop," he told her as he got carefully out.

She followed suit, but misjudging the distance a little, found herself dropping with a jolt.

"How do you know?" she repeated. "And why did you park like that?"

Looking at his feet, and then up at her for emphasis, "You don't really. Not for certain. You didn't even know what you were, and you were in the thick of it, so to speak.

230

"And as far as the parking, I'm feeling just a trifle exposed out here."

Deflating as the desperation of their situation once again struck her, she was about to ask him what he expected to be exposed too, but dropped that question.

Devon had reached into the trunk to get the food and utensils to eat with, and did another quick scan while his head was out of sight.

Sitting down at a picnic table to steady herself, Kat numbly asked, "I still don't understand why I didn't know, you know. I mean, know what I was."

"Like I told you before."

"A—" she began to say.

"Sentinels are usually," and using air quotes again said, "Mental health care professionals that are there to keep track of the multiples — which are called Cauldrons."

"Cauldrons."

"Yes. "Vessels" for the storing of the Soul fragments of the ritually sacrificed victims. That's how they — the Red Circle adepts — get their power."

"Vessels," Kat repeats numbly.

Continuing as if he hadn't heard her mental stumbling, "To make sure that they don't remember too much. Or if they do, to sedate them until they can be... Dealt with."

"Remember— Too much of what?"

"Anything. Anything compromising to the Cult. Any detail which can lead back to the Circle, prove that they do indeed exist."

"But... I wasn't aware—"

"Some Sentinels are fully aware of and conscious of what they do. Like your former boyfriend, Mr. Wolfe. But most, like you and I, aren't," he continued.

"But what if they let you— Let me—

"Yes. Now you're beginning to understand."

"What happens if I am— Just a plant. A trap after all?"

Walking over to her and sighing, he put his hand on her shoulder soothingly. "I don't think that's the case."

"But what if it is? What if I— And I don't—"

"Don't worry about it.

"And if I am— A trap. What do you..."

"Please don't worry—" he began to say.

Stopping herself cold as she finally realized the solution. "You'd have to kill me. Wouldn't you?"

"Like I said, Kath—" he started to say, and then caught himself instead saying, "Kat."

Insistently she tried to push, "Won't you."

"Trust me. It won't come to that."

"But how can you be sure?"

Various families were eating, lounging and laughing close by, when suddenly, Devon grabbed Kat forcefully by the arm. "We've got to get under cover. Quickly."

Startled and suddenly unable to move, she asked, "Why?"

Insistently grabbing to the point of pain, he just said, "Now, Kat." And began pulling her under the car that he had had the presence of mind to park over the gully.

Once under the car, Kat tried to speak, but Devon clamped one hand over her mouth, and puts the other one towards the East, in warding fashion.

Without moving his mouth, he told her, *They're hunting for us.*

And just as he had said that, the roar of an approaching jet began suddenly being felt and heard. The noise of whatever was coming, continued rising in pitch until it reached into being an ear-splitting crescendo. It was flying in both very low and was approaching very quickly.

As families began running for cover and screaming in all directions, mothers and fathers were trying desperately to gather their children into cars, or push them into ravines close by.

In the air, the speck that had been the plane approaching fast, quickly became the shape of a Stealth Bomber; sleek, strange and deadly. And this plane was not bothering to be in anything approaching stealth mode.

But the noise and the altitude were not the only reason why this plane was sending everyone screaming. Crouching under the car, Kat felt revulsion at first like a wave of horror threatening to drown her.

Then she could see — her vision of the undercarriage of the car blurring — exactly Who, and specifically What — was looking so desperately for her.

Lying in the ditch, Kat once again felt herself separate from her body. She felt as if she was being pulled by some invisible force, and that she suddenly *saw* Devon's car and the rest stop parking area below her as if she were flying above it. Then she saw the invisible but now luminous *string* that she was apparently being pulled by.

Then— Just as suddenly, she was slammed into the cockpit of this Thing that was looking for her. She recognized several of the persons there, one of them in formal military uniform but the others not. They were dressed in Dark Robes with — Things — swirling in the inky darkness of the— Fabric?

To her shock, one of the men that she now recognized... was her Father. He was seated just behind the pilot and copilot on a throne of — Something she didn't want to focus on too steadily.

All of the faces were twisted in malevolent hatred, but her father's face was so coldly malevolent that she almost didn't recognize him for a moment. She felt that this... man — her father — was Evil incarnate.

"Are you perceiving them?" her Father asked in a Voice dripping with command and utterly raw Dark Power.

As if she were now floating along the length of this plane, her vision continued on towards the rear. There she saw two other figures, each of them hooded in the black cloaks similar to those being worn by the people in her dreams, with — No, she thought desperately, Remembering.

Finally accepting that they were indeed memories, she let her attention finally rest on the — Something — that (Sat? Reclined? Puddled?) in between these two hooded figures. Something which she could only describe later as The Monstrosity.

IT was something barely recognizable as "human" or what may have once been the possibility of human, with what looked like a head and a face like a human that had been made of molten wax, with the remains of ears, but with no mouth or eyes, a lump of flesh that happened to be alive, and was created (or warped and twisted) by the blackest of magics.

This Thing was a crime against nature, the penultimate Obscenity created by the Forces of Darkness to shout outrage at the Universal. And the worst part about this Thing was, it was not only alive but also sentient — thinking and feeling — in a constant state of deafening agony she could now both hear and feel. She knew that It had been nominally male and that this agony was a tremendous shredding pain that transcended what she thought Pain could feel like.

She did her very best to block it out, physically and psychically — and after what seemed like an eternity (but was really only a few seconds), she succeeded in pushing this naked screaming awareness away, hyperventilating furiously at the effort that it took.

Devon only briefly turned his head in her direction, sensing What she was seeing, but his gaze was unseeing as well. Seemingly a thousand miles away, he battled to keep the Effort of Will that was approaching them at bay; turning it forcefully and completely Away.

Kat's attention returned as the Left Figure sitting next to IT telling her Father, "Not yet," although Kat didn't know how the figure that sounded like a muffled man could know what this Thing next to it was thinking. This Figure didn't feel particularly powerful, but she knew he was one of this — Things — handlers. He also felt as if he were in great pain as well as he communicated with It.

Just as quickly again she backed away from feeling anything, as her Father's Voice threatened in a deeper sounding booming voice filled this plane with chilling madness and malice, "Find them." And adding with even more chilling malice the threat, "Or else."

She could also see as well as feel the two hooded figures shiver violently inside behind him. The Monstrosity even shivered in unison with them as well, although Kat could not imagine what her father could do to It, any more than what he had apparently already done.

Suddenly her Father had a glimmer of recognition flash across his face, that Someone was watching them. His eyes grew wider as he realized exactly who it was that was viewing this.

"Well," he said, cruel victory showing on his face as a wicked smile. "I have you now," he said, gleefully.

But before she could see what else would happen, the air around

236

the Vision began shivering into fragments, and seemed to disappear like a cloud of black sickly-looking smoke in her mind. Smoke as if from a pile of ashen flesh newly incinerated.

Her mind returned, slamming violently back into her body in the rest area beneath the car. While the Plane shrieked sickeningly close overhead and then continued on out of sight into the West, its sound and psychic fury dissipating with it.

The Figure on the Right of IT pulled back their hood to reveal it is a woman. Hesitantly, she bowed her head saying, "We've lost them."

Both of the humans on either side began shivering uncontrollably, each grabbing for their heads, as the left seated Figure tore off its hood as well.

Both of the Figures — man and woman — began violently shaking now, melting and transforming as they sat into two other identical lumps of barely recognizable flesh, and began merging into the One Monstrosity. Three into one flesh.

The Man who had once been her Father, also began shaking visibly, his head now turning red and hideous with rage, but still remaining somewhat human. In a barely recognizable voice, what had once been Human but was now *inflected* with The Demonic Other, growled out a command several octaves lower, "We must prepare for all out kill. Tell Them. They must not be allowed to reach their destination."

The Pilot, trembling visibly and without daring to look in his direction, merely nodded and told him, "Yes, Lord. It will be done." Turning to the copilot and carefully nodding, "Inform them."

Speaking into his helmet mike, the Copilot said, "This is Omega Zero—"

And as The Father began growing from glowing hideous back into merely malevolently brooding, his anger was cooling as his rage bled off into the now solidifying three lumps of smoking ash that now puddled behind him.

Slowly all the families began coming out of their hiding places, with many of the children (and a good number of adults) still shrieking from the shock and pain of the psychic anguish to which they had just been subjected to.

Kat began to crawl out but Devon kept his grip firm, restraining her while still appearing to be in trance. "Not yet," he told her in a voice sounding from far away. "They will still feel you."

Coming back to the present, a look of anger mixed with fear began creeping across his face. Fully back in the present and turning fully on her, "What were you thinking?"

Rolling out from under the car and pulling Kat after him, "That could have been the end of it."

"What?" she asked him innocently.

"Your father. Looking for us."

"But—"

"We don't have any time now left to loose. We're going to have to drive into the night in order to get there. Especially now that you've alerted him to knowing what we're up to."

"I'm sorry. I couldn't help it. I was just suddenly— There."

While looking as if he were thinking the opposite, he finally said, "Well, it's done," and sighing from the exhaustion of the effort involved in shielding them, "At least I was able to block most of their full awareness of how close they were. With some help, that is."

Kat began shaking her head, with terror creeping in once more, paralyzing her with a sudden wave of nausea. "I'm sorry. I just— Did it. I didn't choose to see what I did. It was like I was drawn—"

"Whether you did, or some part of you did, or whether some part of you which is still under his control did... I guess it doesn't really matter. What's done is done.

"But you're going to have to drive most of the way. I need to be able to shield and confuse them should they return. I felt that your father wasn't very happy, and that unhappiness worked against his interests and in our favor. Now he's flying blind because of his rage and its effect on his *human psychic radar*."

"What did he do to them?"

"*That*," he paused, and shivered himself, "Is not something you want to give much thought to." And then he let his voice drift down an octave for emphasis, and said, "Trust me."

Feeling her stomach heave at the implication, she threw up what she had just recently eaten into the gully, as Devon quickly gathered the remains of their lunch and prepared to leave.

Suddenly however, the sound of the voice of Angelus whispered warningly in Devon's head, *Devon...*

Heeding the (unheard by Kat) silent command in his head, he cut himself off with, "I still can't explain much more of this to you before we get where we're going."

"Why?" Kat asked, although she knew the answer.

"Because we're still in very grave danger. And for all intents and purposes, we still have a long way to go."

"But where are we going to?" she asked insistently.

"For our safety. I can't tell you, especially after your recent *connection* to your father." Reaching over and caressing her nearest leg comfortingly, "You'll know soon enough when we get there."

Suddenly he asked more quietly, "Can you drive for a while?" and walked over to the passengers side door without waiting for her answer.

Although she wasn't feeling up to it after the last few minutes, she grudgingly sat down behind the wheel.

TWENTY-ONE

Over the last few hours of driving, The Rockies had grown from the hint on the horizon from before, to being a solid image rising out of the now rolling hills of western Kansas. They were a line that separated the growing dusk from the barely lit surroundings that Kat was driving through.

The sun was almost on the horizon of the mountains in front of them, and the rolling farm lands that they had been cruising through the last few hours now had long shadows behind the tree lines in the direction away from the sunset. Those shadows were quickly becoming deepening night once more, and she wasn't looking forward to it.

Without realizing it, the scene in front of her had become mesmerizing, and dangerously so.

Kat could feel her attention slipping. Her view of the road in front of her ban blurring and shifting darker suddenly.

There were shadows appearing alongside the lit highway that

had nothing to do with the illumination of the five story tall light poles with their lights perched high.

Images seemed to swirl just outside of the edge of her sight, popping up and then when she turned to look in their direction, disappearing in a blink.

Her vision was growing watery and hazy, and she was about to wake Devon out of his trance for him to drive. "I should let Devon drive," she thought she said out loud. Even the "muscle" of her mind was becoming as blurry as the outside.

Devon had been riding *psychic shotgun* for a while, sitting beside her. For her part, she was not saying anything that would distract his focus away from the vigilance that was needed.

His eyes were half-lidded, but his mind was on full psychic red alert.

He had gone once again into a *Council Meeting* miles back, fighting off some of the suggestions that Dr. Runyon was too dangerous to bring into their stronghold.

If she were what you think she is, he *said* to them, *we would both be dead now.*

You, my friend, would be dead now, Gregory told him. *Or worse.*

He was ready to beat back any attack that might be sent against them. *She has not fallen yet*, he told them. *She is very strong, this one. Or else I wouldn't have risked everything to help her.*

But Devon was beginning to regret that last night in the motel, now becoming unsure of how much his growing affection was clouding his viewpoint. For now though, he was still willing to give her the benefit of the doubt.

She will be one of the greatest of our Order, he had told them, closing off any further discussion.

But he also remembered that Angelus had remained silent during the entire Council. And the look on her face had not been a very comforting one.

The Darkness was now actively pursuing them. Were they only lying in wait ahead for some attack? Hopefully, They would believe that Devon and Kat were continuing on West, and not be knowing their intended destination.

Devon asked Kat suddenly, "Are you doing ok?"

Shocked back to the present, Kat responded with a "Yes," even though she had been very close to not being Ok in the least.

I can handle this, she thought erroneously, and bent her attention back to concentrating on the road ahead.

But am I? she asked herself after his question had brought her back to the present. He had brought her back from the brink of what she was feeling as if she was almost falling into.

The road ahead had begun getting blurry again, and she was feeling as if *Someone* (and she hesitated to even think clearly of him or think his name, even now) was still looking for them. Looking *for her.*

I should just pull over, stop the car, and walk away, she thought, just as she was beginning to feel mesmerized by the road again. *I'm dreaming, and I'm about to fall into the worst kind of nightmare. One where I know I'm in it and I can't get out of.*

But she continued to drive. Looking over at Devon, she could see the weariness that was creasing his face even now. He had driven her half way across the country by now, and except for his *sleep* in the car and whatever sleep he had gotten in the motel, he hadn't really slept for days. *Perhaps even weeks. I need to keep up my part in this*, she thought, as her attention began drifting yet again.

Before she knew it, she had slowed down to a crawl (or so she thought). The other cars were passing her by, but no one was seeming to notice.

Her gaze was starting to drift. Her seeing of the road was getting blurry again. *I have to wake him up to drive*, she thought. *And Now.* And then she kept on driving.

Then the blur of the headlights in front of her began blurring even more. Suddenly, it was if a cloud began forming ahead of them. Except that this cloud was glowing, as if it was lit from a fire within. A storm cloud, but without a *storm.*

As she felt as if she were slowing to a stop, a Figure began forming in the midst of this fiery cloud. A figure she recognized. Then this resolved into a face filling her vision.

That Face. Her Father. But He was no longer the Dark and

244

Malevolently Angry Father. Taking over her full vision.

"Daddy?" she almost asked, but didn't quite.

Instead, He was smiling softly in her direction. *Benevolent,* the image seemed to whisper. The way her father had almost never been during her *real* life.

Without his lips moving, she heard that Voice commanding her, *Why run, Daughter?* he suddenly said (without saying anything). *You cannot win in this. In the end, your little boy toy will not prevail against myself and those of us that are surrounding me now. His—* he began to say with rising anger, his voice betraying him.

Quickly gathering himself back into the image of the Good Father, he continued more softly, *His friends will not help you either. Your Destiny is with Us.* And raising his arms as if to bring her back into the fold, he said, *Come back to Us and your special place in our future. All will be forgiven. You will—* and his voice began cracking again at this, *Come back and take your Rightful Place among the True Rulers of this world. It is inevitable. You should not try and fight your Destiny.*

And just as suddenly, Kat realized that he was not even talking in her direction. His eyes wandered, as if he was talking to a crowd and not just her. *He still doesn't know where I am,* she thought, with a little bit of glee.

But then, just as suddenly, he looked directly at her. His mouth forming into a smile that made her shiver.

*There you are, Daughter. I **see** you now,* he told her. And then looked away again.

That part of her Power came to the fore again, and willed this Vision to disappear into the dusk that she was truly in.

She suddenly snapped back to the present, realizing that she was still driving. And the car was still going seventy miles per hour. She had not slowed down for more than a few seconds, and her Vision of her Father was only that; an Illusion. In fact she realized, it was a quite Desperate Illusion.

That other Part of her heard more than saw, her fathers Voice return to raging. *You will not evade me for long*, he screamed at her from wherever he was, his full Malevolence snapping back as he lost any *sense* of where she was.

The weary part of Kat was trembling. The full furor of his Dark Intent hit her, full force in her chest and her forehead, and almost left her crying in its frightening intensity.

But her No Longer Dark Part, calmed her and began taking over the driving once more. *Dissociation can be a good thing*, she thought suddenly, as she consciously relented to that *vanishing*.

And some time later, she *awoke* to Mountains scraping their blackness across the night sky. With the million lights of a glowing Denver in front of them, separating the darkness from the flight.

TWENTY-TWO

Devon had come out of his Trance and taken over driving again just outside of Stapleton International Airport on the outskirts of Denver. Other than an emotionless "I'll take over from here," he hadn't spoken to her since.

He did not ask about her *encounter* with her father, and she didn't bother to tell him. In a way she sensed that he already knew, but she didn't want to press it or even want to discuss it.

Even though he was driving, she felt as if he were still in trance and working to keep anything from psychically *latching* on to them.

A little while later, they were passing the city limit of the town of Boulder, Colorado. It was both quaint as well as cutting edge.

"I've heard good things about Boulder," she said to break the silence.

"Yes, and no," he replied quietly all of a sudden, shocking her that he had.

"This is not our final destination," he then said. "Be careful for what you sense and react to here. It's not the "quiet little town" it seems to be."

Since the 1960s, the remnants of the counterculture and what was to become the New Age movement had flocked to Boulder as a haven. With the mountains close by for the rugged of spirit and plenty of small shops with presents from the edge, it had become a Center for the New Age.

Not so soon after that however, it also attracted a decidedly not very "peace and love" kind of faction that followed, drawn to the more darker aspects of the drug revolution and soon opening up to the darkest aspects of the rest of life as well.

Halloween in the 80s, had morphed into an annual "Devils Night" celebration. The Dark, always attracted to the Light like dark moths of evil to any flame, were mistaking it as a way for Them to gain control over others. And seeking for a way to corrupt the Light.

In the years since, there had grown to be a balance of powers, as powerfully ancient traditions had moved to Boulder and taken up residence there. Devil's Night still came every All Hallows Eve (Halloween) though, regardless of who or what of The Light moved in to restore that balance.

As Devon and Kat drove into town, it seemed like your ordinary, sleepy little blue skies Colorado town, even though it had become very late in the evening.

Surrounding them were Victorian Houses the likes of which she had never seen before. Ornate and many gabled, Kat sat back fascinated, and let Devon drive. "I've never been this far West on the ground before," she said dreamily.

Devon had had to respond to her though with one of his increasingly ironic regular looks and had had to tell her, "I'm sorry, my dear, but you have. You just don't remember it, that's all."

"What else don't I remember?" she sighed suddenly, as she asked herself rhetorically, "How much more of my life has been hidden?"

Not bothering to answer, Devon just drove. Stunned but not questioning anymore when he made these announcements, Kat continued silently riding in shocked silence, trying not to think so hard about it anymore. But it wasn't helping her sense of well being in all of this.

Arriving at the center of the New Age district (which was filled with both coffee and crystal shops), Devon pulled into a parking space.

"We've been driving for a while. Want to stop and get a quick cup of coffee before we go on?"

Suddenly feeling very sleepy, she nodded a "yes" to him.

"I guess that means we still have a long way to go yet. Don't we?"

"Not far, but far enough," he told her, reaching over to run one of his fingers down her face lovingly. "Come on. A quick rest stop and back in the plane again."

Nodding solemnly, she took a deep breath of the crisp mountain air when she had finally managed to get her legs to stretch outside of the car. Stretching her arms above her head as well, truly cat- like, she looked over to find an admiring Devon leaning against the car top. She smiled for the first time since their first night together and waited for him to join her on her side of the car.

Finding themselves walking closer to each other than they had in days, Devon surprised her by reaching out and taking her hand in his. Feeling a thrill at this small gesture, she leaned into him as they walked, taking comfort for the first time since that night at the motel from his presence.

They hadn't gotten more than half a block before they turned the corner onto the street that served as Main Street, where the greatest number of shops were. Enjoying themselves openly for the first time in days, they continued on in this warm silence.

Gesturing to a particular small coffee shop, Devon turned abruptly, suddenly having a very bad feeling.

Turning his attention away from the shop and towards the tree studded median of this mall, his eyes caught a glimpse of a figure walking, hopping lightly along up to stand on a concrete and wood bench there. His view of this figure was accompanied by a swirling black mist that unfolded like dark wings harboring a vast number of *Somethings* that Devon knew were captured souls caught in the web of powerful Black Magic. Here was one of Kat's Fathers lieutenants, in the dark flesh himself.

"Perhaps this wasn't such a good idea," Devon leaned in to whispered to her, stopping and starting to draw her back towards the car.

Ironically, this mans appearance was closer to that of Jesus in modern faux Old West garb, with long hair and neatly trimmed to a pointed spaded end, beard. It was also similar to the "Country Gentleman" version of the Devil himself in most of the Old West and Southern tales of The Beast. The type of man that women would swoon over, and men gave their respect to. That's how "Old Scratch" had lured them in.

Except that this *country gentleman* stepping ominously into the common area was obviously a Preacher, winding up for his "pitch." His black wings unfolding to reveal even more power and Dark beings just inside for those that could see, his gaze was anything but soft and pleading.

Sensing Devon's grip tighten to *ferocious* as well as feeling the *Something Else* that had suddenly appeared close by, Kat tried to loosen her hand. "What is it?" she whispered, although a part of her already knew the answer.

His grip was getting too much for her to stand, but his focus didn't allow him to realize it. "Shhh," was all he told her, his focus reaching for maximum strength of shielding.

Stepping up onto his newly christened stage of bench and tree, this Dark Preacher began.

"Brothers and sisters," he howled, with a Voice as much magic as real. "The End Times are here. Prepare ye the way of the Lord! Behold, I come to you with terrible tidings wrapped up in the Good News."

Even those surrounding him hesitant to listen to such a message by a Fundamentalist minister, suddenly found themselves turning and being pulled in, gathered round to listen to him. Many of them had faces that were conflicted as to why, but seemingly unable to stop themselves.

"An Ill Wind is blowing in from the East!" this Preacher continued, looking first in the direction of, and then finally directly at Devon and Kat. "The Winds of War are about to break upon all of you! Are you going to be ready when the Lord comes to smite the wicked? Are you, brothers and sisters?"

More men and women, some with children in tow, were leaving the shops and boutiques, as if *called* by Jesus himself. Some appeared to be being forcefully dragged to hear this "message."

Lowering his head and now focusing all his malevolence in Devon and Kat's direction, Devon could see some of the entities under the *wings* of *Darkness* surrounding him, reaching out and some leaving the Darkness there, coming out in search of their prey.

Devon whispered to her obviously straining, "We have to leave. Now," and began energetically pulling her away.

Looking at this Preacher not that far away, Kat hesitated. Feeling drawn to listen to him in spite of her self, some part of her began struggling to hold her here as if also heeding his *Call*.

Breaking away from the battle that she could feel Devon was waging with this Preacher just long enough to exert some will in her direction, Devon said again his Voice dropping low into a Command, "Now."

Feeling both the stranglehold that this "Preacher" had on her and the competing and vying for her attention resolve coming from Devon, something welled up deep inside of her. Kat could feel that Other Part of herself reaching out to comfort Devon in one instant, and ready to join him in his battle of Will with this Preacher in the next.

At this, a number of the wraiths around the black hole of the Preacher began flying out to join the battle, sensing unleashed power coming from Kat.

Her hands slowly leaving her side and rising, she could feel the chill of raw Power emanating from them as she raised them in the direction of the approaching Entities. Much like that she had felt just before she had lashed out at the car hurtling towards her in the Hawthorne parking lot, just a few just days earlier.

Both feeling afraid and also utterly calm, she allowed the Power rising in her to do what was necessary.

Suddenly seeing the black clouds hurtling towards her, her hands rose up and once again directed what she could now see were beams of light in their direction. Being struck by these beams, these black clouds of Dark Energy retreated quickly; some of them withering away into ash before they could.

But at this, the Preacher broke off his rant, sensing a Power he needed to counteract. Turning directly towards Kat, he also let his hands begin rising like black birds ready to strike out.

"BEHOLD!" he cried, almost shrieking with a face now looking more like a demons. "The very Forces of Darkness are here to lay claim to your souls," he said, pointing in Devon and Kat's direction.

As if bidden by God Himself, many of the individuals began turning as one and walking in the direction of the Two. Their looks changed from an almost rapture, to one of blankness, with a smattering of eyes turning quickly and malevolently Black.

"We can't fight all of them," Devon told her in a strained whisper. "NOW," he Commanded her, and with all the strength he could spare, began backing away.

But "Katherine" was no longer there. Her face and her hands glowing brighter and brighter, she began walking away from the terrified Devon, seeming Intent on some other purpose.

She began approaching the now rabid hoard sent against her, Light flashing out of her hands and engulfing many of the Dark zombie-like Minions. Many of these faltered with their eyes loosing their black, and stumbling, came to their senses, looking around themselves suddenly in a daze. Seeing raw Power flowing from Kat many began stampeding this way and that trying to get away.

254

Devon began working to add to her influence, but many of the Dark Spirits began swarming towards him. With most of the Minions awakened and fleeing in a rout, Kat turned her attention towards the Dark Sparks attaching him.

Flicking his fingers in the direction of Kat and Devon, waves of blood red dark sparking energy pulsed towards them, intending to kill.

But Kat, raising her hands ever so slightly in this Evil's direction, flicked her fingers in the same way in Its direction, shattering his pulses completely, breaking them from dark into fragments of Light sizzling as they fell into dust and blowing away towards his feet.

Shocking the Preacher just as suddenly with a stricken look of lose on his face, he quickly and carefully blends into the growing shades of growing inky darkness around them and in the fleeing crowd.

Her hands began widening their gap, as her Power began rising to create a halo of White Light around her. Clapping her hands together, her power began dispersing like a cloud of energy becoming a field leaping at the Dark Forces. As this cloud continued expanding on towards the still defiant Preacher, a lot of the Black Sparks around him began flashing out of existence.

Her cloud of Power finally engulfed him and his attitude changed from mighty to frightful, knocked back as if by a strong wind. His influence cracked as he stumbled back, and what remained of the frightened people surrounding him began fleeing.

Rising up in his own uncertainty now, his face began transforming

255

from Demonic to dismayed, fleeing himself now in the face of Kat's energetic prowess.

However, reaching the car, Kat stopped. Walking back around the car and getting in between Devon and this Devil, her hands rose again instinctively and she began walking in the direction of the Preacher and his Minions. As she did, the white Glow of her hands began spiking into bright pools of radiant Light.

Some of the Beings of Darkness came to an abrupt stop and turned, fleeing. The Preacher however, did not stop, but came striding in their direction as if he had the upper hand.

Kat's hands became bright sunlight illuminating the dark night that seemed all around them. The Energy in her hands began reaching out towards the Minions and the Dark Sparks from the Preacher, stopping them in flashes of light, extinguishing them into ash and falling motes of dark.

At this, the Preacher stopped his forward movement, beginning to start turning away. He had not expected this show of force from these two, and hesitated.

Kat began walking purposefully in his direction as what was left of his common folk Minions continued turning and fleeing in terror.

As she turned however, the skies above them suddenly appeared to her as cloudy. Backing up with him, she began to run and then stopped. Her face and her hands glowing brighter and brighter, she began walking away from the terrified Devon, seeming Intent on some other purpose.

She began approaching the now rabid hordes sent against her that had been commanded to rejoin this battle, Light flashing out of her hands and engulfing many of the Dark zombie-like Minions. Many of these faltered with their eyes loosing their black, and stumbling, coming to their senses, looking around themselves suddenly in a daze. Seeing raw Power flowing from Kat, many began stampeding this way and that to get away.

Her hands began widening their gap, as her Power began rising to create a halo of White Light around her. Clapping her hands together, her power began dispersing like a cloud of energy becoming a field leaping at the Dark Forces. As this cloud continued expanding on towards the still defiant Preacher, a lot of the Black Sparks around him began flashing out of existence.

Her cloud of Power finally engulfed this "Preacher" and his attitude changed from mighty to frightened, knocked back as if by a terribly strong wind. His influence cracked as he stumbled back, and what remained of the frightened minions surrounding him began fleeing.

Rising up in his own uncertainty now, his face began transforming from Demonic to dismayed, fleeing himself now in the face of Kat's energetic prowess.

With her white light energy lashing out now, the Preacher began to turn to flee. Catching him in her power, he cringed and began to start collapsing in on himself, crumpling into a black mote himself. With one last scream in terror, this seemingly powerful Minion of the Beast seemed to flash out of existence.

Devon began working to add to her influence, but many of the Dark Spirits began swarming towards him. With most of the Minions awakened and fleeing in a rout, Kat turned her attention towards the Dark Sparks attaching him.

With another clap of her hands, these last Dark Sparks glowed and became ash, floating away on an invisible wind.

Turning and collapsing from the effort exerted, Devon luckily reached her before she hit the ground. "Come on," he said, "Let's get out of here while we can."

Grabbing her to steady her, Kat began coming out of *her* trance. "Are you ok?" he asked her.

"Yes," she said groggily. "Why— What happened? Sighing in relief, he opened the door and helper her in.

"I thought I'd lost you."

"What—" she began to ask, and then began to remember, regaining full limited self consciousness. "It happened again. Didn't it?"

Looking in her eyes intently, Devon finally felt satisfied that she was all right. "Yes, it was like in the parking lot at Hawthorne. I've never seen such raw power exerted by someone like that before. At least... not by someone of The Light."

"The Time has come indeed!" Devon leaned in to whisper in her ear.

258

"What do you mean?" Kat asks innocently.

"We need to get to where we are going to; and fast. It has begun. He recognized you, and the Dark Assault will be coming now. In full strength."

As the clouds above them began to have hints of red lightning edging them, Devon following suit but still straining to protect the two of them, from what was still not very far behind, got them to the car.

Closing her eyes for a moment now safely in the drivers seat, she let our a wracking sigh. "God, I'm so tired."

Smiling in spite of himself and their situation, he said admiringly, "I guess so. You just went up against a very powerful Mage, and you bested him."

"Mage?" she asked, appearing to drift off.

"Are you going to be up for this? I need you to drive," Devon said, concerned through his strain.

Back at the car, Kat got in the drivers seat, soon followed by Devon, still deep in his concentration. "They'll be coming for us in strength now," he told her, as if still far away. "We have to drive like the very Winds of Hell are at our backs. Can you?"

Shaking her head to clear it, Devon took the shotgun position, returning to being deep in his concentration. Without answering, Kat gunned the engine, spinning tires and backing up quickly, preparing to take off, driving like she had never driven before.

She could hear what sounded as unearthly, shrieking screams

259

mixing with the sound of sirens starting in pursuit, as they reached the outskirts of town heading deeper into the mountains. The full moon was quickly rising behind them the East, with the forces of Darkness now howling up behind them as well.

Turn here and continue on this road, he told her inside.

With Boulder now far enough behind them and the tall trees with their earth energies shielding them, Devon visibly relaxed, his breathing becoming less strained and his face draining from the strain he had been under. "Drive on this highway until I tell you to," he whispered, his voice barely audible to her from his exhaustion.

Looking at him with a very worried expression, Kat fought the urge to ask or talk about anything while he recovered from what strain she could only imagine.

They were now deep in the mountains, the road rising at a rate that worried Kat given the age of the car she was driving. The full moon was rising through the trees and the canyon behind them, giving an eery glow to the even taller cedars and pines that lined the hills surrounding them rising steeply up on both sides on this now fully night drive. The smell of the woods and the energy of the trees surrounding them as they drove them, helped to revive them both.

She could still feel Devon concentrating beside her, aware that they weren't out of the woods and into the clear yet. She could feel the rising wrath and frenzy of the Dark Energy behind them in sharp pursuit. And she could also still feel that part of her that was beyond her understanding that was focusing energy on helping him to shield them as well.

It felt strange to her that she had never felt this inner strength coming out of her before the last few days. She seemed like a newly emerging person, even to herself, ever since that Deep Part of her rose up to save her in the Elevator.

Why had she not felt or known about this part of herself before, she wondered to herself..

"Because the Forces around you were working to keep them in check," Devon replied suddenly.

Jumping, startled, she turned to him for a second. "God," she blurted. "Please don't do that to me now. Give me some kind of warning."

Softening, he relaxed some more and gently placed his hand on her right leg, giving her a little squeeze of affection before retreating.

After a while, he said wearily, "Pull over. I'll take us the last stretch up from here."

Pulling over onto the gravel, she noticed a sign for another side roadway up ahead in the now moon-drenched semi-darkness. Intuitively, she knew that this was where they were going to turn.

Getting out of the car for one last stretch of her legs, she walked around the hood with heat pouring off of it to get to the passengers side.

Also suddenly realizing it, she knew that she had *helped* this poor old beaten car get them this far, this quickly. She sensed that, when they got where they were going to, that this car was going to need a long, if not permanent rest. Like some horse that had been driven far beyond its normal life span.

Settling back into the seat, Kat was also realizing that she herself was just as exhausted as Devon looked. She thought, *I hope it's not that much further*, and then promptly fell asleep.

Falling almost immediately into a *dream-like* Vision.

Suddenly she was back in Boulder, and the "Preacher" was no longer even fully human in her eyes. Now he looked like some long dead zombie demon with deep set burned out dark eye sockets for eyes with red piercing pits deep set in them, like laser beams seeking out targets to destroy.

And the Entities that she had just glimpsed, transformed into fully malevolent Spirits like animalistic black holes themselves, lashing out in a frenzy seeking to literally devour anything that got in their way unprotected.

She *knew* both the Preacher (what was left of him) and all of his surviving Minions were now desperately seeking out her and Devon's whereabouts. She felt them touching like black crows here and there on the mountainsides in their journey, casting out for Kat and Devon's scent and catching whiffs of it, becoming a snowstorm of Dark Fury whipped into further frenzy.

Reaching out in all directions though, they were far behind, even though they could apparently sense her and her *dream seeing* of them. They and the more violently boiling *fingers* of Dark Force were in a frenzy from all directions, seeking to literally devour anything that got in their way unprotected. Thousands of beings of demonic fury seeking out death and destruction behind them.

Then her Vision switched back to the roadside Rest Area where they had almost been caught. Once that image came to her, They caught the psychic *scent* and aligned into a coherent pack pursuing Kat and Devon up the mountain.

This Vision switched and wavered once again and she found herself back in the Bomber where her Father was seeking her out with the aid of his Monstrosity and Adepts.

Only this time, the image that she *saw* of her Father was now even more terrifying to her than that of the Preacher, in that his physical presence had not so much changed, but grew Darker with layers added to his image that she hadn't seen before. Layers of Other—

But the feeling roiling off of him was that of such pure Evil as she could not keep looking at him, but glanced back at the Monstrosity. It was as if she could see image after image of different Demons that he had conquered over the years. All overlaid with her now barely sensed image of her Father as a dark *anchor*.

Realizing that he was just as twisted and deformed by his centuries of abusing power as that Thing that he had apparently created for his own purposes was, didn't help her feel any different about the man who had brought her into this world.

He was no longer human at this point, but was so much more Demonic Other that she couldn't stand what she was feeling. She could see the metaphysical overlay of the Beast-Dragon like non-human thing that he was becoming, (or had indeed already become).

This had the image of That which she didn't want to think about at this time, but realized she knew far more of than she had been able to acknowledge to even herself.

A massive chill of revulsion ran through her body as he seemed to suddenly look directly at her, and deep inside of her, drilling with Hatred down to the very core of her being.

He was working to break her — Kathryn, or that Something Else that was inside of her fighting the evil Intent that had been brought to bear on her in the last week — body, mind, and soul. He was seeking to rip out that Part of her with Power that Kat felt wrenching and shredding her at the same time.

Waking with a start and taking a sudden, very sharp intake of breath, she straightened herself up from where she had slumped and noticed that they were turning onto an even smaller gravel road.

Looking around her, she also noticed that they had ridden deep into the mountains, and they were now very high in the Rockies. To her right, she was looking out on the vast full moon drenched Midwestern plains below. They were very high indeed.

"And your senses are also very much sharpened," Devon added to her reverie.

Not startling her as much this time, her senses were somehow getting used to his seeming to know what she was thinking. She didn't reply, but tested him saying *Oh, yeah?* in her mind at him.

But he kept driving without replying this time, whether he had heard her or not. His mind was now intently focused on the elsewhere they were driving towards.

Rounding another bend and seeing a break in the trees, she was sensing another kind of break. All of a sudden, she felt as if a weight were being lifted off of each of them.

"Are we there yet?" she asked playfully (knowing that they were).

Relaxing entirely and enjoying the last half mile or so, he turned to her with a gentle, but exhausted smile. "Yes, Dorothy. I don't think we're in Kansas anymore."

There were no signs saying, "Welcome to The Community" when they finally crossed over the final psychic threshold, but Kat knew that they were "there."

They turned another corner and passed under the remains of a large Old West style gate and lentil sign, that was now devoid of almost anything except rotting wood. But she could feel that there was something else there, some signs that the untrained eye could not perceive, as if there were a spell protecting the last threshold to... What?

Part II
Entering the Darkness Within

TWENTY-THREE

Passing on into a final clearing, they came into a very large open space riddled with torches drowning out the moon light. She could now see that there were numerous buildings of various sizes spread out around a common area that was the size of several football fields but without any bleachers. Devon pulled the car up to a large rounded dome-like building that seemed to be the focal point of the entire complex.

Looking around her, Kat asked, "Are there actually any people that live here?"

Smiling without a word this time, Devon stopped and got out of the car, walking over to where she was emerging and took her hand tenderly in his. "Oh, they're here all right. Most of them, that is."

On the point of asking him Where?, she took in this massive building that he was about to lead her into. She remembered it from one of those earlier visions of Devon. It felt as if it were some kind of a church, but there were such feelings of peace and well-being radiating out from it, that it took her breath away.

She found herself crying with the sense of profound Peace, that she almost didn't notice a small group of people beginning to emerge from it. That it almost wiped way the last few days of terror. Almost.

Kat couldn't make out whether these were men, women or both. They were all dressed in robes of a deep purple that seemed to shimmer in the flickering torchlight. And there, in the middle of these, was one of them who was crowned by a white overlay.

The One in White began raising their arms — palm up — but not in welcome so much as in warding, and Kat felt herself freeze at this.

She also felt as if she were being scanned as much as Devon had often done, but this time it felt to Kat as if this scan were reaching very deeply into her very soul. She couldn't figure out whether this felt as if it were a scalpel peeling away her outer layer in utter pain... Or whether it felt like ecstasy in the act of being laid bare to the soul.

After what seemed like hours of this, this Figure lowered Its hands.

Devon walked Kat up to— *This Man*? she thought, and extended his left hand into an act of both obedience and reverence, and taking it to his chest, bowing to this person.

Rising from this gesture, "Dr. Kathryn Runyon, I wish to introduce you to the leader of our Community," he said formally. "This is Angelus."

And then stepping back and bowing — as if he had just introduced her to royalty — he left Kat standing awkwardly in front of this
268

hooded figure who said nothing. *But, oh that nothing*, Kat thought.

Having become accustomed to being frightened by anyone veiled with a hood, she now realized where a large part of that peaceful feeling had come from. This... "Angelus." Without even trying, Kat senses that this is one of the most powerful Beings on the planet and she's immediately cowed. Having become accustomed to being frightened by anyone veiled with a hood, she now realized that This "Angelus" was where a large part of that peaceful feeling had come from.

This figure didn't feel like anything she had ever encountered before. She felt that she was in the presence of a saint, or someone very much like it. Only, this was... Different. She felt both completely at ease with this person, as well as being totally daunted by being in Its presence. This was God, as much as The Beast was so totally Other than.

Those ancient looking hands once again reached up, only this time they drew the hood back away from Its head. Kat could finally see that this person who was standing in front of her was actually a She, (although she felt that that distinction didn't ring completely true, either).

In a way, Angelus felt as if she were both a woman and a man as well, and in some strange way She transcended both distinctions. *Curious,* Kat thought.

"And not entirely untrue," the figure "Angelus" finally said,

269

breaking her Silence.

Feeling suddenly unsettled again, Kat asked again aloud (in a voice she clearly thought to be a "thought"), "Is every one here going to be reading my mind?"

"No, my dear," Angelus said walking forward. Those hands extending her hands towards Kat's, seemed to settle on them as lightly as a hummingbird, even though Angelus was still feet away from touching her. This gesture calmed Kat's inner turmoil almost instantly.

"Normally, we are not that intrusive," she said softly. Then she added with a much more forceful intent, "Only when necessary."

Wise cracking without thinking about it, Kat retorted, "Well, that's comforting," immediately regretting the comment.

"And entirely understandable," Angelus smiled comfortingly, "Considering what you've been through. As well as what you've been subjected to," she added with another small, and much more mysterious smile.

Suddenly, Angelus felt very much like a woman to Kat. *A much older and deeply wiser woman, but a woman nonetheless.*

She felt herself moving in to take the hands that Angelus offered as Kat relaxed her guard. Angelus in turn reached out and embraced Kat.

Kat moved into the embrace like a hungry child, feeling as if she had never experienced anything like it before. Even the embrace of Devon back in that dingy motel room just a day before (now feeling more like years ago now), didn't feel like this.

270

She began crying softly first and then found herself sobbing uncontrollably, as if the years of the Dark Mysteries were lifting and heading towards being released and forgiven. As if from the very Being and Essence of God Himself.

She felt herself begin the releasing process, shedding layers of all of her anger, fear and hurt, in the embrace of this woman that she had seemingly only met just moments before. Kat felt as if they had known each other for years; even lifetimes, perhaps.

She could also feel more so than hear, Angelus telling her that she was safe now. And slowly, after standing in this embrace for what began to feel like decades, she began to release her hold on this strange but comforting woman, stepping back.

Sobering up, Kathryn wiped the tears from her face with her now dirty blouse, and laughed self-consciously at this show of what felt (to her) as un-adult like behavior.

Except that when she allowed herself to lift her eyes to look at the older woman, Angelus was not looking critically, but lovingly, at her. Softening up, Kat even smiled a little in return of the warm Madonna-like mother smile she was receiving.

Releasing Kat, Angelus turned towards Devon, telling him aloud, "You have done well, Devon. May you never be so sorely tested again." But to him She spoke formally without speaking, *Go now. Rest. Your arduous and harrowing journey has ended. Go and get the rest your soul is craving.*

And Devon, bowing deeply, said a silent *Thank you, Ancient*, and turned away towards one of the other buildings.

Turning to Kat, he caresses her face and tells her, "This is as far as I can go with you right now."

"Will I—" she starts to ask.

Interrupting her, he says, "Yes, but not for now," and walks away without looking back, while leaving her in the presence of this mysterious and daunting Figure.

Nodding to Kat, The Ancient gestures towards a bench that Kat hadn't noticed just a second before. Beyond it, the hallway leading into this building is dark and foreboding.

"Do not fear. You will see your Devon again," Angelus told her. Kat resisted the temptation to turn to watch Devon walk away. In her mind, she could feel that he was desperately tired and he needed to rest.

Sitting down and placing her hand on the bench next to her, Kat feels the Command of *Sit*. When she does, Angelus begins telling her, "First of all, Doctor," becoming formal, "You are still an Unknown. We do not know as of yet whether you were "allowed" to come here, or you were *meant* to come here."

Asking in a trembling voice, as if she thought that had been settled, "You mean, you're still not sure yet whether I'm a double agent or not?"

"I believe the current terminology is *mole*." She says with a slight bit of irony in her voice. "Before we can truly trust you, we need you to allow us to give you a few certain tests."

"Tests?" Kat asked apprehensively.

"To determine your true nature, as it were. Whether you have indeed been sent to us by The Light… or by — The Other Side."

This was sounding ominous to her. As if should she *fail* these tests, she might be killed.

Reaching up to take her hood fully down, Kat could now clearly see that she was indeed a woman. Standing and placing her hand palm up at her side, "Come." Kat could feel that she was supposed to place her hand — and her trust — in this woman.

"You must work to clear out that which is your Dark Past once and for all, and step fully and completely into The Light. This will happen in the building behind us, which we call the Flight House."

"I'm sorry… The What?" Kat asked incredulously, as she heard "Fight" house in her mind.

"It is called the Flight House, but it is flying in the *spiritual* sense and not in the physical."

"Spiritual? As in… What's going to happen to me? Are you going to perform an exorcism on me?"

At this, The Ancient did finally laugh. "Perhaps, nothing. And perhaps… Everything." Emphatically holding her hand out once again, Angelus grabs Kat's hand and begins walking away now, dragging the younger woman into the dark maw of that door.

Reaching out again, Angelus formally and forcefully took Kat's hand as she stood and began leading her into the open barn door of what she heard in her head was *The Sanctuary*. They crossed the threshold and Kat felt as if she had crossed over into another level of safety.

Turning away from Kat and heading back towards the door from which they came, Kat felt compelled to follow. "This is a Refuge," she said as she did. As Kat followed to be at her side, Angelus also said, "But in a way, this is also a Stronghold. A Fortress of Intent."

As they walked into the warm darkness without fear, Angelus tells her, "Yes, you are very powerful, indeed.

"All will be explained," is all the Ancient replies, as Kat feels a soft and silent rejoinder of, *Soon.* "Come," Kat felt *commanded* again.

Walking through the sudden darkness of this birth canal-like tunnel, they crossed over yet another psychic threshold into a huge open area inside. Her eyes adjusting quickly, Kat was taken aback by the large number of men and women, and even a few very self-aware looking children and teens, that were gathered just inside. *There must be hundreds of them*, she thought, as she looked over the wide expanse of the interior of this domed building.

Then the room went completely dark. As if she had walked from a fully lit room into a fully dark one, Kat blinked against the sudden transition. *Is this the first test?* she asked herself.

Her eyes adjusting to the difference and began to open wide. The

274

"Room" that she found herself in, was huge. She could now see that there was a dim light from the torches she had seen gathered around outside filtering into windows that were high above her. It only made the space look even more enormous — and open, and menacingly... Her mind was confused by more than just the size of this room.

Stepping into the center of the room, still following the dim figure of The Ancient, light began building seemingly out of nowhere. She felt as she reached the center, as if there were a spotlight from above, building in strength until it became a blinding brilliance.

Covering her eyes with her arms, she found that she still could not block out this Light.

Just as suddenly, the Light began becoming less intense, so that she let her arms slowly drift away from her eyes.

But this only startled her even more. Instead of being in a building, at night... She appeared to be in the clouds. During the full light of day. With the *ground* being far below her.

Feeling truly disoriented now, her feet felt as if the ground had dropped out from underneath her. Flailing her arms and legs, as if she needed to fly, she found that she was not falling after all, but floating.

Her heart suddenly let her know that it had been racing, ever since she had stepped into that blinding Light. She felt an anxiety unlike she had ever known, even in the replaying of the scenes where she "remembered" her "fights" — first with the Demon in her patient's body and then Kirsten in the therapy room, in the parking lot, and then with Tom.

"This isn't real. This isn't real," she told herself, trying to calm herself down. "This is just some sort of—"

Dissociation? A Voice asked suddenly.

"Magic trick," Kat replied.

"Magic can be a trick. Yes," the Voice replied again.

In her mind she said, *that must be The Ancient.*

"Just so," The Ancient replied back. And as soon as she says this, a circle of sitting figures floating as if on their own individual clouds appear around her.

"Not all appears to be as it is," The Ancient tells her, looking up from her place in the Council.

"This is the first test. And also, the first lesson. You have already seen much. Devon has also shown and told you much."

"My feet are still solidly on the ground of the Flight House then?" Kat asked, bewildered.

Almost smiling at this, The Ancient looked up and said, "Who told you the ground was solid?"

And just as suddenly, the clouds and the Council disappeared, as did the light of day, and Kat felt herself plunging into the Darkness.

Punctuating the Darkness that she found herself in, were points of firelight probing beyond the black-hooded Multitude of Figures surrounding her at the stump of a woodland Altar, a raging bonfire next to it.

A screaming child appears out from beneath the robe of one of these Figures, placing it in the middle of the stump. She watches as the hand of another child appears in front of her. A jeweled Dagger dripping with bloody emeralds is placed in that little hand—

And all of a sudden, Kat realizes that the "hand" she is seeing… is hers. Where the hilt of the dagger is now being place into.

The raging Chanting begins building once again to its inevitable feverish pitch, as her younger Self plunges that Blade into the suddenly silenced child below her. Closing her eyes at this, the sound of the crashing Multitude also comes to a crashing stop.

Opening her eyes, the adult Kathryn Runyon finds herself lying on the ground, sobbing hysterically in the darkness. Alone. With no one surrounding her.

"This is only the first step," she hears the disembodied Voice of The Ancient telling her as she falls asleep continuing to sob.

Coming back to the present, Kat looks around to see the large number of people that were the Community… vanish. The members of the Council are now the only ones left, and they have turned from kindly to fiercely evil looking beings, floating on red-tinged clouds. But the clouds were not tinged by any sunset, but by the pyres lit from below. The earth below her now was lit by so many pyres that were everywhere; sacrifices being given to—

"Surely you did not think you would be allowed to get to a place like this. Did You?" the man named Gregory, a middle-aged black man with a rim of fire appearing as a halo above him asked.

Kat turns to the still angelic looking Angelus, who slowly begins turning darker and morphing into something resembling The Monstrosity. Only this Monstrosity is still the Leader.

"We are your true Family," she hears, coming out of the Monstrosity. "Come back to Reality, Doctor!" And with this, the Monstrosity morphs into the (now) demonically grinning Jimmy Hagan. "Did you didn't think that I was *only* a **Guard** now? Did you?

Feeling herself being broken down quickly, Kat begins sobbing at this attack.

"All you need do is Come Back! Come Back! Come Back to fulfill your Destiny!" she now heard her Father saying. "Give up on Running. You can't Run from us. You cannot hide in such a pitiful group of demons as these. Come back to your True Path!"

Crumbling now at all the Cries coming from everywhere around her all at once were shouting, "Come Back! Come Back!" Kat was about to break down and cry out with a "Yes!"

But instead of *Yes*, what she said instead was a quietly resounding, "No."

Feeling the White Heat of the Other rising up inside of her, she felt that Power rising from the Core of Who She Truly Is. Rising up, ready to display her full Power against this Dark attempt to break her.

But instead of sending ripples of Light out against this Dark Uprising, she took a deep breath drawing in her strength, seeking to

278

destroy It once and for all.

The White Light began turning all of the Demons around her — into dark clouds now lit with white, dispersing everything surrounding her into a glowing mass of Light.

As Angelus stepped out of this cloud, she raised her arms to embrace Kat. "Forgive us, but you are the most Powerful Being to enter here... Ever.

"We had to make sure."

Caught between anger that she had been tested so sorely and threatened to rise once again... And the relief that she now knew which side of the divide she lay on, "Then I'm—

"Yes, Daughter. Welcome to The Community of Light, Kathryn," Angelus announced with a whisper that sounded as if it rebounded off of the walls and ceiling. "You are safe here, by the love and devotion of All of those around you who have helped you on your journey to be here now."

Looking up, she could once again see the sea of shyly smiling faces lit from within that were surrounding her; indeed had apparently been surrounding her throughout her ordeal. Like meeting Angelus outside this hall, her heart melted at this reaction, with her tears beginning to flow freely once again.

Beside her once again without a sound, Angelus floated back into her awareness. "Come, my dear," she said, taking Kat's hand tenderly. "I will make a "wild guess" as they say now, that you might like a warm bath and some fresh clothing."

Turning to the older woman, Kat almost melted on the spot. "God, that would be nice," she said with more emotion than she intended and the suggestion merited.

"This is Lilly," Angelus said, as one of the younger Community members shyly stepped up to her side. "She will take you to where you need." Lilly *looked* to be a teenager, except for the *look* in her eyes.

Looking around her, she suddenly remembered that Devon was nowhere to be seen. *I suppose he knows this place well*, she thought, feeling a little more hurt now than she thought she might.

Was he reporting back to his "superiors?" she suddenly thought. And then another thought came that she wasn't sure was hers, *Don't be ridiculous. These **are** his "superiors,"* it said.

Kat looked around suspiciously, but saw that everyone around her was once again in deep meditation. And that the mysterious "Angelus" had once again floated far away and was taking a seat on the soft packed earth that was on the opposite side of the room from Kat. It *felt* to Kat as if it were *her* (Angelus's) seat, as she gracefully (seemingly belying her years) turned and floated into place.

Kat felt suddenly both bereft and alone, as well as completely welcome, as all of those around her grew quiet in body and mind. With separate seeming sides inside of her fighting for dominance, she felt both drawn to walk away and also drawn to sit down in the silence around her.

280

I'm not ready for this quite yet, she thought to herself, and found her body instead turning and walking away.

In the birth canal seeming hallway that led back to the outside, she said to the girl Lilly walking softly and quietly beside her, "That bath does sound nice." To which the younger girl smiled shyly at.

Stepping outside once again, she found herself standing in the soft shining light of what seemed suddenly like a billion stars beaming their light down from centuries past. Suddenly the stars seemed much closer, and the days of panicked running (even the specter of The Preacher), began receding into the more distant past. This was indeed a sanctuary, she finally felt, as the faint sound of humming began filtering out from the building behind her.

Now she felt as if she were looking forward more to sleeping in a clean bed than even that hot bath, as she moved towards a large building that had lights lit in it across the field. The warmth of those lights beckoned to her now even more than the supposed sanctuary of her apartment ever had.

That bath having been forgotten in her need for sleep, her body was exhausted as it had other ideas to occupy her mind. After having been shown her newly appointed bed and then taken to where she could have that bath, she was beginning to feel as if she was in heaven now, with the peace that pervaded this place.

Later, lying back in the feathery soft bed in the dorm style room that she had been shown, Kat wondered if she was going to see Devon again. Her heart had this deep ache now at the thought that she might not. Even the blessedly welcome hot steaming bath that she had just luxuriated in, couldn't heal that thought.

But her body, exhausted as it was, had other ideas to occupy her mind. She found herself drifting off soundly into the warm fields of a deep sleep lacking any disturbing dreams to interrupt her night this time.

For the first time in weeks, or perhaps even years.

TWENTY-FOUR

Waking up gently this time without any hazy memories of dreams exploding into nightmares breaking through, Kat sat up suddenly. Were the nightmares a thing of the past now that she was finally here and seemingly protected? Or was this merely a rest before the storm? Her *final* test last night... Last night? Time had become such an unreal thing since her life — what she had once thought of was her life — had imploded back at Hawthorne.

Kat lay back in the soft bed watching the play of sunlight on the ceiling above her. There were trees swaying outside that were blocking some of the sunshine, waving hypnotically and calmingly in the presence of a crisp, gentle mountain breeze she could feel blowing through the window close by. The scent of the pine trees just outside drifted in the windows, filling her lungs with their peaceful aroma.

Not in any rush for the first time in days, she let herself laze in the fragrant covers floating just below her chest, not feeling any need to rise or to cringe. *I could lie here like this for days, drifting in and out of sleep,* she thought, and then let her mind grow soothingly blank once again.

She was almost ready to drift off back to sleep for another few days, when all of a sudden Devon's finally smiling face appeared in her mind.

Kat wondered once again if she was ever going to see Devon again. Her heart had this deep ache at the thought that she would not. Even the blessedly welcome hot steaming bath of the night before that she had luxuriated in, couldn't heal that thought.

But her body had other ideas. She found herself drifting back off dreamily into the airy fields of a deep sleep lacking any disturbing dreams to interrupt this time.

She awoke with a mild start, realizing she had indeed gone back to sleep. The light was decidedly much lower and no longer in evidence on the ceiling, but coming in low from off in the West. But a hunger in her stomach was now however very much coming to her mind as evidence, making her wonder exactly how long she had been asleep.

Dressed now in the flowing off-white robe that she had been given the *previous night,* she was off in search of both food and Devon. And Kat was unsure of what order her priority was for either at the moment.

Later after she had eaten (more she thought than she should have — because she found she was famished) she was starting to get upset that her "other priority" hadn't put in an appearance yet. It bothered her that Devon hadn't even left her a note. Was he really gone? Now that his "task" was completed, did he feel that it was better to just disappear?

Walking across the great expanse that was the common area of this village towards the second largest building, she was again struck at both the size, and the (seeming) emptiness, of this place where fate had brought her to. *Where are all the People I saw last night today?* she wondered, as she slowly walked across.

Suddenly, as if from out of nowhere, she found Devon at her side. Very little surprising her at this point, she tried not to jump when she realized he was there.

"Well, good morning, sleepy head," he said, although it was obviously no longer any where close to morning. "Did you sleep well?"

"Yes," she said. Then stopping and turning towards him, "But just exactly how long have I been asleep?"

"Oh… For days," he said playfully, although a hint of concern was lurking just below his smile suggesting to her that he wasn't joking.

He was now dressed like everyone else in the flowing purple robe that passed for a uniform in this place. Even the children wore a modified version of this.

"No, really," she pleaded.

Sighing, as if he were afraid that she would ask, he reached out and put his arm around her waist. "A day and a half now," he told her, nuzzling into her hair. "You had us worried there for a while. All of us except Angelus, that is. She told us that you just needed to rest. That a part of you had exerted more in the last week than you had in your entire life."

Shivering involuntarily for a second, Kat moved in closer to him as they continued walking.

"But... Here you are," he said cheerfully. "Healthy, looking rested, and—"

Turning sober, she corrected him with, "But, it was touch and go."

Turning sober himself, he agreed. "Yes. It was touch and go for a while. The Red Circle exerted great energy towards turning you against us during that time. It's probably a blessing that you don't remember any of the battle that ensued."

Blanching again at this, she could feel that it was true. And that as much as she wanted the battle to be over, it wasn't.

Turning cheerful again, (almost forcedly so) he said, "Let's go get something to eat. I don't know about you, but I'm starving." And disengaging from her waist, slipped his hand into hers for the remaining walk.

She didn't bother telling him that she had already eaten, but was just glad that he hadn't put in a "disappearance."

While he was looking away from her, Devon closed his eyes as they walked, extending his senses deep into her body and psyche to make sure she was as recovered as she looked. He occasionally turned to smile broadly at her (also to gage her reaction) and was finally satisfied at what he saw and felt.

The Main Dining Hall was a large affair too. In a way, it was almost like it was a monastery to Kat though. Or a military base. She couldn't quite tell which at this point.

"Not quite as enormous and cavernous as The Flight House, but close enough," Devon remarked mysteriously.

"The Flight House." she asked.

"That's where you saw everyone that first night; where you met Angelus."

"But why is it called the Flight House," she asked, more curious than disturbed.

"That's for later," was his only response. "Let's not talk about anything so serious for a while," he finished, tantalizing her with yet another mysterious element to this place.

They had been sitting down while Devon eat "for a while" now, when Kat turned to him and asked him once again, "So, why is it called the flight house, Devon?"

Sighing, as if he were not really ready to tell her, he grew sober again. Stopping and starting to speak a number of times, he finally settled in for the explanation.

"It's called The Flight House, because it's where we all have to go when we first come here, to take the journey into the darkness that was our life before," he said without further explanation.

"Before..." she began, trying to lead him on. "Before, we got here?" she asked teasing out the answer.

"Yes," he said, taking another bite of his remaining food to stall.

"Why do I get the feeling that you haven't told me much of anything before now?"

Obviously weighing internally how much he even wanted to tell her now, he paused before continuing. "Because it might have only frightened you more than you already were," he finally told her.

Stopping and turning to fully face her and taking her by the shoulders with both hands, he began looking deeply into her eyes. "You see Kat, you've only had a glimpse of what we're up against. Some of them are very powerful, and you have much to learn."

She almost asked him, *More powerful than The Preacher? Than my Father?*

Kat was growing concerned now, but she worked to keep her expression still innocently quizzical. Seeing her reaction, Devon suppresses a smile. "Despite your rather impressive abilities to deal with some very rough characters recently."

Then growing more solemn, "And, I haven't told you even a small part of what I know."

"And you're not going to tell me any more," she stated with certainty.

"You'll know more than you want to in a short time. More than you'll ever wish you knew about this world." Dropping his hands, he returned to silently finishing off his plate.

Letting the discussion drop with a sigh, Kat turned her attention to doing the same, helping him to finish the remains of his food off. Both of them eating in an uneasy silence now, she suppressed her other pressing concern.

Were they going to be able to continue the deeper part of their journey they started back in the motel.

shadows and **LIGHT**

TWENTY-FIVE

Devon had been showing her the property since the night before, and she had let go the discussion about what she didn't know but felt was coming, laying low for now. "Let's take a walk. Shall we?" Devon said, getting up from the table. "Perhaps it's even time for some answers, I suppose."

Leaving the Dining Hall, Kat was curious about this place. *Beyond the high, lofty goals of the night before, that is.*

Strolling arm in arm (now that danger wasn't actively pursuing them), she had let go the discussion about what she didn't know but felt was coming laying low until now. Walking by Devon's side, she was suddenly struck by the feeling of "normal," and being "at home" that she was feeling, that had felt like such foreign concepts to her before now.

Then she realized, "It's so quiet here," Kat remarked suddenly. "All these people, and no one's talking. And yet there's this feeling of peace—"

"Oh, there are plenty of people talking. Just not speaking."

"I expected laughter and joy," Kat sighed. "But everyone's so—"

"Somber?"

"Yes. It's as if no one knows each other and they're just not—"

"Content not to be engaged in idle chatter?"

"God, you're making me feel like—"

"You're just not used to it," Devon says and stops to caress her cheek.

"The no need to talk?"

"The peace. There's no need for conflict here. Everyone here has had enough conflict before they got here."

"Yes. But all these families…" she said, crying inwardly.

"Many of the families you see here, are families of choice, not birth."

"If they can get beyond the horror—"

"Everyone deals with what brought them here differently. You'll understand, and hopefully soon."

She could feel the breeze blowing lightly on her face and through her long coppery hair, and because of the silence, also heard the rustling of the pine trees everywhere. Lifting her head up, she once again took in a deep breath of the crisp, clean air, and looked into the deep blue barely cloudy sky above.

"When you become more acclimated, you'll be hearing conversations taking place all over." Grasping her hand even more

Robin Chappell

lovingly, "Come. I have something to show you."

Devon finally allowed himself to smile. She couldn't help but follow him in smiling. "Where—" she started to ask, but he just lifted his free finger up to his mouth with a silent *Shush*.

Walking further and passing through into a clearing of especially deep fragrant pines, she finally allowed herself to take a really deep breath of ease for the first time.

They came through a clearing and Kat found herself standing at the edge of the Mountaintop they were on, looking out on miles and miles of clouds and land that stretched off in the distance seemingly forever., she found her breath catching at the beauty of it all.

"I've never seen—" she started to say, breathing deep with a shudder that turned into sighing deeply. She remembered once again what he had told her about not remembering places she had been to, and decided not to press the issue for now. "This is such a strange place; so strange, and yet so beautiful."

Clasping her hand even more tightly in his than he had before, she could feel his concern and growing anguish. "Consider this a rest before the coming storm. And know that this place is being guarded in ways that you can't even understand yet. But you will, and hopefully soon."

Great. More mysteries, she sighed inwardly.

Turning towards Devon and stepping closer, she asked hesitantly,

"But what *am* I doing being here? Besides being protected, I mean."

"If you knew what we're doing, you might not want to go any further. But you'll be up to it. Angelus—"

"Gives me the creeps, in some way," she interrupted, shivering without any breeze to react to. "She's so motherly one moment, and then the next—"

Laughing ruefully, Devon said knowingly, "Angelus has knowledge and power that are way beyond your understanding. And, she's older than you can imagine.

"It's been rumored that The Ancient — Angelus — has been alive for hundreds, if not thousands of years. No one knows for certain."

"But... How is that even possible? I mean—"

"It comes from Dedication to Spiritual Practice. It's said that by learning how to control physical reality, we can live forever. If we wanted to, that is."

'Why wouldn't you? Want to live forever, I mean."

"We already *do* live forever," he said.

"We do?" she asked incredulously.

"Yes, we do; just not in the same body, that's all.

Lifting his hand in the air to trace an infinity sign, it glowed brightly in the afternoon sun, as he repeated it several times, "World without End, Amen." And continuing to trace the symbol in the air, she noticed that each time he did, the trail ended in the Center, and started

294

again on the other side.

"Each body is a finite loop. When the Cult tries to live forever in one body, it breaks the cycle. That way they never learn from their mistakes, only getting caught up in them even more. They get caught up in the material world, and end up stagnating."

"So do they live forever?"

"No. A very long time is not forever. Even with all the ritual magic, their bodies do eventually break down. Nothing material is forever. That's not its purpose. That 's the purpose of Spirit."

"So then, why?" Kat asked.

"Because that's what reincarnation is for. Most of us need many different forms over many centuries to get to the point where we can see the One True Form, the One Being that is God. To know that We are all God. That there is only One Being."

"Have you?"

"Yes. And you will soon see your other lives as well. If—"

"Do I want to?"

Not smiling suddenly, Devon continued. "But those of the Red Circle live for a long time, too. Only they do it by killing others to control the life process."

"That's what the Multiples — the Cauldrons — are for?"

"That's one of the reasons, yes."

Turning to stand in front of her and holding her at the shoulders, he began gazing deeply into her eyes. "It's also said that your own father is probably as old as The Ancient as well; if not older."

Gasping in realization at the toll, "How many children have—"

"There are some things it is best not to think about," he told her gravely.

Feeling a sudden chill run between them, Kat felt him begin to withdraw. As if there was something that he was not telling her.

Releasing her and walking away, Kat stands where he left her, feeling stunned at the thought of her father. And also at how she had unconsciously helped him over the years at this evil, blood-soaked task. A severe shudder suddenly racked her body.

"Am I going to become like her?" Kat asked.

Hesitant again, Devon turned to look off into the Rockies. "I don't know," he eventually told her, his voice wavering, betraying the depth of his concern for her.

"Am I going to become a monster? Some twisted tool that doesn't feel anything?" she asked, and then also hesitantly added, "Like my father?" *Like the Monstrosity*, she caught herself thinking.

Laughing awkwardly at this suddenly, he turned to her and said, "Now *you're* being melodramatic."

Kat felt her face become deadly serious.

Looking at her, Devon saw a dark cloud that seemed to pass over it, leaving an involuntary shiver running through her body behind it. Devon pretended not to notice, maintaining a forced smile, but inwardly cringed.

"I hope so. I don't want to become a monster. Either for the Light, or the Dark," she said, echoes sounding of something below the surface that disturbed Devon deeply. He hoped that she hadn't felt what he saw.

Lightly but with a difficult to hide concern playing behind it, he said, "You won't."

Lightening up at this, she managed a smile, however faint. "If you say so," she said, and mimicking Angelus added with a husky voice, "My dear."

And then, not so lightly she added, "I won't worry."

"Good. Then I think you'll be just fine."

Brightening considerably, Kat returns her gaze to looking toward the new horizon. "But speaking of Angelus," she continued, her thoughts returning to her fears, "Why haven't I seen her since I woke up?"

She looked at Devon who was doing his best to keep smiling, "You will soon," he said. *A little too soon, I'm afraid*, he thought, glad that she couldn't read his mind yet. "She just has a lot she's dealing with at the moment."

But as soon as she turned away, his smile began fading into a very troubled look.

"Like my arrival here," Kat said, with an edge to her voice.

Unable to keep the full concern out of his voice this time, he merely answered heavily, "Yes."

Breaking the heavy silence that descended between the two of them, "They're really desperate to find you, sending all that firepower They were sending."

"But why? I still don't understand why I am such a—"

"You are the result of centuries of their breeding program to create someone as powerful as you are. But it was their mistake that you weren't, in the end, *controllable by* them. That's why they're unleashing Hell itself as it were to find you. And destroy you."

"Oh," was her only reaction possible.

Turning towards her very affectionately, "But They made someone that is beyond their powers. *That* is why *you're so special*.

"Your father is — for all intents and purposes — the Anti-Christ. The Beasts commanding General on earth."

"The Anti-Christ?" she asked incredulously. "You're—"

"I'm afraid not."

"That's why you said if you told me—"

"Yes. You might be too afraid of what was coming.

"But you are a very powerful being. Something that they did not count on when they sent the Sentinel known as The Preacher against you. You and I should not have been able to fend off the attack. But you, my dear, did. You beat back one of the most powerful Mages that they had, and sent him running."

Coming to a standstill, Kat was finally understanding the immense severity of what she was apparently born for.

"I'm sure it was quite a shock to them, to find out just exactly how powerful you indeed are."

"And they didn't know already?"

Amused by her sudden puff of ego, Devon reminded her, "Yes. And... no. But don't let it go to your head. Ego is how they capture you. If you let it feed into your pride, you'll be more likely to cross over to the Darkness.

"The Darkness feeds on Control. Trying to Control the very fabric of nature and what passes for the illusion of reality, is how they live."

"The illusion of reality" she repeated. "And don't you and the Others—"

"Lightworkers?"

"Yes. Don't you—"

"Not like the Darkness does. We seek to be in harmony with The Light. To work with, and not against, the Grand Purpose."

"Which is?"

"God Knowing ITself. That's what the Evolution of All Life is about."

"And what am *I* supposed to do in all of this?"

"You were something that they created, and then they learned the hard way that they couldn't control. You did something that you weren't supposed to be able to do."

"Control. And that something is?"

"You're one of the Chosen; One of those who chose to come into this life at this time, to do something that—"

Amazement turning to amusement as she interrupted him with a sarcastic laugh, "What? Like Israel was the chosen of God, you mean? Like that?"

Smiling despite himself, he told her, "Yeah. Something like that." Walking away from her, she began pursuing him.

"The— Chosen," she continued to scoff. This was really too much for her. "Is that all you're going to say? We're—" mad she stopped and made air quotes, "special? Is that it?"

Without turning, he told her, "Yes. Because we Remember." Turning and walking back to face her, he took hold of her gently on both arms. "We — all of us here — have been advanced spiritual beings for many lifetimes. We've chosen to come back to help prepare the rest of the world for the Transition."

"The..." she started to say and then stopped.

Slipping his arm gently around her waist, he paused before continuing. Choosing his words carefully, "The Shift that I told you about on the road. The transition from the physical level to the next level of evolution."

"The Spiritual."

Letting her waist go, "Yes. And those who follow the Beast—"

"As in, Satan."

"Yes. As in Satan… Baal… Beelzebub… Old Scratch. IT has gone by a great many names, but ITs not really anything like—"

"And you were going to tell me this when we were in a safe place. I'm assuming that this is as safe as it gets."

"Yes," he said, a little too grimly. "This is about as safe as you're likely to be on the planet. As in the safe house we stayed at, there are those of us here that are expending great energy at this time shielding this Community from outside intrusion."

"Like a force field from Star Trek."

"Exactly," he said, stroking her face lovingly. "Only we use our abilities to help shield and protect this location, in much the same way as I did with the illusion I created in the truck stop restaurant."

His face crisscrossed with both worry and love. He took her in his arms for a few moments before continuing, not wanting to explain further.

Impatient for him to continue, she said into his shoulder, "I wish you didn't have to lay it out for me like this, but part of me is resisting knowing."

Sighing, he said, "Yes. I know." Separating himself from her, he looked deep in her eyes for another long moment.

"Well?" she asked impatiently after the moment became too long for her taste.

"Well, I have been telling you some along the way. But I had to wait until we were sure that you weren't one of them."

"And you're sure of this now?" she said just a little too coldly.

"Do you think that your *remembering* in the Flight House was for your benefit only?"

She had a sinking feeling that they still didn't fully trust her, even now.

"I'm sorry, Kat. But we had to know."

"And you do now."

"Yes. And we also know that they're gathering their strength for coming to get you; coming against all of Us." Stopping and looking her directly in the eyes, "The final battle has just begun."

"All because of me," she said, dumbfounded.

"There's always a last straw to everything, Kat." Caressing her face suddenly, "And you were the last straw; the one they couldn't afford to loose."

Dropping her hand suddenly from his, she told him coldly, "I think I'd like to be alone for a little bit. Before my, whatever — trial, challenge — begins."

Creating his broad smile of a minute before, his hand began to stray toward her face, but Kat caught it before he went too far. Wanting ever so desperately to kiss him and allow his caress, she forced herself to turn away instead, returning to looking off into the distance.

Instead, nodding approvingly if sadly, "I think that might be a good idea," he told her. "This is a very healing spot. Arthur will know where to find you when they need you."

Merely nodding vaguely in his direction and continuing to drink in the scene before her, she waited patiently for him to leave.

Sensing that she needed this time to be alone, to begin the process she needed to undertake soon, Devon smiled and walked away.

But his smile began fading quickly as he leaves her to herself. He had seen troubling things in her face and in her mind, and he needed some time to figure out exactly what it meant.

Turning to look once more in her direction before returning back to the main campus through the clearing, he also probed her mentally and psychically to get some information to contemplate.

Instead of feeling her open to his higher senses though, he worriedly finds a shield up preventing him from knowing. Something that she had not had in place before. He wondered whether this was a new form of attack on her, or worse yet, a strengthening of her Dark Side gaining prominence.

Whatever Godness Wills, he thinks, thinking once again that their liaison in the motel room might have been a grave mistake.

After a while of sitting by herself in the late mid-day that was quickly turning to dusk, Kat looked up to see Angelus standing just a few yards away. She hadn't heard any footsteps, and was afraid that she has dissociated once again. *But I hadn't*, she thought. *I felt her coming this time.*

Just so, she heard quietly in the back of her mind.

Kat looked up and saw Angelus standing in front of her, then just as suddenly, she also realized that Angelus wasn't standing on any solid ground. She had just walked off into "thin air" about four or five feet past the cliff's edge and appeared to be floating there. "What did I say the previous night about this thing called *solidity*?" she asked, walking towards Kat and back on to "solid ground."

Only this was in what Kat called *reality*. *Unless I'm being hypnotized or mentally manipulated into believing what I'm obviously **seeing***, she thought. "Is nothing real?" Kat asked, afraid to hear the answer.

"And how do we know that this is reality?" Angelus asked her verbally.

Moving in silently and sitting down effortlessly beside Kat, Angelus remains silent for a long while, barely acknowledging Kat's presence.

"Reality is a relative thing," Angelus replied after a while. "Why do you still question what is possible, and what is not? Have you not performed miracles? Moving cars around with your mind?"

Angelus turned quiet, leaving Kat to continue looking out over the *illusion* of the great distance in front of them. They stayed silent for what seemed to Kat to be a very long time. *What is she expecting of me*, she thought.

Just as Kat was beginning to feel unnerved by this silent presence, Angelus turned toward her just enough for Kat to feel that she was being regarded intentionally and about to be spoken to.

Finally, Angelus said quietly, "So I assume that you are feeling better?"

Unsure as to whether it had been a question or a statement, Kat replied slowly, "Yes," feeling as if she were once again being tested somehow. "It's nice to get out of the car, to not feel so much in danger," she replied guardedly.

Turning fully towards her now, Angelus smiled her Mona Lisa like smile again, a gesture that Kat felt was more for her benefit than out of any warmth towards her now.

"Not exactly true," Angelus said in reply to this unspoken feeling.

Not sure of exactly what to say being alone in the presence of this woman who did not somehow feel completely human, Kat hesitated. Finally, she asked, "What is it that you're expecting of me? Am I going to be tested every day I'm here? Or do I get some kind of a merit badge at some point, so I can relax?"

Feeling, more than actually seeing amusement on the elderly woman's face this time, Angelus replied to Kat's anger with a light touch. "I am sorry you feel this way, but you do understand something of the danger we potentially face after your encounter with the Entity known as The Preacher back in Boulder. Do you not?"

Sighing and knowing that what she was saying was unfortunately very real, Kat deflated. She was both still hurt and understanding at the same time. "Yes," she replied, sighing.

"There are many things that you need to learn about yourself, Kathryn. And there are many things that we need to learn about you as well."

Suddenly standing, Angelus began walking away from Kat. Reaching out her hand to Kat, she stood and followed over to where The Ancient *stood.*

Looking down suddenly, Kat realized that *she* was now not standing on "solid ground" herself, but that she had somehow "walked off the edge of the mountain." As with the first "test," she felt herself begin panicking and looking for "solid ground" to retreat back to.

Relax into the illusion, the Older Woman told her. *Relax and find your footing, even in the illusion.*

Kat's mind reeled at this, and then just as suddenly, found herself and Angelus standing on the ground she craved to be on. *Or the illusion of it*, she thought. Reaching out her hand for emphasis, Kat hesitates before reaching to take it, at Angelus' side and ready to walk away.

"You have seen — and done, the Impossible." Gesturing to her feet, "This is you, yourself, making this possible, because all things are possible. The Incredible is merely a state of mind."

Angelus whispers suddenly, "Isn't it beautiful here?"

Turning towards The Ancient, Kat notices for the first time that she had walked over to take the Elder's hand once again, not noticing that as she did so, she herself had walked off the cliff's edge. Looking

306

hesitantly down, she noticed that the edge of the cliff that she had been standing on had dropped precipitously past where her feet had walked.

Gasping and fearing to stare below her, "How did I... Why didn't I..."

"See the drop off?" Angelus asked her ironically.

"Yes," was all Kat could whisper. As if to talk any louder would break the spell, leaving her to fall.

"Ah, the world of illusion," was the only reply that Angelus would give.

"So you were controlling my mind so I wouldn't see that I was walking off the edge?"

Sitting down on a non-existent rock, Angelus merely smiles for several long breaths. "Your attention was merely focused on me, so you neglected to notice the *mountain* fall away.

"So you didn't—"

"We don't work that way, my dear. Hopefully Devon explained to you the difference between Our Ways and those of The Cult?"

"You mean, about free will?"

"Yes, and that We ask, but do not compel. We seek to awaken, but not to influence."

Suddenly having lost her fear of the height she saw *below her*, a tear began coming to Kat's eyes. "Will I ever be ready to go beyond this past of mine?"

"Not yet, my dear. But hopefully soon." And taking Kat's hand, she walks the younger woman uneasily standing on nothing, leading Kat back to *reality*.

Angelus held out her other hand once more to the still in shock Kat. *Come. It is time*, Angelus *spoke*.

In a moment or two though, she sighed, stood turning to follow, finding once again that this mysterious older woman had vanished as she had appeared. "Was she even here at all?" Kat asked herself. Maybe that was how Angelus had seemingly defied gravity. She had only been a projection in Kat's mind after all.

Angelus communicated, *Come, young one. It is time*, in a way that Kat was unsure of whether she had been spoken verbally to or only in her mind. Not wanting to go anywhere, she stood her ground, continuing to gaze out at the mountains in front of her.

Once again, she heard the Voice in her head, *Come*, and she continued up the path, eager to get the next test over with.

TWENTY-SIX

Without knowing where she was to go, Kat found herself walking through the compound once more, now filled with families and lots of children.

As she passed through these idyllic scenes, she couldn't help but feel twinges of jealousy. Here were whole families who had found their way here, now seeming without concern or tragedy registering on their faces. It seemed unfair to Kat.

But as she began passing a mother, father and young son, the child — *Four? Five years old*? she thought — this "child" turned in her direction. Kat found herself at first curious, and then mesmerized, as she felt herself falling into this supposed child's gaze.

Kat found *herself* once again in the Dark, even though it had been daytime (although fading), just a moment earlier. Then she heard screaming in the distance, and realized she wasn't just *in the dark*, but was again reliving one of her Dark memories. Except that it didn't have the same feeling of horror this time. She felt detached somehow, as if she were watching a movie.

Then she became aware that "She" was breathing heavily, and trying not to breathe at all. "She'" felt her heart pounding. Then she felt that "She" was not alone. That there was another Presence pursuing her, a Presence intent on one thing: Death.

Then suddenly, without any warning, she was once again Kathryn Runyon, staring into the altogether too wise for his years stare of the "Child" in front of her.

And then she realized, that the *memory* for which she had just been frightfully in the body of, was not hers, but that of this *Child* in front of her. This *Child*, who just a moment ago she was thinking of as the "son" of the parents he was with, had been through the horror that she had been through. No doubt from a very different age that she became aware of her own situation.

Only Kat was now an adult remembering. This child she realized with horror, who was only recently in the midst of this altogether real horror, was at an age when other boys who hadn't been part of the bloody history that she and he had been a part of, were barely aware of the world around them. "The World" being one full of wonder and horror, was only a thing on TV or in the Movies. And he had already been to the depths of the worst of what this world had to offer.

Her jealousy quickly turned to shame, as she had assumed the scene in front of her was an idyllic one free from care and concern, when it hadn't been any where close to that at all.

How many children were still in that nightmare, she wailed inwardly, feeling herself crumpling in on herself? *How many would have a childhood like her that, once they became an "adult," would like her past disappear into the haze of nightmare and dissociation?*

She came back fully to her "now," finding herself suddenly staring into the eyes of a wise beyond centuries Being standing in front of her in the guise of a child. He was now nodding silently at her in acknowledgement of her late realization, and she felt more than anything else his "voice" say to her, *Courage.*

And smiling with a similar Mona Lisa smile to that of The Ancient, without another word or gesture of acknowledgement, this "Child" returned to playing with these adults who Kathryn now knew were not his real birth parents, but were the parents that this extraordinary "child'" should rightfully have been born to.

He went right back to acting the part of four year old boy he appeared to be as Kat turned away and continued on her way walking through the throng.

When Kat finally found herself at the large entrance of the building known as the Flight House — (*This was a Stable*, she finally realized. *A large training stable. And that center space was where the horses were trained.*) — she came to a standstill. Without any artificial lighting inside, it had the feel of a tunnel leading into a darkness she did not want to explore.

Picking up one foot after another, she made her way into the maw of her awaiting future (and past).

Inside, the darkness began clearing as she made her way further in. She could make out features that she had apparently been too exhausted that first night (*What night was that?* she thought) which had brought her here. With each step she could feel the air grow heavier around her.

She hadn't felt this way that "night before" (which in truth was actually three nights before). Then, the air had been filled with the collective energy of all the people that Kat had been surprised to find in the now empty cavern that was the main space under the large dome.

Now however, the emptiness she was feeling and the weight of everything that she had discovered about Her Life were pressing in on her like the walls of that trash compactor in Star Wars.

"Am I ever going to get through all of this to some other side?" she asked herself to fill the emptiness of the huge space she had walked into.

"That depends," a Voice behind her said.

Whirling quickly around and jumping out of her skin, she found Angelus standing ever so close behind her. Her heart beating frantically, she whispered, "God, I wish you wouldn't do that."

Angelus reached out and put her left hand on Kat's shoulder and Kat felt instantly, and mysteriously, at peace. "How do you do that?"

Kat asked in awe.

Gently letting her hand drift back down to meet the right one that had stayed in a position of prayer at her waist, the older woman simply smiled that enigmatic smile and turned, walking away.

Kat was both calm and felt a sense of unrestrained anger rising up deep within herself. She struggled to control the Darkness rising, and fought with herself for what seemed like minutes before she regained control.

She *knew* the Older woman was now some distance away, had felt the rising tide reaching up to drown her, but Angelus had kept on walking without concern. *Who is this person?* Kat thought, and then rushed to catch up with her.

She followed in the serene wake of this Angelus, through a door down on the opposite side of the Main Room that Kat had not seen before now, and down another corridor. She had followed the barely moving figure until they stood in front of what had obviously been a horse stall previously. The Ancient turned serenely to Kat and gestured inside, not immediately following Kat into the small space.

It was lit only by high windows that only seemed to have glass blocking out the elements. Kat found the room both comforting as well as daunting, with feelings of opposing qualities rising up from the sawdust on the floor around her.

She turned once again and found Angelus directly behind her. She congratulated herself inside for not jumping this time, but also felt that that part of her who Knew had once again known without letting the more shallow Kat know. *God, this is getting complicated*, she thought.

"So..." she said aloud just for the heck of it. "What *am* I supposed to do here?   Are you going to take me on some kind of like, shamanistic journey? Hypnotize me? What am I supposed to be looking for; remember?"

But that enigmatic smile just continued to infuriate her, as the older woman said nothing, only gesturing to the two rustic chairs that were in the center of the room. Angelus sat in one of them, and after circling it in fear for a minute, Kat finally (and warily) sat in the other one.

Angelus closed her eyes as if going into meditation. After a few minutes of this, Kat sighed and did the same. No swirling colors, no vision of her past came to her; only darkness. After a few minutes, she opened her eyes again.

Angelus had stood silently and was standing at the closed door. Kat felt herself get anxious and then felt tears forming at her eyes.

Feeling abandoned and without any sense of dignity, Kat allowed herself to call out to the figure about to exit, "Aren't you... Isn't someone going to help me in this? What am I supposed to do?

"Tell me, Angelus," Kat pleaded, and then repeated child-like, "What is it that I'm supposed to do?"

Without turning back, she heard the voice of Angelus whisper (as if she were whispering into her ear), *You will know*, and then continued on out the door in silence.

Almost beside herself now, Kat sprang out of the chair and crossed to the door. Finding it locked as she suspected, she began pacing back and forth from end to end of this small room, turning it into a circuit of the four walls.

Her abused child began quickly coming out from the closet that it had been locked in for all of those years began crying. The thirty-something year old woman was quickly finding herself changing into her three year old self. She wanted to cry out Angelus's name like a child cries out "Mommy!," but found That Part of her holding herself back.

Returning back to the Adult self and drying her eyes, she returned to pacing, beating back the tears. "Ok," she finally said once her Adult had started gaining on the Child, "I'm going to know. I'm going to know. I'm going to—" And then suddenly, with the inner chaos about to burst over the interior dam once more, she cried to the ceiling, "Just what the hell am I supposed to know?"

Stopping and feeling as if she was about to sit down and cry again, Kat stood and took a deep breath and began to make a conscious circuit of the entire room once more. She slowed her steps to a more meditative pace, working on clearing her head of the past week, and all her fears and expectations.

Stopping after the third round, she succumbed once more to the Anger rising inside of her. *Yes*, an internal Voice said, *Feel the Rage, the Power...*

The loneliness? another Voice asked. *The sense of loss? The anguish of knowing you are not loved?*

Plopping herself down in the dusty semi-darkness, she decided to give in to the little girl inside and began sobbing, rocking, and whispering defiantly. "Why me? What'd I do wrong?"

Suddenly rising and shaking her hand at the heavens, "Is this some kind of cruel joke? Are you laughing up there? Why did you put me in this—" screwing her [mind/courage] up, "Goddamned... Mess," was all she could come up with. Ironically, she was never one for cussing.

Sitting back down to cry, both the Inner Child and the Adult struggled to see which one would gain the upper hand. The no longer Dr. Kathryn Runyon was now finally finding out what it was like for her patients all those years, dealing with the internal battle that didn't seem to have any victories.

She slumped into her diminishing sense of self, exhausted from this short inner battle, wondering if she was really up to delving any deeper. She was an adult, but she was also an iceberg, and she was deeply afraid of what lay below the Dark (and Demonic) icy surface surrounding her.

Finally exhausted to the point of laying down and going to sleep, she sheepishly looked up at the ceiling once again and said a soft, "I'm sorry. But my whole life is a lie. My whole past. What is there left to do? What—" And laying down, began drifting off into the Sleep she wished she wouldn't wake up from.

But before she did, she began seeing in the deepening darkness above her, hints of ghost lights of red descending and felt them flickering, then cascading, down over her face. *Even here, I'm prone to the darkness seeping in, trying to have power over me*, she thought.

Inside her head, she felt the Red Light at play with no holding back. But it wasn't playful at all, but seeking it's way deeper inside, seeking to destroy her. Flashes of the angry fire begin licking at the deep recesses of her mind, tearing at any outside influence that the Community was presently exerting to keep her safe.

The Flashes began growing above and around her in the darkness, lashing out at her now and causing her to writhe in pain in this *sleep*-like trance.

The Flashes began to try to drown now, becoming a raging tidal wave of Hate. The Memories that had been kept at bay before, were now craving for her attention, and demanding it insistently.

Tired of fighting off whatever might come, she allowed herself to begin floating deeper into the Darkness, like a drowning victim in water over her head surrendering to the inevitable filling of the body with water.

Down. Deeper. *Let us in*, the memories demanded, clawing at her like a thousand knife points nicking her skin.

The Jewel incrusted Knife was suddenly there, floating above her on a haze of malicious Intent.

The screams of countless Children, echoing, become a tidal wave of Pain.

A Face, coming out of the Darkness, full of rage and inhuman Utterings that a part of her recognized as the true Face of her Father. The blind rage, the consuming Hatred and Malevolence that had kept him alive...

Suddenly shooting up and out of this Nightmare that was all too Real, Kat sat up finding herself alone in the shadow filled dusk of the ancient and huge Hall. *How did I get here*? And amidst a Community of a thousand souls, she felt more alone than ever.

Aching inside with a gnawing pain she wondered whether would ever go away, she was close to giving up hope and letting go her body, "Why don't I want to give in?" she asked the darkened air.

And as if in response, she heard the whisper of Angelus again saying, "It is her choice."

"What?" Standing up and looking around in every direction, she sees that Angelus is not here. That she is still alone.

Resolve came from the depths. As much as she felt hopeless— "I can't succumb to the Darkness. I can't let Father win," she said defiantly. And unlike the character of Darth Vader in Star Wars, she knows that her own Dark Father had chosen his path consciously, with full Intent. Also that he had placed himself beyond any redemption that Kat can imagine.

But she also knew that she was not ready yet to face the Demons

318

lurking not so deeply within her own self either. She felt as exhausted as she did the first night she had arrived here.

Feeling as if there was nothing she could do but unable to walk out of here defeated, she plopped herself back down on the dusty floor again. Caught between the wracking frustration around the feelings that she doesn't know what to do with, and the fear of what would come to her even if she did, she sat on the knife edge between laughing truly hysterically at the absurdity of her situation and sobbing uncontrollably without being able to stop for what she's seen of her life so far.

As the shadows around her deepen, she stands and begins a series of futile gestures that only serve to direct the shriving energy that she doesn't know how to deal with.

Pacing again. Sitting down. Popping up to pace again. Praying walking. Sitting, sobbing. And then praying.

And finally exhausted, lying down and wanting to die, and get it all over with once and for all.

As the shadows became dusk and then darkness around her, she began to notice a flickering of lights playing on the ceiling again. Rubbing her eyes, "That's it, I must be going crazy now."

After a few minutes more, it was becoming evident that these ghost lights were coming from the outside of the building, increasingly illuminating the dome of the room. Watching the lights play as if they are fireflies in the summer night, twinkling against the field of early evening stars, Kat starts becoming mesmerized, drowsing off in spite of herself. Eyes gently closing, then fluttering open again, their weight finally taking over.

Her eyes closing quite solidly now, the gentle white reflections from the ceiling succumb to changing color, returning to the Red Lights that begin playing over her from another influence now, changing her tear streaked face away from gentle into malevolent, increment by increment.

Inside, her mind reels. Thrust into the Darkness once again, she is nowhere near the Community. She is back in the deep forests of the Ozark Mountains. In the land of Ritual Killings. In the Darkness of a place and era that had so much illusion masking the depth of Horror that was going on.

She now knew why the camping trips. She now knew why the gapping holes when she thought back on these days.

Feeling like she is floating above a fire and frenzy that she knows all too well, Kat suddenly feels herself falling. Right into the middle of this Circle of swirling lethal, devastating energy. To where a much younger but still copper-haired Kat Runyon faces her, mirroring to her what she didn't want to face.

These eyes she now found herself looking into were as Black as the darkest night, reflecting the malevolent Red of the pyre she was now apparently standing in the middle of, vacantly staring out in her direction unseeing but with a hint of malevolence about her.

This is who I am, some part of her thought dispassionately.

No, another part of her said. *This is who you have been, but it is not Who you Are*, this Voice told her.

Startling out of her vision with a sharp intake of air, eyes wide with most of the whites showing, she gives in to the violent sobbing that she feels. Sitting up and pulling her legs to her chest, she begins rocking violently. "Nooooooo," she says in the singsongy child's voice of desperation she has heard so often from her "patients" in the past.

"Oh, God. What kind of a God would allow this?" she asks, looking up at the ceiling and pleading again, her voice rising in anger at the witness of the un-god-like atrocities that she and those around her have committed in this life.

"How can you let this happen, God?!" she says, shaking her fist at the ceiling once more, and not finding the words to put to the depth of disgust she is feeling, just said, "Goddamn you." And, "Maybe my father is right. Maybe there is no God. Maybe there is no right, no wrong, only taking what I want."

Her body snapping back and forth now with the fury of her anger and the depth of her hopeless feelings, Kat's body snaps erect as if pulled up by her throat. Sobbing uncontrollably once more, she can't believe how wretched and vile she feels.

And she's coming as close as she has ever felt to that chasm that represents the desire to die.

An hour or so later, a deathly exhausted Kat is now sitting calm again. The candle light from outside is now quite bright, belying the Darkness she feels inside.

Outside the Flight House is a field of Light being held by a large number of the Community seated lotus style there. Holding Kathryn's consciousness with theirs, the flickering candles in hand sconces are floating like lily pads in a sea of Light to help protect her and aid her in dealing with her Inner Darkness.

Fingers of the Community consciousness occasionally reach out and push away the tendrils of Outer Darkness creeping in like a dragnet vine to drag Kat away back into the Field of Darkness, bending its strength and effort to return her back to the Dark Fold.

While inside and mostly unaware of the battle raging silently outside, Kat has the white ghost/candle lights flickering across her face. Closing her eyes and surrendering to the waiting onslaught, she thinks, *I give up. Take me and show me the worst that I've done.*

This time, Kat feels herself rising slowly out of her body, partly under her control and partly totally out of control. She feels herself traveling without traveling, going into the past without going anywhere at all. She feels her Soul truly taking flight.

Floating on a sea of consciousness, she drifts, and then, caught like a child in a whirlpool, begins getting drug down into Darkness.

Knowing that she is an adult, she also knows that she is the Child, the version of her younger self, standing there with that bloody Blade of Hell itself in her small hands. She feels it weight, both physically and metaphysically, knowing that this Blade has bitten flesh back to the time of Jesus and beyond. Has known the darkest nights of history. Been wielded by the Darkest Souls that have walked the Earth, and...

Fleeing from that knowledge, she returns to the child that she once was — the child that lives within her still. And the child that she must *kill* in order to live. Or is that let live in order that she must die?

Inside the young Kat is slicing in slow motion that she can't stop, slicing the air and then the squirming body of the sacrificial child on the altar before her. As she had unfortunately done many times before. Killing her innocence once more, with the sacrifice of the Innocent on the bloody altar before her. Both wanting to stop that Blade, and knowing that she can't do anything to stop it, no matter how much she wants, her present self watches in horror as the event reaches its bloody conclusion.

She watches in horror as the Blade enters into the small body, the forces of Darkness swirling and lashing around her reach like snakes into that body, slashing and tearing at the moorings of the Soul there, until it detaches from that small body, leaving only a beating heart in decline and lump of flesh that will live on only as fuel for this madness.

It writhes and twists as it leaves the former shell that it rode into this life with, as the Chanting reaches newly frenzied heights, rising beyond the physical again, bringing Chaos to life.

This Soul shivering and splintering into shards of Dark Light as it leaves, is quickly turned Red as the Darkness around it works on it to ITs Own Purpose. Coalescing into a form that for a second, begins looking like a Dark Dove hovering and teetering on the edge of tearing away from its Dark intended destiny and escaping, finally becomes engulfed in sufficient Dark tendrils of pulsing red energy to claim it and pull it glinting like the Dark Diamond it is to become, descending in the raging pyre light—

—Into the figure of a naked teen-aged girl barely past her first period, who is also writhing in agony on an adjacent altar to the now unmoving form that once was a child, the dead body of which is being lifted and carried off to feed the Dark Blood pond that is the source of this Magic close by.

As this soul fragment enters the form of the Girl, her body shivers violently, as if she had just been stabbed and shriven of life herself. This melding though, instead of being the end, is only the beginning, and rising like the fragments of houses in a tornado, some twenty other different Alters already in residence take turns rising out of the vortex that is this "child," writhing until coalescing once again into a glowing Dark Crystal mass of a whole descending lava-like back into the host Cauldron.

Taking a deep shuddering breath, the Girl rises from the altar and, seemingly calm, begins walking over to a group of other naked girls and women standing just inside of the whipping and writhing figures of the inner Circle.

As the teenager reintegrates with the other Cauldrons, a middle aged woman at the other end of this group separates and jerkily turns to take her place on the Altar, lying down vacantly obedient to the Dark Task to come.

Jerking herself, Kat feels herself ripped back into the whirlpool of madness, both drowning and not, being torn apart and yet feeling more whole than ever. Gasping for air to wash away that Madness she had witnessed her younger self preform and internally sighing that the ordeal is almost over, she feels suddenly dropped as if from a great height, seeing Darkness and Light in a Dance that is both maddening in its complexity and in the end, deafeningly simple.

Feeling and seeing Darkness descend and herself into it, she is sure that the next stop down this rabbit hole must be being dumped back into the safety of the Flight House.

Instead, colors and fragments of the madness swirling around her begin coalescing into Faces, each rising one at a time gasping out of the BLACK.

The faces of the Slaughtered.

The faces of those that she — she now knew with certainty — had been the executioner of.

The face of yet another infant wailing, one of the hundreds, maybe thousands, killed by her. And by how many Others like her?

Suddenly replaced by the terror filled face of an elderly Black

Man she knew she once knew but now could not name, eyes wide in shock and fear, as well as defiance.

Next, the face of a young twenty-something bleached blond woman with piercings and facial tattoos, who professed to being a Lover of the Beast — shouting "I love Satan!" — that They then took her for her word, was eyes blazing white, filled with the terror at the reality of her fantasy being fulfilled—

And the Faces continued on more and more rapidly, until—

Kat returned dropping violently back into her body and into the deep darkness of the Flight House at 2 a.m., her lungs heaving till she thought that they were going to burst from her chest, the terror she had experienced in all of those faces of the Dead and Not Dead, vying for dominance in her streaming tear-filled eyes.

Standing weakly and silently dry heaving through her sobbing tears for the Multitude that she had slaughtered, unsure of whether to kill herself here and now, or wait for later.

"My God. How could I have killed that many people and never have remembered it? God, where are all the bodies? How many thousands..."

She reviled herself for having done it. She reviled herself for having been so used against her will. She... Felt that she could go on hating herself to the end of time and it would still not seem enough.

"I should walk out and let them take me now and never look back. How can I ever be redeemed," she asked between sobs. 'There aren't

326

enough tears that I could cry for all of you. How can I ever be forgiven?"

Walking towards the door, she paused before leaving this darkened space. "Will I ever be ready?" Will I ever be clean again?" she asks tearfully, tossing it off into the darkness knowing that she won't get an answer but needing to say it anyway.

Doubled over in her grief and stumbling blindly, Kat somehow managed to find the exit leading her outside. Maybe it was the chill air of a now fleeting reality blowing that led her.

Reaching the outside, she found The Ancient, standing emotionless waiting for her there. Sure that she would cut her down for her part in all that madness and unforgivable death and destruction, Kat was prepared to fall at Angelus' feet and await her death.

Instead, the seemingly ageless face looked at her with what could only be compassion. After all the destruction she had done.

"All of those here before you," Angelus told her, gesturing to the Hundred or so other Community members still seated in silent meditation around and behind her, "Each of them have gone through much the same as you have just witnessed yourself having done."

Unprepared for this of all things, she stared for a minute before finding her voice. "But... There's hundreds of men and women--"

"Yes. There are," The Ancient said. "So you are not alone." Lifting both of her arms up in a welcoming gesture Kat never would have thought anyone capable of again, Kat just stood there.

"But, you don't know what—"

"You've just been through? My dear, I've witnessed it thousands of times, time after time."

Gulping, Kat could only find, "Witnessed," to say. And then, "But..."

"Come, Daughter," Angelus emphasized. Unable to handle the kindness in this older woman's eyes, Kat toyed with walking away and disappearing into the night. Instead, she found herself collapsing into those still open arms and sobbing furiously into the shoulder of this enigma in rough cotton clothe.

"Such is the World as it is, Child. When Jesus Wept, he saw all that you have seen, and More."

Separating herself from the Ancient's embrace, Kat asked numbly, "Tell me that's the worst of it. Please?" *No More* echoing like a recurring bell tolling the impossible.

Without answering, Angelus turned wrapping one arm around the still cringing Kat, and gesturing towards the sleeping quarters with her other.

Kat reluctantly allowed herself to be led like the child she was feeling, walking exhaustedly away. Leaving the field of flickering candles illuminating the Others still holding vigil for All of the Dead behind her.

Repeating "More," once more, Kat found herself stumbling, walking over the even ground. Catching her and helping her continuing to walk, Angelus seems like a giant to her, even though the other woman was a mere six feet tall.

She wanted to see the hope and the lightness, and feel the joy around her that the People here who had known just as much Darkness as she had, seemed to radiate.

It was time for her to join the land of the loving, and let the battle in front of her go for now. It was time for her to turn herself towards the Dining Hall, walking along with the fellow travelers on this Dark journey, where she could feel the glow building towards a very late diner... And Bed.

TWENTY-SEVEN

When she suddenly wakes up, it's in the light of daytime.

Staring vacantly into space over an as yet to be touched breakfast, Kat appears to still be in the mind numbing shock of the night before. The depth of the horror at how many she had killed was sinking in, quietly and ever so desperately.

Devon starts to approach her, unsure of reaching out, and begins to touch her shoulder. But Kat flinches, unseeing, still in the midst of her unwanted recollection.

Instead of sitting down beside her as he would like to, he sits down across from her at a safe distance.

After a few dead moments, she begins to raise her head in his direction with desperation starkly in her eyes. "My God, what have I done," she says to no one.

"What many of us here have done as well. The only difference with you… Is who your father is."

Collapsing her face into her hands and then finally releasing her pent up anger, fear and self-loathing, she begins sobbing again. After a while, her sobbing eased up, and she said, "And Angelus told me that this was only the beginning."

Burying her face in her hands once again, Devon rises and slowly makes his way around to her side of the table. He pauses before getting too close, but Kat finally begins reaching out for him, and he moves in closer. He reaches out and draws her in, cradling her closer, as the activity continues on around them.

"Is this going to get us in trouble?" Kat asked him, sheepishly peaking out over his shoulders.

Laughing lightly, "This isn't some fundamentalist Christian school, Kat. We're all adults here."

"But the children—"

"Have all seen far worse than someone being comforted with a little bit of tenderness and affection in the dining hall."

"I mean—"

"Nothing is hidden here. Only Darkness is forbidden."

Shyly smiling finally, she folds back into his arms, getting as close as she can. Drawing comfort to soothe the pain of the memories. "Nothing?" she asked playfully.

"Well," he whispered mischievously in her ear, "I wouldn't throw you on the table, and 'do that which undoes evil' here, but…"

This brought a laugh to her finally. "I would hope not!"

A little later, they were walking slowly in silence in the woods where he had taken her before, and where Angelus had helped her to find the "nature of reality." Still pale from last nights visions and waking nightmares, she occasionally finds herself stumbling. But this time, Devon is there to catch her.

Devon for his part, was patiently waiting for the approaching storm of questions and incriminations to break. Knowing what she is feeling, he feels both the compassion of one who has done the unspeakable too, as well as the fierce protectiveness of a man in love.

Knowing he needs to keep his distance in this matter, both personally and "professionally," Devon wages his own inner battle preparing for the inevitable.

Finally and flatly, Kat asks him, "So you went through that too?" Almost as much accusation as question, she waited before pouncing on him, sure that she was going to pounce.

Walking a fine line still as to what to tell her, he finally came up with, "It's different for each of us. But—" admitting the inevitable, "Unfortunately, I did."

Angry now and ready to pounce, she burst out with a very hurt, "And you couldn't just warm me?! I mean... My God, Devon."

Stopping now as well as heavily sighing, he turned and stopped in front of her, gently brushing her arms to calm her. Her face told him to back off, but he didn't want to. "What could I have told you? To prepare you for... That?" he asked.

"Oh, I don't know," she said with as much acid as she could

manage in her still exhausted state. "I guess you could have — described... Told me...

"Oh, God," she finished, flailing around in her tornado of mixed emotions and torment. Collapsing into his arms sobbing, she finally failed to stay angry. "Please tell me that it doesn't get much more worse than that."

"You already know the answer to that," he said lovingly. "You just don't know the particulars yet."

Pushing him away again with a play of emotions across her face, she asked, "How much... I'm not sure I want to—"

Moving back in to kiss and soothing her hair, "None of us did." Pulling back from her this time. "But for most of those here, they didn't have any inkling of what they had done in their life. You and I at least had some idea, being brought to that awareness with working with our respective clients. But many didn't.

"Till the Dreams began, that is."

Separating from her and reaching out his hand for her to follow, she reluctantly reaches and grabs for his as they begin walking.

Their hands reaching and intertwining, "It'll get easier."

"How."

Turning and moving in very close very quickly, "Once you learn to forgive yourself. That's the only way to move on."

Barely smiling and turning to continue further on into the woods, she finally says, "I'm not sure I know how."

"I want to show you something," he told her, taking her into a thicker area of the woods. Entering into an even darker area, they came through a hedge into a brightly lit glen that Kat hadn't even expected to find there. With a very different kind of altar in it.

"Natural rock, natural moss," he said playfully. "Much softer that way. And leading her to it, he lay down and patted the rock next to him.

"A place to do that which undoes evil," he said with a not too pure at heart smile.

Laying down on the rock next to him, she suddenly realized what he was proposing.

Blushing, she begins going through several different emotions in rapid order. Finally asking, "What if we—"

And rolling over he began kissing her, silencing her question with a kiss. And his hands betraying the monk-like feel of the robe that she was wearing.

It didn't take long for her to forget her question.

With both of them lying there naked in the afterglow in the warm afternoon sunlight, it was quickly one again turning into mid-afternoon. A shiver ran though her as she heard Angelus tell her once again, "Time is the greatest illusion."

Of course, she had heard of the Eastern belief that All life was an illusion. "My life, certainly," she told herself verbally.

"All of Life," Devon said suddenly, causing her to jump.

"I wish you wouldn't do that," she said after catching her breath."I can't read minds. Remember?"

Only because you're fighting it, he thought at her. And verbally said, "There are a great many things you have been fighting."

Kat couldn't but help to ask. "Wasn't this kind of dangerous? I mean, anyone could have—"

"But they didn't. I would have heard them if they were."

"And politely warned them off?"

"There are certain "perks" to hearing other people's thoughts. You know?"

Rolling over to face her and sitting up at this though, he added, "However, we should be getting back. You still have an *appointment with destiny*."

"Meaning?"

"Dark secrets still left to unfold. And the time is coming when they will attack us as well."

"Will we win? And what does that mean to win?"

"Not what you think. Not what they think. Grabbing his robe and hers and handing hers to her, "I'm not sure if everyone is ready yet, either."

"Meaning, me," she said, matter of factly.

"Meaning... all of us."

TWENTY-EIGHT

Approaching and entering the Flight House later, Devon enters the large meeting area reluctantly. Seeing the Figure he seeks off in the distance, he quietly approaches the apparently meditating Angelus, sitting very still with her eyes closed. Respectfully waiting for her to recognize him, he waits for a good long while, standing in the semi-darkness.

When she does finally open her eyes, she nods in the direction of the floor beside her, waiting for him to speak when he has sat.

Sitting down next to her but not too close, he finds his head in his hands. "I don't know if she's up to what lies ahead," he finally tells her.

"She will be," Angelus tells him quietly. "She has been through much already."

"That's not all, Ancient--" he begins, but she quiets him with a lifting of her hand.

"You needn't say it. It's etched into your face.

"What am I going to do?"

"You will learn. Of course."

Finally turning toward him and placing her hand firmly on his shoulder, comfortingly yet distant, her smile is still gentle, but he sees a firmness behind it that frightens him.

"My heart says one thing, but my head says no."

Telling him, "Listen to your Heart, Devon. The heart never lies. Your head will mislead you, but your heart never does."

"But how will she be changed?"

Her face softening, Angelus begins to have a motherly expression that has a touch of irony in it. There is obvious affection for Devon registering there, even beyond her general aloofness. "That is up to her as well."

"In other words, you're not going to tell me what you've seen," he tells her, his voice betraying a little bit of anger involuntarily. "Are you?"

"You know by now I can't, Devon. Even if I wanted to. If you want to help her, be by her side. But you must surrender to whatever comes, as she must as well."

Becoming distant again, Angelus returns to her contemplative attitude, leaving Devon to his own decision.

Sitting another moment only, he stands and quietly leaves the room. As he does, Angelus opens her eyes briefly to compassionately watch him leave. She sighs when she is alone, and returns to her former contemplative distance.

TWENTY-NINE

The next morning, Kat was woken up by the rustling of the hundred or so beds being arisen from. It was barely five o'clock in the morning and she had looked forward to sleeping in. Apparently though, this wasn't standard Community practice.

Throwing back the covers much less ceremoniously than her neighbors, Kat was cranky. And not above allowing that to be heard.

Turning to the young girl next to her still in her white flannel nightgown, she began to ask what everyone was up to. But before she could, this woman of about twenty with long blond hair said, "We greet the Sunrise every morning with meditation in the Commons." And turning, began walking towards the bathroom/shower areas, as if that explained it to Kat.

Who, deciding that was not in her plans this morning, flopped back into bed and pulled the sheets over her head to drown the sounds of the rising activity all around her.

Stepping outside about twenty minutes later however, she was dressed in her robes and being drawn by the chanting — and the energy — coming from the Commons. She was amazed that the large field had so many people in it so early. All shapes and sizes, all races, all ages. As if humanity were represented here in the best of all possible forms.

Why hadn't I seen this variety before now? she asked herself.

This is one of the last vestiges of very high development which had removed itself from the world, she heard in her head. Both humbled and awed, she wandered among the crowd like a small lost child looking for a parent.

Wandering into Devon walking quietly and purposefully towards her, she is startled suddenly, realizing he was in front of her.

Without speaking to her, he gestured her towards the edge of the throng, and once out, took her by the hand, leading her towards the Flight House.

Once out of range of the field of meditators, he whispered to her, "I don't think you're quite ready to join the morning Sun Salutation just yet. Matter of fact," he chuckled softly, "I hadn't expected you to be up for this mornings activity anyway."

"Neither did I," she told him warily. "I fully intended to ignore it. Didn't happen though."

"I see," was all he said.

Entering the Flight House doors, he relaxed, sighing. "It takes some getting used to at first. Trust me, I know."

"They all seem so... I don't know. Advanced. And I'm—"

"Just beginning a journey that some of them have been on for most of their lives. And others, only for a few short years or months."

Sitting in the dust mote-filled corner feeling overwhelmed, she said, "I just don't know about this, Devon." Sighing broadly, "I mean..."

"Kat. We didn't choose this life for ourselves once we were in physical form. We did however choose it before we came in."

Unable to wrap her head around this lifetime much less other lives or before this life, she cried out, "But, why?"

"That is the way of the world," was all that he could tell her.

Leading her back to the small side room that she had been led to by Angelus the day before, Devon began opening the door and holding out his hand indicating that she was to enter. Kat hesitated to walk back into this room that she could now see were lined with bare walls painted in a glowing yellowish-white, and looked around for a chair to be sitting in. As her eyes adjusted to the light level, she could once again see the two chairs, in the center and facing each other.

"Ok," she said to herself, hesitant to sit down. "This seems like some sort of interrogation room." Looking up at the ceiling and feeling like the room might begin closing in any moment, she did her best to regain some sense of peace that she had had here in the last few days.

"This is another test. Isn't it?" she asked herself as much as the room. "I'm supposed to be calm, collected, and ready when whoever is supposed to take that second chair comes in." But she couldn't find that peace right now.

In her head she heard a disembodied voice say, *She's not ready yet.*

Another one said, *She has to be.*

Kat resisted shouting out to the ceiling that she was ready. She could feel that she wasn't. "I'm not a prisoner," she said quietly. "I can walk out whenever I want to."

As soon as she said this, the door opened. There was no one she could see on the other side that had opened it, and she started walking towards it.

Stopping herself though, she felt her mind calm down and her hands go out to the nearest chair. 'I have to be ready,' she thought, and sat down.

No sooner had her back side touched the chair than the door closed as mysteriously as it had opened. She closed her eyes, and took a deep breath, feeling her body relax and her mind open as she did.

The first lesson once again... is peace, the Voice said sitting across from her. She opened her eyes as slowly as she could find the patience to, and saw Angelus sitting in the other chair. As if she had just materialized in it from outside.

342

"All things are possible once peace is found inside," she said. "Welcome to your inner life, Kathryn Runyon.

"It is time to learn more about space, time and other knowledge," the Older Woman said, "And Prepare you for the conflict that lies ahead."

shadows and LIGHT

THIRTY

Later that afternoon Kat was still in the main room of the Flight House, standing in the middle of the room where Angelus had left her.

During the day, the size of the room had not felt daunting to her. It seemed large to her, but was in many ways, was just another large room.

She had wandered around it, wondering when Angelus would appear again, ready to test her. As she waited patiently in the center, she watched the shadows changing on the walls around her. "Am I only supposed to be at her beck and call to be tested?" she asked.

A short time later, she realized that she was getting impatient. Looking around, she also suddenly realized that she no longer saw a door in any of the round walls. Walking over to the wall where she thought that a door should be, she began pounding on it. Pounding on the walls—

As she transformed into a teenaged Katy Runyon, banging on the walls of— A prison cell? Collapsing into a corner that appears in front of her suddenly and crying, she also just as suddenly gets up and walks over to a wall and laying her hand on it, pushes through the wall and walks once again into the Big Hall.

"Who am I really? Am I just another Multiple?"

The now no longer "Dr." Kathryn Runyon sits down in the Flight House alone, reluctantly ready to confront her bloody past fully, and without fear as much as she could. Like she had been doing with her former "patients," only this time it was her all alone to confront those fears and memories.

Without Devon or Angelus to help her to face her inner conflict, she knew that she did not have the courage to come here and confront such an internal evil.

"How much more bad can it get," she asked the air again. "I'm not even sure what I'm talking to. Are you up there, God? Or... What?"

There was both a feeling of great emptiness at what she had done and a great self-hatred. Even if she had been manipulated into all of it against her will, she still held herself to a great responsibility for all of it.

She was more determined than ever to find some small Light that she had done to offset the Darkness. Sitting down in the dusty cavern to wait for some vision if any to comfort her, she closed her eyes which were still wide and afraid.

"Show me something good that I've done. Please? Let me know I've done something right in my life."

First there was only darkness in the inner cavern to match her outer condition. Then a flash of brilliant Light startled her to open her eyes, but she found that she couldn't.

The blinding light though quickly began fading to reveal the treatment room of one of the first institutions that she practiced at. Really not much different than that of Hawthorne, she had forgotten how grey the walls had seemed to her then.

One of Kat's past "problem patients," was a young woman in her late 20's by the name of Valerie. Valerie was a "problem" patient in that she was not wanting to acknowledge her condition. After many sessions where the other Alters had come out and were taped being separate individuals, Valerie was still on the couch and in denial.

Though in her 20's, she appeared to be a teenager because of her upbringing. She liked to dress in high school aged clothes and thought of herself as a cheerleader. Which had presented problems when this "teenager" started "coming out" at her job. She had also had bouts of "missing time" and as a result, was often late for work. She had been recommended to an Institution when these incidents started to become too regular and she was fired from her job.

"No! This is not... Who I am."

Being early in her career, Kat hadn't gotten tired of hearing the stories that her patients brought to her. But Valerie was different. She claimed that she had no stories. That there were no "others" other than herself.

"Who are you then?"

"I'm... My name is..." Struggling, she finally came up with, "Valerie."

Looking at her notes patiently, she looks back up to the girl. "You've had six other people come out of you. I've shown you the tapes of those sessions. But you don't remember any of what happened in those sessions."

Still having a perplexed look on her face, she went blank for a second. Kat was sure someone else was going to come out, but the light returned to her eyes. She smiled sweetly, as if nothing had happened.

"So, who were those other people?" Dr. Runyon asker her. "You saw that it was you who was speaking on the tapes. Yes?"

Clouding up again, the older Valerie spoke again. "But... I can't be..."

"Look, Valerie, I know what you're going through. All of my patients usually go through the same thing. It's just—"

And then more desperately, "But—"

"But we've been at this for almost a year now. You've seen the evidence. Why do you still need to deny it?"

"But I can't be — one of those — things. I'm a girl—"

"No, you're a Woman. You were a grown Woman until a year ago, until the others inside you began coming out. Your psychiatrist told

348

you there was something wrong with you, and you didn't believe her either."

"But..." she said, and began crying again.

Taking a different tact, Kat gets up from her chair and walks over to her Patient and hugs her. Valerie breaks down in her arms and begins sobbing uncontrollably, wailing like a small child, "Mommy?!"

A short time later Kat is once again in her chair, and Valerie is talking calmly, once again a Woman and not a child.

"I'm sorry I've been so much trouble, doctor. I just—"

"It's ok. You needed to break through past your history and..."

Sighing and on the verge of tears, she begins wiping her eyes as Kat hands her a box of tissues. "I think I'm ready... Oh God, I don't — what do I need to do?"

Returning back to her chair, Kat sighed a "Thank God" sigh and said, "Let's start with Michael. He was the first to come out. Tell me what you know about *him*."

Changing from the core to another alter, a twenty-something awkwardly gawky man appeared to come out of this woman who had just a few minutes ago been denying the existence of anything/anyone else inside of her.

"Can't I tell my own story?"

"Michael?" she asked.

"Yes?"

"You've already told me your story. Now I need Valerie to tell me your story."

"Why? She can't... She don't—"

"Don't you understand? She needs to be the one to tell me."

Sighing his resignation, he allowed a petulant "Oh, ok."

And switching back to Valerie, "Ok, doctor." Closing her eyes to cry again, this time Kat only handed her a tissue box.

"What is it you want me to do?"

"Go inside and tell me what you see."

Closing her eyes, Valerie grew petulant and defensive quickly. "There's only darkness. What am I supposed to see? Demons? Horrible creatures from my deep and dark past?"

Trying a new tact on the young woman, "Ask yourself, *Who's there*?" Kathryn told her.

Folding her arms defensively around her chest, Valerie was about to tell her Psychiatrist something nasty, when her hand went up to her mouth. "Nooo," she began to wail at nothing.

"What do you see? Who do you see?"

"No one," she said, her petulance reawakening. "No—" And suddenly gasping, asked, "Who are You?" Without opening her eyes.

"Who are you seeing?" the Doctor asked.

"He's— There's no one there."

Changing her whole face and posture, the definitely masculine voice of Michael comes out of her body. "She sees me. She just don't want to tell you. Tha's all."

350

"Who else?" Kat asks.

But shaking again from "boy" to "girl," Valerie comes out to accuse Kat of tricking her. "Who were all of those people?" she squeaks.

"Who do you think they are?" the Therapist asks, waiting patiently for a breakthrough.

"Why are they inside of me?" Valerie asks, hoping for different answer.

"Inside of you? You can see all of them now?"

Closing her eyes again, Valerie's demeanor changes drastically. "Inside of me?! Doctor... They can't be inside of me. There's like twenty or thirty of them. They can't be me."

"You've seen the tapes. Now you see them; inside of you. Now do you see where the problem has been, Valerie?"

Beginning to cry softly, Kat hands her the tissue box again. "But... But, they're me?"

"Not exactly," Kat told her. Recognizing that the Patient is not alone in their own head was the first breakthrough that each patient needed to go through. Of course, there were many more breakthroughs that would need to be dealt with, but this was the first real hurdle.

Valerie went on to explore all of those "Others" that were in her inner world with her, eventually deciding to say goodbye — the process known as "Integration" that would help for greater self-knowledge and progress to come later on.

As Kat reawakened to her present life in the Flight House, a smile was now on her face. "I'd forgotten the small victories," she told herself.

Kat was reluctantly ready to confront her bloody past fully, and without fear as much as she could. As she had been doing with her former "patients," only this time it was her, all alone to confront her past.

She knew intuitively why Devon had left her like he did in the stall, to begin the task of confronting her literal demons inside. But part of her still resented that he had done that.

But without his leaving her to face her inner conflict alone, she knew that she did not have the courage to come here and confront her internal evil.

Crying now, she told the room,"Ok. I guess I'm ready to face my Dark Side again.

"What else have I done," she asked the still air. A deep shudder ran through her as she felt the inner storm coming on. There was something there, that she — didn't really want to face it.

She finally knew that part of her just wanted to disappear back into the Cult, back into the madness and hatred there. She knew that she would have been disturbingly unhappy knowing there was something else there just below the surface that she couldn't put her finger on. But she had lived most of her life blissfully ignorant of the horror she was a part of.

352

"Do I really need to see what I've done? Do you really have some destiny for me other than Darkness?"

Sitting down in a ragged huff, she closed her eyes and asked cringing, "What is it. Show me the worst of my sins."

The fallow darkness around her didn't answer. For a few minutes, she sat and waited, cringing less and less. Both fighting the urge to run, and opening up to it and trying to control it at the same time.

After what felt like another eternity, she shifted and began to lay back into the dusty floor. As she did, the Darkness threw its hangman's bag onto her mind, and she began suffocating.

Out of the Darkness, the spike of the Pyre shot through her. And another. Until she felt she was being stabbed by a thousand blades of terror.

The blazing, raging preternatural pyre became her whole field of vision. Stabbing red. Burning into every cell of her... Body.

Transforming into the body of a teenaged Katy, banging on the walls of a — prison cell? Collapsing into a corner and crying, she suddenly realizes... She calmly rises, and walks over to a wall and, laying her hand on it, begins pushing through the solid wall, and through it—

And into—

Blinding red. Etching pain. And suddenly...

Stabbing, blazing light of another kind. Intensity falling around her. Sunlight. And then—

Back to the pyre; the chanting around her gutturally pounding her into submission. Crying in the wilderness of pain and excruciating sound, and... Others.

Looking around the circle, she realized she was looking up. She was looking at the ugly monsters moving back and forth, back and forth. Dults with no clothes on. Red. Hurt.

Standing in the shadows, the light feeds further into a reddish glow surrounding the sacrificial Pyre. The adult Kat is seen shimmering in the present, as the child Kathryn is in the center of the Chanting hordes.

One Man steps forward, unveiling his face and body to reveal himself as her Father. Raising his arms and making signs that flash bright red in the flames of the Pyre, those around them begin removing their hoods, revealing Powerful Men, current and former Heads of State and the uppermost Government. All of them Chanting the guttural Words of Destruction to set the scene and lay this Darkest of Magick s down.

And into the middle of this Pyre rises the shimmering form of That which they are Calling. Coming to give ITs Power to this task.

As this Ancient Blade of terrible Age was and the immense Power it wielded descended towards its intended end, she suddenly knew that there were many more like it, all around the world. A thousand tiny, but also powerful blades of Utterly Evil Intent, ready to slice and shiv the Infinite from any tiny finite body laid in front of Them.

354

And then the sunlight stabbed into her awareness again.

Pretty day. I got my pretty dress on. People. Losta people. Grown ups. And other... Young.

She was going back and forth, between Child and adult. It was becoming a roller coaster. Up, down. Grown up, baby — child.

And she goes through the wall and out of a car door into... Another time. 1963. Three years old and holding her hand out to be grabbed by her father, blocking the bright sun for a moment.

Moving away, the sun returns, stabbing. Blinding.

Looking down at the grass, she saw her pretty white dress. Her... No, they don't go to Sunday school.

Lotas peeple. Waitin'. For what?

The nasty noise. Peeple singing, but not singing. Making bad noise. HE was gonna come. IT. She didn't like IT. She HATED IT. IT was BAD. Real bad.

And all the grone ups were shouting, dancing, calling to IT. "COME," they shouted. But she didn't understand what they were shouting, just knew they were calling — IT.

And IT came.

IT... Was the Beast. Not peeple. Not animal. Not live, but dead. But live, too. An it was like a snake. Or a lion. Or... Or a Snake. With big horns like a bull. IT was... Something else.

She knew it wasn't human. This was no Angel. Her adult was screaming inside her to—

RUN! GET AWAY! NOW!

But her child self knew she would not run. And knew that she also didn't have any clothes on. And also knew that she was part of the reason that everyone was calling to IT.

This was big. Something big was going to happen. They were all calling to the IT that came. Came into being in the center of the pyre, stepping out of the raging fire.

IT was— (her adult knew now) — an Alien. The Devil. The thing that had fancied itself both the Devil, and God as well.

IT made us — humans — do *things*. To keep it alive. Feed it. Make it strong. WE were the reason IT lived. And all those that WE had killed over years and years beyond the memory of those here.

Gathered around her were (the adult in her now knew), the rich. The powerful — Politicians. Famous people. Stars. And, the truly Powerful, Names. Names that every person living at the time would know.

And they were all here, calling to IT. Calling to The Devil. Calling the Devil into their midst. And IT came. Horrible, hateful, EVIL pouring off of it, being IT'S very being. A monster.

And this was the reason for her being as well. This THING that had come to be worshiped by these rich and powerful names ruling this world. Doing IT'S bidding. Killing in IT'S name.

It looked like a goat. No, a Ram. the adult said. Except that it wasn't an animal. It was... Beyond this world. The real Ruler of this

356

world.

At this knowing, the inner Kat Runyon quaked in fear and hatred, the scorched ash of her former innocence.

She wanted to kill IT, but knew she couldn't. Then she wanted to kill herself. But knew she didn't. Knew her whole life was spent worshipping this THING that had ruled humans from beyond the dawn of history. Almost every night.

She deserved to die. She was internally disgusted with who and what she was, had done. And knew that this night was preparation for the unspeakable act she was to witness and participate in the next day.

This was the preparation and magical prelude to the Killing of a "King," who ironically was also one of them. Us. Good and very bad. In the same person.

Only he wanted to be Very Good now. That was not going to work for *Them.*

All of a sudden someone points in the direction of cars in the street, to a — motorcade beginning to turn that fateful corner. The Presidential motorcade. John F. Kennedy's Presidential Motorcade. She now realizes where she is and what is about to happen. It is Dealy Plaza in Texas, one fine day in November...

The blinding light again. Day. Daytime in Dallas. The ritual slaying of the leader of the "free" world. "Time to kill the Kennedy," one of the older men joked at the end of that night before.

"And then, to rule. Openly," Another said.

The grass was terribly green for it had been a good spring and not a long hot summer. And the sun was high and bright in the sky. And the adults around her; some out here to greet the President, and others to put an end to his life. To bring down — break down — the collective mind into a million pieces of horror. Make the whole country accept the rule of the Few.

"Time to kill the King," the Man next to her said.

Looking up her tiny arm to the Man holding her hand — her Father — she saw a strange light in his eyes. A strange light the adult now knew was *glee*.

He was there to make the ritual happen. Take in the energy of the full force of Darkness gathered surrounding them now.

In Dealy Plaza, Dallas. The Bad Men with Guns, on the tops of the buildings, poking their guns out of windows. Behind her in the trees around the Plaza, and on the nice grassy hill behind her and her father. Waiting in shadows made by both trees as well as the spell of magick.

The faces of men that her daddy knew. That she knew.

And then suddenly, people around them began shouting. She could make out the wave of sound that was beginning to wash over the area.

"The President is coming! The President is coming!" they shouted.

And the Silent Ones around her, bending their minds and magick's to do this task of bringing down the (supposedly) most powerful man on the planet.

"Here they come," someone else close by said. This person was gleeful, but not hurtful. They were only here to truly see "Their President."

"Look. Governor Connolly's in the car with him," another Voice said close by.

She saw the big car turn the corner so far, far away. In between the big people. Saw it driving so slowly down the street. Waves and waves of men, looking this way and that.

Her father then took the umbrella he had carried, and raising it, opened it fully in the mid-day sun. The Sign to begin.

"Let the Darkness prevail," he whispered quietly, and then began Chanting up Power with Great Intent.

Kat looked up at her father, ready to smile. But what she saw there suddenly made her want to cry. She saw a Demon at her side, smiling broadly while it chanted the Invocations of Dark Power, to bring a Nation and a World emotionally to Its knees.

There are many people around her, some waving American flags and cheering, and others silent and laying in wait. For what?

As this big car comes into view and is about to make a hard turn and drive by in front of her. Little Kat is beginning to jump up and down like the excited others in the crowd, but a hand restrains her. The Hand of her (seemingly younger) father — looking down at her very grimly. With a psychic impulse, Kathryn is ordered to stand where she is. She watches her father walk off, leaving little Katie standing by herself. She looks over to where the motorcade is about to pass right in front of her.

The Little Girl inside of her began to wail at what she was feeling. She was a conduit of power that was focussing on the large car with the President and his beautiful Wife approaching. And she was not just a Little Girl.

As the Motorcade began getting closer on the last leg of this Destiny, everyone on the street were all smiles. But the Action taking place surrounding her, began to grow the shadows beneath the trees to hide the true purpose of the day. Clouding what was to be the Final Act in a centuries long "Working."

And just as soon as the car was about to pass where her and her daddy were standing, other shouts began to be heard. Shouts of loud bangs not making any words, but being carried on silent WORDS.

Finding their mark.

And the glad shouting of just seconds ago began to be shouting of pain and despair. And horror. And disbelief.

The Car began to slow, as the Chanting starts to crescendo, with — shots beginning to pepper the air surrounding them like popcorn going off. POP! POP! POP! One after another. Some of them were physical bullets, and others simulacrums of Power, sending birds scattering. Magic Bullets, indeed!

Flashes appearing from the Grassy Knoll behind them. From the tops of several buildings surrounding them. From the hill by the railway bridge to their right.

The Handsome President began clutching at his throat and his wife began asking 'What's wrong?'

And more bullets strike him — and the Governor in the front seat — and the blood and brain from the slain King splattering Katie and her white dress nearby. White for the occasion to collect the energy of Madness and Power.

Then the people in the front of the car, began turning, and the man sitting in front of the president began twisting and turning as well. Kat wanted to scream out to *Move*, but all she heard was her little girl self wailing at the pain of the Raw Power moving through her.

She felt herself shout *Stop!* And her father began turning towards her, ready to strike her down where she stood.

"Someone's shot the President!" someone shouted from nearby.

She looked up into the eyes of the Demon who had been her Father, and felt — something — shoot between them. He slapped her with power, and she was silent, as she watched the car start speeding past them. Followed by the Darkest of Shadows trailing behind it.

And hands and arms began pointing towards one of the buildings close by. Including her fathers hand.

And as the car began speeding up to fly by them — her father and — he told her, *Look. Look on the face of the fallen King.* Except that she knew now that she was the only one to hear this.

And she now could feel the blood that had splattered her pretty white dress. With parts of the dead man passing quickly in front of her.

Only now, she was seeing it in slow motion. The First Lady looking around her, not sure of whether she should be jumping out of the car that now held her dead husband, or—

Looking at her for a split second, the Widow caught sight of the Man and the Little Girl. Looked into the eyes of the Little Girl, and her horror grew wider and starker and—

She was gone. The big car was gone, speeding up and away (now that the deed was done).

And her father beside her said, "Such a wonderful afternoon for a Killing of the King. Wouldn't you say, my dear?" and began leading her away.

Crowds scrambling, Federal Agents (some) running, and others merely standing there. A loud whine of a chorus of cacophonous voices literally rises to a scream. The glad shouting of just seconds ago began to be the shoutings of pain. And horror. And disbelief.

And The Darkness had slammed shut on her vision. It was night again, and the Pyre was blazing. The faces of the (mainly) men and women around her were bathed in sweat. And Power. Eyes blazing with the glee of what they had done.

In the next several days though she knew, that glee would fade as The People Mourned, and the crashing madness that had been intended to happen for that Day, did not descend. The Intended Madness did not allow them the Power that they had worked towards for so, so long.

The King was mourned, the Power still stayed in precarious balance, and—

Then, Katherine was snapped violently back into the present, her breaths raging raw out of her lungs, and her eyesight both squeezing into darkness as if she was going to faint, and tearing her apart from the inside.

"What did I do?" she asked herself with spikes in her lungs and her heart. "What was I a part of?"

Another Voice that she had not heard before answered her quietly, *You were the Instrument of Darkness.* She thought she heard the accusation hissing violently in this Voice.

But what she was truly hearing was Pity. The modern day Kat Runyon, began gasping for air in the darkness in which she was sitting. Unable to catch her breath at what she had participated in, she began to be caught between severe sobbing and maniacal laughing that she could not stop.

After another eternity, the sobbing had slowed into the dull roar of madness and unfathomable pain. How could she *not* have known? The greatest killing in history, and she had been unaware of her part in it.

Lying back still sobbing and choking on her memory, she turned to one side and began curling into her fetal position, wishing she had never been born.

What had she done? Why had she not remembered it till now?

Because I did not want you to, came a Voice booming out of the Darkness, telling her gleefully.

Sitting up suddenly, she was now caught between sheer terror and utter hatred and desire to kill again. Except that the Voice that had spoken so lightly and dismissively, was not a physical presence.

She felt the rage and Evil Intent rising in her. She would kill him with her bare hands this very second if she could.

"But you can't. Allow yourself however to feel the feelings though. Feed that Fire. Feel the Power that can be yours," her Father told her out of the Darkness.

"Give up on this White Light Bunny horse shit, Kathryn. It does not serve you. You do not serve it. Come back to the Darkness. Where you belong."

Standing, furious, she lashed out at the Invisible in the Darkness. "Show yourself... Father. Or are you afraid to?"

Flames of red began licking out of the Darkness in front of her, coalescing slowly into the form of a face. Slowly but surely, the image of her Father began to materialize and resolve in front of her, as if with great effort.

And in the midst of the darkness, a Cheshire Cat grin was forming, slowly bringing the rest of the body into form with it.

"Come back to us. Take your rightful place by my side. The Master will welcome you back. *If* you take Him back."

364

And finally resolving, there was her Father. Standing in the center of this Sacred Space used for meditation on the Highest Good. He was wrapped in the monstrous Flames of the Pyre in front of him, with the hint of That Which he served echoing in them and surrounding him, staring at her now. She almost tried to hide from this blatant Presence, that was enfolding the figure of her father like a burning wall of Living Flame.

Her Fathers Eyes were not solid Black like most of his Minions, but were now two unbearably piercing Blood Red Fire Stones flashing like lasers looking to set Fire to and burn everything within the reach of their Gaze. Like the Preachers "eyes" had been.

Suddenly Kat felt so small, like a rabbit in the presence of a fierce Hunter, as her Father began growing and feeding on her fear and using them like the Pyres his Minions used to bring this, their Beast, into the Flesh.

"Not so powerful now, your White Light Bunny powers. Are they Daughter?"

She could both feel as well as see a firestorm of waves of lacerating Energy beating at, and threatening to blast the more than solid walls of the Flight house into rubble.

This Being of Great Darkness began moving towards her, wave after wave of Dark Energy flowing in her direction, working to either turn her into a tool like her Father was, or destroy her utterly. Once, and for all.

"You still have a choice, Daughter," he said, with a voice like a rising wind that, for now, was not at its full power. "Come. Be *That* which you were created to be.

"Your Master will take you back," he said cooly. And then with a little more evil intent, "Or the Master will Take you back, against your puny Will."

"Your *Master* has always been your master, Father. Not *mine*." She wanted her voice to sound defiant and strong, but instead even to her it sounded small in comparison to his booming Voice.

"No. You are wrong. He is Your Master, too."

"Never," she said as defiantly as she could.

Her fathers face softened, and all of a sudden seeming sunlight began playing across it. His smile suddenly became that of the loving father, as he purred, "You can come back and be my daughter."

But this illusion was not stable for long, as his true nature was never really far from the surface.

"This Light Bunny nonsense is a world of Lies. This world — My World — is the real world," he began shouting once more, as tendrils of power reached out to wrap themselves insidiously around her body.

Feeling more assurance that she actually felt she had, she stood taller. "And if I don't?"

"I have the Power to destroy you," that Voice began to rise in strength again. "If you will not take my hand and your part in our Master's final crushing of this world."

366

Pointing one hand at her, palm downward, burning Red lighting flashed out of it, and enveloped her. "This is nothing compared to what my Master has to bring to bear on you and your puny excuse of this pitiful Group of Demons."

She felt herself being taken by her father further into the Darkness, into some future that was both far away and very near.

She first saw herself walking quietly through this Community she had come to love.

But this time she was using her mind once again to set fire to all of the buildings here, slowly and methodically burning the entire place to the ground. And all those she had been coming to love and trust? They were fleeing before the fire of her wrath.

She saw herself walking through the ashes willed by her and her Masters Wrath, like some Dark Vengeful Goddess, her eyes and body on fire a with non-consuming fire, as she strode out of the still once Community and towards—

With Kat shivering in the darkness, she saw the Capitol Building in Washington DC rising up in front of her. *Am I flying?* the current Kat thought suddenly. *Or is this just an illusion too?*

"They..." he says with all the full Intent of sudden disgust (as if *he* were the wronged one), "Do not know the meaning of True Power. They are weak. Their—" he began and putting as much as the full venom of a servant of the Devil could put into it, began thundering, "Petty little *god* is weak. We are the ones that control this world. They control nothing."

The next vision that she saw was of a large leather Throne-like chair with its back to the her. She recognized from the photos that she had seen,that this was the Oval Office in the White House

This massive throne of a chair began slowly turning around towards her. Sitting there in it she was fully expecting to be a gloating version of her Father himself, in all of his Dark Glory.

But to her shock (quickly turning to horror), the Figure sitting there was not her Father. It was another version of— Another *Her*. A Her whose coppery red hair had been burned to coal black, as if the color had been blasted out of it by the overuse of the Dark Arts.

This other *Her* was a shriveled husk of a woman, far beyond what her age was now, looking dead of all emotions, with a pair of dead eyes, (also burned black into obsidian but without any luster to them). This other *Her* was dead for all intents and purposes, having had any last glimmer of compassion or anything resembling what she would have considered to be left of humanity, scorched into a cinder.

"This is my glorious *destiny*?" she asked, not expecting to get an answer.

This other *Her* had served her Father's and The Beasts wishes to her emotional death. That other *She* had been a servant of Darkness and nothing more. A Tool which had been used up. *She* — or **It** now

— had served Its purpose. It was no longer needed and was lost without any purpose or meaning. A living husk to what she was now.

This other version of President Kathryn Runyon, was reigning from the Oval Office like a deadly Queen of Darkness, threatening to turn into a statue of Malice. They had bred her to be the Anti-Christ, and this was her intended final destiny!

This was the price of her servitude. Having gotten the last of The Beasts final plan through, This was what her Father had created her for. *This*, and only *This*.

As Kat now watched in horror at this vision they had for her, she looked into her own stone cold eyes, eyes the shiniest of obsidian, piercing in their hatred. Of all the things that she had seen in her visions, this was by far the Darkest. And it frightened her the most.

"That person isn't me," she whispered.

"This is your true destiny," the Father whispered, as if the statement were an incantation. "Fulfill it now, Daughter!" he said, in Intent and wrath. "You *will* fulfill it."

"Or what? You'll kill me?"

After rising once more into the air and away from this living nightmare that she would become, she saw the outside world. It was also as dark and devoid of life as her other Self in the Oval Office had been. A hell of living Flame was burning what was left of nature away. As Dark and devoid of life and pity as her other Self had been.

As she looked up into the night sky, all she could see were the shadows of naked singularities from black holes filling it. There were no stars. And as she continued to watch, even the naked singularities began falling from the sky and burning out. What was left was only a black featureless sky devoid of stars, or any light whatsoever.

She felt that all of the other Guardian Alien Races that had once been here guarding and protecting this cradle of life and possibility, were now long gone. They had long since fled this planet that was now hopelessly moving towards being dead.

This was the World that The Beast wanted. **IT** was dying now, and **IT** only wished that this World that **IT** had ruled over for so many tens of centuries, would die along with **IT** as well.

Like the Story for which it had spun Itself regarding it being an Angel railing against heaven, **IT** had even lost most of **IT**s Lieutenants to other Star Systems, fleeing from the Hell on Earth that **IT** had been so intent on and had finally succeeded in creating.

Slamming suddenly back into her current Body again hard, she was reduced to sobbing unconsolably and seeming to her, without end.

After what had seemed like weeks, she finally came back fully to the present, and saw the ghost lights of the candles lit from outside of this room and the Vigil for her that it had represented.

With Kat still huddling in the darkness, the darkness begins having patches of lesser darkness showing now. These patches began glowing with colors as Kat stops shivering and starts to straighten up.

"They—" Her Father says once again with full and utter disgust, "Do not know True Power. They are weak. Their petty little—" and here his Voice dropped into icy depths with, "*God* is weak. It is *We* who control this world. Not They.

"Turn your back on the White Light Bunny," her father told her.

"But I thought that the Anti-Christ was supposed to be a man?" she asked, both taken aback and truly not understanding what he wanted from her in this.

Pausing with a look between disgust and dismissal, he laughed sharply, spitting out, "The Anti-Christ?" Laughing more derisively, he said with all the irony he could instill it with once more, "Oh, my dear, that's such a ridiculous concept. How can there be an Anti- something that never existed? More White Light Bunny God trash. That's all that that myth — that that supposed man... was."

Pausing herself not knowing what to say next, she then realized something. Asking cunningly, "Then why do you hate it so much? Why spend so much time dismissing something so ridiculous? That is, if that is all that this is. Just "White Light Bunny" nonsense."

Turning piercingly cold and derisively dismissive at the same time, he merely told her "Come," as if he were loosing patience with her. "We have so much work left to do."

Standing firmly, she prodded him, "You didn't answer my question. Why do you have to fight so hard against something that doesn't — didn't — exist?"

And pressing the point now with all the spite she could, she said dismissively, "Father."

Pretending not to have heard, "You will open yourself to me now, Daughter," he began to shout.

"And if I don't," she asked in challenge.

With his Voice dropping several octaves in menace, "Then... You will regret it."

Calming visibly, she watched him as he obviously took a different tact. "This is your true destiny. This is what We have worked for all these years. Fulfill it now, Daughter!"

"You still didn't answer my question," she said, repeating her question more defiantly, "And if I don't?"

Having lost all desire to pretend patience, he merely told her, "You *WILL* come back." Transforming further into the Dark Father — his face now growing more and more fire red and twisting internally, morphing until, with his Voice booming, "**NOW**."

Her Fathers face begins resembling his true nature: that of The Beast. Waves of energy begin pulsing out of this now alien, reptilian form.

With dark tendrils of Power reaching out and hitting Kat, she begins writhing in sheer agony, as her body begins feeling as if it's imploding in on itself. Her organs expanding and all of the molecules in her body breaking apart and loosing their cohesion, "You were meant to be a man," her father gloated, "Not some poor little White

Light Excuse of a simpering female.

"As soon as you were born we should've sacrificed you to Our Master. The full intent of your Power would have fed Him for generations to come.

"But we had to put far too much Majical Intent into your creation for that to have been wasted on a momentary gain. If we had known what you would become... Your sacrifice would've been an an acceptable Working."

"But you didn't," Kat said, now throwing as much of her Intent in as she could before she died. "And I wasn't born a man. You haven't had as much power over me as you thought. Have you... Daddy!" she threw at him out of her agony.

She watched as the man who had given her life, gathered his abominable Dark Strength around him to finally take that life.

"I am not the minor Minions you have dealt with before!" he whispered, as his words continued sliding down to the register of what Kat sensed as only a moving of lips. But His dark Whispering soon began to rise into the Heard, climbing once more to the crashing crescendo of—

Malice. His arms splaying wider by the second as he was pulling in Power into the swirling mass of the Darkest of Energies he was collecting around him, gathering It all into the singular ball of dark and furious force that he was going to use to destroy her utterly.

"Do what you will," she taunted him, feeling the Power inside of her she had felt rising up in her before. *Is that part inside of me strong enough?* some part of her worried.

As she heard, *Know Thy Strength* echoing around her from both inside and outside of her.

Bringing his hands together in a furiously powerful clap of Dark Energy, he finished with a thunderously Loud, "Be. Gone!"

Looking down at what had once been her hands and the rest of her body now only turning to ash, she saw her self beginning to come apart excruciatingly cell by living cell. And then she continued to be literally torn apart from the inside out, those cells began dispersing into the molecules, then atoms that made them up.

And Pieces of her began to smolder from the inside out, flaking off her body and flying away like ash, as screaming in terror and pain, her flesh continued flying away until only muscle and then only skeleton remains.

PAIN! she cried in pure agony from deep inside. The only Word that could come to this ripping and shredding agony.

Her body one heaving mass of blood and molecules each being shredded, until there was only that Word, PAIN! Screaming, Feeling what was left of her atoms beginning to shred from the inside out. She felt as if every atom in her body was suddenly on fire, and each one was burning from their core. The Pain was so excruciating, she almost cried out to him to—

"Stop? All you need do is ask, Daughter. Fulfill your Purpose and

374

come to my Side. Embrace Your Destiny, and this pain will be gone forever. You will never suffer the Doubt of these insignificant fools and their petty little Godling that is the essence of Nothing."

"No," was all she could say through the sheer terror and Pain, with what voice she still had. She couldn't stop it from happening, and she could barely think that one Word again.

Looking up at him in very conscious defiance now, she repeated that one Word, almost silently, "**No**."

"Very well, then. You have failed your test and failed me and your True Master. I pity you and your fate. Worse than Death indeed!" he roared, the echoes shattering the Walls surrounding them, burning them down into ash and rubble.

She felt her body ripped apart, sub atomic particle by quark now, sheered from anything that would hold them together. Her body dissolving in the Fire lashing out from his fingertips, centuries worth of Pain shredding her body, mind and Soul.

No, she said. Not knowing whether she *said* it or not, she said it again. *No*.

At which point Kat felt several things at once. She felt her own energy collapse in on itself like a star collapsing as it died. She also felt her body wrenched in an unbearable Pain beyond even her previous imagining.

She both saw and felt herself dissolve into Nothingness, while still being aware as she did. As the pain finally ceased, she thought, *I guess*

I'm dead.

The rest of her charred to fly away, leaving only glowing embers of Spirit releasing from the Body, as she finds herself in numbing Darkness.

As she felt the last of her essence floating away like smoke from the Fire in front of her, she felt— Peace in that ordeal. At last.

She was floating in a sea of nothingness. A Darkness so complete, she could barely Feel, much less think. There was nothing to see. Nothing.

So this is death, came the thought. *Nothingness.* Tossed into the Void. Darkness till the End of Time.

Loneliness. Where was everybody — anybody — else? Would she be alone in this Void forever? That would be a fate worse than Death, indeed.

I Surrender, she thought, with her last "breath."

Only there was no breath to breathe. No light. Only Darkness. Forever.

And then, an overwhelming Sense of peace began taking over a mind that should not be there.

What had once been a solid room around her, began dissolving into an overwhelming Presence of LIGHT. She sensed rather than heard, a VOICE that was not a voice, telling her, I AM WELL PLEASED. BE NOT AFRAID.

Is my suffering done, she asked in thought, now not needing a Voice—

YOUR SUFFERING IS DONE. BUT YOUR TASK IS NOT COMPLETE.

Must I really go back? she asked.

YOU ARE PREPARED NOW TO DO WHAT YOU WERE MEANT TO DO. BE NOT AFRAID.

Are you... God? she suddenly thought to ask.

YES. AND NO. THAT WHICH IS, DOES NOT SPEAK.

Are you Jesus then? Can I finally get some answers?

YOU HAVE ALL THE ANSWERS YOU NEED INSIDE OF YOU. THE REST OF WHAT YOU PRESENTLY CALL YOUR LIFE WILL BE THERE FOR YOU TO FIND OUT.

Suddenly, she knew that she did know The Answers.

AND THERE WILL BE MORE UNDERSTANDING TO COME, the VOICE said with finality.

And then the Light began to show, faintly at first, as if her mind — was that the only thing she had left? — was fooling her in her lack of feeling — Anything.

And then she could Feel it. Purpose.

That's right, Daughter, she heard a Whisper.

Terrified by the sudden Other, she took an — Inbreathe? Something? There was always Something.

377

There is Nothing. And there is Everything at once, the Voice said.

Not her fathers Voice. This one was soft, as if the first breathe of life after the Darkest of Nights.

They crafted you for their DIRE purposes, Daughter, the Voice said. *But it is time for you to claim your Higher Purpose.*

Please, she thought. *Let me just stay here in the darkness. Let me rest. No pain. No—*

In the growing Light penetrating the darkness, she felt her Consciousness rising up to meet it. Choice. Choosing. Being.

She felt her Intention and reason for being rising. She was feeling stronger and not the victim of her Fathers Rage and Dark Power. She felt that Part of her that had *protected* her in the past, before recognizing it as... Herself.

Hands began forming, once again, atom by atom, and then molecule by molecule, out of that Nothing. Closing her mind like she would her eyes, she willed a Body — here, a Body — to be rising and forming out of that Nothing. All of those atoms and molecules that had been scattered into the Darkness, she began pulling into Form again. She began pulling herself — together — out the Formless Field of ALL THAT IS and ALL that EVER WILL BE.

Whispering, "No. This is my destiny." She felt both elated and as if she could sleep for ten thousand years. Having found something in herself that she didn't know she had — the positive to beat back the negative, she sighed and told herself and whatever Darkness was still listening, "You have no power over me. Over us. I've won."

She felt and Chose to bring her Self out of the Darkness, scattering that Darkness like dried up leaves blown by a winter wind. She Willed herself into Form again, back into the Flight House. In front of her Father. Stopping the destruction of the Flight House and reversing it, pulling the physical Reality back together.

Her strength of Will now Gathering more and more Strength and Intent, she began pulling the scattered "ashes" of her Soul together, glowing brighter and brighter, coalescing into... Power. Feeling the Power that was her Soul, rising out of the ashes of defeat at her Fathers' Dark Intention.

But then, as the embers of Spirit begin cooling to float away, fragments begin flashing into brilliant motes of sunlight and coalescing again. And the whole of the destruction process reversing again, until...

A Cheshire Cat grinning Kat begins emerging out of the growing regenerating form. Returning to her original state, but now glowing internally until her whole form is pulsating with Light, the brilliance almost blinding.

Lessening in intensity till her body's form is once again visible, a now relaxed and deeply breathing Kat turns the tables on her Father. As she crosses the line back into *solidity*, she tells him, "Now dearest Father, I commit you to Your doom."

Her hands floating up and her Energetic Aura expanding until it touches the image of her Father, who is now the one with fear on *his* face. His image beginning to shiver, his is now the look of horror as Kat feels the Power in her growing even stronger than his.

His image begins to melt, shatter and burn off as hers had, and now shivering to the point of breaking, shattering into a million shards of glass, each one representing one of the lives that was shed to allow him his thousand years of life.

These thousands of other souls began coalescing into one giant blinding orb of Light in front of her. She felt the pain, and now the triumph, of each and every one of these fragments let loose, as they collected into one triumphant shout of joy and freedom.

Opposite this collection, time and space coalesced into the blinding strings of Reality known as the Tunnel of Light that each soul sees on its death. As One by each One of these soul fragments thanked her silently and entered into this Tunnel, free once more.

She now saw her Father, both raging further than he had before, but this time with the definite look of Fear in his Eyes. The flashing burning lasers that had been lashing out there were themselves now shattering, burning those eyes into the Black Coal pits of his much less powerful underlings.

"Noooo," was all he could say.

His Hands held up high against her onslaught, as sickly green and red as he had mustered before, the Power there began being beat back by the rising wind of her pure White Hot energy beating back all of

380

his strength until—

His Rage began quickly turning into screams of anguish and pain as his power was being forced out of his body, crumpling from inside out, with the onslaught of Kat's Energy and Intent.

The Master that was her Father, was quickly being turned into a lump of energetic lightning being beaten down by the Daughter.

At the last flashes of whirlwind exchange, the mighty Master was now just an old, and cringing man showing the age of his centuries of "life" finally.

When the "Battle" was over, Kat was tempted to blast him with his own type of power. But instead, told him, "No, I'm not going to stoop to your level."

Attempting to gather his own power back as she relented, Kathryn told him, "No." Raising her hands once again in his direction, "Use the last of your Power to leave here. Be gone," she said, and then added the final blow, "Daddy."

"We'll be back," he said ominously.

"We'll be ready," she said forcefully in response, and reaching out with both of her hands, she clapped them together loudly and forcefully, as her now beaten father disappeared in a cloud of dark smoke. Taking his fearful and also now very frightened Master, along with him.

Walking out of the Flight House, she saw what she now felt of as

Her Community. All of the Faces, young and old, were collectively beaming a glow of Love at her, with Angelus at the forefront, moving in slowly with hands outstretched. "Welcome Home, Daughter of Light," she said, in a voice both quiet and one that Kat knew All of the Community could hear.

"You have died and been reborn to Us. And for Us.

"It took great courage to come back and face the full strength of your father," Angelus whispered to Kat. "And drawing on the energy of the Universe is no small feat for those of us still in human form."

"Is he really gone?" Kat asked hollowly. It took effort to just keep herself from plunging into sleep.

"For now," she said, with compassion echoing in her voice. "But this was merely the first major assault. Even when you and young Devon fought against the Preacher in Bolder, that was only a minor quirmish.

"When he next returns, it will be with an Army of Adepts and all of their Minions that they can gather."

Looking up at The Ancient, Kat dared to ask, "Should I have come back?"

Placing her palm again over the younger woman's head like a benediction, "Godness Willed it, and you heeded the call.

Rising and drawing the younger woman up with the mere force of the energy emanating from her hand, Angelus wraps her arms around Kat, and begins guiding her towards the sleeping quarters. "You have time to rest.

"You have done well. But—"

"They're coming," Kat said abruptly.

Unfazed, the older woman merely agreed with a nodded, *Yes. I know.*

"So he'll— They'll be back?"

"Oh, yes. We will have a short time to prepare, but when your father and his Dark Minions return, they will return in full force. It will take every ounce of combined strength to defeat them here."

"I was hoping that doing what I did to my father would at least give me a rest."

"Oh, it has, my dear! You were wonderful beyond our wildest expectations," Angelus told her.

"But you still thought I would be turned."

"We feared that you might. Devon however, insisted that you would not."

"Speaking of which..."

"Go inside, and you will know, child."

And The Ancient did what Kat least expected once again, reaching out and enfolding Kat into the Older One's embrace. "You have won a great victory today. But the battle goes ever on. It is the reason that we are here in flesh."

Embracing Kat, she sighed into her stillness. "Come," she finally said, although she couldn't tell if she had actually said it. "Now it is

383

time for you to rest."

Back at the dormitory, Angelus left her with "There is nothing further to say. The time has come to act," Angelus said, turning away from an exhausted and perplexed Kat.

"Nothing to say," she repeated. Where was Devon? This time over all the others, she needed to fall into his arms.

Her elation at her victory over her father was quickly fading. She knew inside although she didn't know how, that they were all in very grave danger now.

She could feel the forces gathering like an approaching storm. It wasn't going to break tonight, but when it did, it was going to be a raging one, full of sound, fury, and everything else that they could throw at this place.

Come now. It is time for sleep.

Kat was feeling both exhausted from the effort that coming back took, as well as feeling as if all of her nerve endings were on fire simultaneously and she was shedding Light. The last of the Community members had filtered away from their Vigil and off towards the Dining Hall or the Living Quarters. She couldn't see Devon anywhere among them.

Sleeping the rest of that night in the most restful sleep that she had ever had, Kathryn was still lying in bed, watching the play of light and shadows on the ceiling above her cot. "How long have I been asleep?" she asked no one in particular.

"Another two days," a Voice answered. "I take it you had a dreamless sleep?"

She very slowly leveraged herself up in the bed to see a smiling Devon sitting beside her.

"The Beast is gathering Its Forces now. We still have a little time."

Standing but still gazing lovingly at her, he said, "Rest for now. The Battle of our Lifetimes is a few days away."

She wanted to get up and eat something, but her body wouldn't respond. She went back to staring at the play of light on the ceiling.

Turning and taking her hand suddenly, Devon said with affection, "Everyone will be waiting in the Flight House for us."

"Everyone."

"Angelus has said, the time has come."

"That was too easy," Kat says, feeling the absolute exhaustion now more than ever.

"That was only the beginning," Devon suddenly whispered in her ear. "There is much to do now. We will have a short time to prepare, but when your father and his Dark Minions return, they will return in full force. It will take every ounce of our combined strength to defeat them here."

shadows and **LIGHT**

THIRTY-ONE

Angelus had silently summoned all those in the Community to come to the Flight House at noon. "Everyone," Kat repeated. She had heard the Call as well.

Devon and Kat were walking on the grounds trying their best to have the illusion of a carefree day. Kat felt a tenseness in the air that even Devon didn't need to tell her was centered around her.

The grounds were filled in the meantime with everyone silently going about their business until the appointed time.

Entering the Flight House several hours later, Kat and Devon crossed over the threshold of the Big main Room. She was still amazed at the number of Community members gathered there. Everyone was already seated on the ground, quietly waiting for their leader to speak

The majority of the other Community Members were sitting on the floor in a silent semicircle, apparently deep in meditation. Kat had never seen them all gathered in an inside space before, and was both excited and frightened at the number. There were more here than she had seen gathered in the whole compound. Plus many others that had arrived since, were now gathered here.

All were sitting on the floor in a huge, silent semicircle, apparently deep in meditation. Without a word, Devon took Kat's hand and began walking in, guiding her in her hesitancy to the front row center spot. Kat got the feeling that as she had been the center of the psychic focus, she was now to be the center of the physical focus as well.

Kat saw a lot of people who she had grown to know in her few short days here, but also many that she did not know. Members had been showing up over the last day or two, as if Angelus were assembling an army. One of the few times that Devon spoke to her, he said, "An army of Light to meet the coming Darkness.

"We'll go for a last walk, after The Ancient has spoken to us."

"Last walk. That sounds mighty final to me."

"It may be. Who knows? If Angelus knows the outcome to this, she's not saying."

There was now almost a thousand people in this room now, an amazing number to Kat. *Of course everyone's dressed in their purple robes*, Kat thought. Then, *This is a large number of people*, she thought in Devon's direction, knowing that he could hear her. *But is it going to be enough?*

There are many powerful masters of the higher arts here, he thought back. Ever since she had returned from death, she was amazed that she too, could hear others thoughts. When she wanted to, that is.

And this isn't all of us, Devon told her silently. *There are very powerful Elders in our Order, who have been alive for many years. They are guarding this place in ways that you are only now knowing how to imagine.*

The Forces of Darkness will underestimate our abilities, much to their detriment.

"What will we do to them? And what are the Forces of Darkness going to try to do to us?" she asked quietly aloud, leaning in to whisper to him.

They're not subtle, he thought to her. *They'll crash and burn as they come, because that is all they know how to do.*

We need to go into the silence now, to prepare for what The Ancient has to say.

Even after her experience on the Other Side of this Life, there was still a part of her — most likely her inner child — that was nervous.

Having relived what the Other Side could do in Dallas, she couldn't help but wonder how they would bring their power into this. *Could they kill us outright?* she thought. And then remembering back to her father and what he did to her before she "resurrected" herself back into her Body, she didn't need to wonder. And this time there would be even more "fire power" brought to bear, she realized. They would try and kill off Anyone in this Community, much like her father had shown her in that vision of *her* doing the destruction.

But then she remembered, *That is not my Path. I am here to join, not to kill.*

At this moment, Angelus glided into the room and over to Her Place and sat. The Seven Council members were sitting in a mirroring semicircle facing the rest of the Community. Raising her hand, as if to silent the conversations that had apparently been going on around her, she began to speak.

The Ancient was rising once again.

"The time is come," she said, looking at each of the individuals gathered, glancing but also penetrating especially as her eyes landed on Kat's. "As most of you are aware, the Dark Ones are building their strength for their final assault on our Community.

"The time that most of us have prepared for — some for their entire lives, others for just a short time. I cannot guarantee that All in this room will survive. I do know that all of you are prepared for this last act of your lives. Should those lives end here, this night, they will be done in the Highest of Spirit. You will not need to return unless you desire to."

Turning in Kat's direction, "Some of you have endured much. Some have already paid the highest price and know that there is nothing to fear. If anyone else is not up to the Onslaught that will soon be upon us, you are free to go with my blessings."

When no one stood to leave, she continued. "I cannot foresee completely the outcome of this coming conflict, but should we prevail, I do know that the Power of Darkness will be greatly diminished. The World may even begin the healing process to rise of out of the Darkness it is currently in.

"That said, let us now begin preparing for whatever is to be. Godness Wills It."

And almost the entire Community repeated it after her, "Godness Wills It."

Rising suddenly, Kat asked Angelus, "Forgive me. But how — I mean — what are they going to do? And what exactly are we going to do to resist it? Are they going to try to kill us all?"

"They cannot kill That which cannot be killed," Angelus replied mysteriously. "Surely you know that personally by now."

"I'm sorry, but—" Kat began.

"You should fully understand that," Angelus answered. "You knew — part of you knew all along — how to protect yourself." *How to bring yourself back from death,* Angelus told her silently. Angelus continued. "That is why you are here with us now."

As silence was returning to the hall, a low barely audible hum began vibrating around them. Kat self-consciously squirmed in her spot, not really feeling comfortable yet with this type of Power. Even after her return from oblivion.

Eventually calming and closing her eyes, she began breathing deeply and rhythmically with the Others around her.

She saw Blackness as colors begin swirling, began taking shape in that darkness around her. A brilliant Light began illuminating the darker landscape around her. With the shadows still in dominance. Kat, who begins smiling serenely, whispers to herself, "Yes. I see now. Oh..."

Putting his arm around her, he leans in. *I know. Trust me I know.*

The strength of the Light began to displace the darkness, as more and more minds and souls began to be in tune with each other and the energy surrounding them.

But she knew just below the surface, that that wasn't the case. The air was humming with the crackling clear magic of the Light, preparing this place against death and destruction. She could feel the expectation of something great and wonderful developing in the psychic *air*.

Several hours later, a number of Community Members were exiting the Flight House now, among them Kat and Devon.

"There were more people in there than I have seen before. How many have come from Outside?"

"Quite a number. Our Community has grown by quite a lot, and we will need every one of them tonight."

"Yes. I can feel the strength building. But will it be enough?"

"Godness—" Devon began to say, as Kat interrupts him.

"Wills it. I know. But will it?"

"You are one of the most powerful among us. You were able to turn away from the Darkness that your Father tempted you with and rise again out of the ashes that he consigned you to. There are Others of equal or even greater abilities who are bending their wills towards protecting and defending this Place of Peace even now.

"It will not be the "fight" that your Father and his other Adepts think that it will be. Know that, and we will prevail. Others are Knowing that. You need to set aside your doubts, and remember the strength and Spirit that you showed to your Father. And also Know that there are those here that have abilities that even The Darkness knows nothing about."

"And then... It happened. You began letting go and began being where we were. Opening up to your true Self once more—"

A half an hour later, Kat and Devon were still walking in silence. The full moon was making their way easy, even if both of them hadn't had the heightened senses of the Aware.

Kat was both elated and felt a sickening drop in her belly.

"So I didn't..." Kat began but was reluctant to finish the sentence.

"Kill you father?" Devon asked as he smiled. "No. Diminish him greatly? Yes,."

"So I really didn't…"

"Relax," he said, both bemused and proud that she was concerned about this. "I don't think that even Angelus would be able to kill your father. We would all be hard pressed as a community to kill him."

"So then, we need to kill him once and for all."

"You diminished his Power. He feels vulnerable now, unlike he has for a very long time. And his Master now feels vulnerable as well. Unlike he has probably *ever* felt."

"But... Why? If he's evil, why wouldn't we—"

"Even if that were our way — which it isn't — you know the answer to that. If you didn't, you would have tried to kill him while you had the chance. But you didn't, and who knows? Maybe you might have been powerful enough to—"

"You're joking with me. Right?"

Directing the conversation towards another path and leaning in, "Your father has much of the energy of The Beast coursing through him at this point. He's been a loyal servant of the Beast for centuries upon centuries, and as such, is a very powerful being. Perhaps almost even immortal now."

"So..."

"So we wouldn't try to kill him even if we could."

"But, why..." Feeling confused, Kat tried to reconcile in her mind both the conflicting desires to try and kill something that evil, and her growing awareness that she shouldn't even think of it. It was mind spinning conundrum, if she tried to focus on it for too long.

"So, what so we do?"

"Don't be fooled that what happened here the other day will permanently end the Rule of Darkness. But they have been shown that their game of power is not what they thought it was. And *that* is, in and of itself, a victory.

"And now you have broken away from that past, and all of the horrific things that you have done. The Infinite is very forgiving of what we have done in the name of our Fathers."

She saw his smile radiating in the moon lit darkness, "Only with you they obviously bred more than they bargained for."

"So... What am I to them now?

"Obviously, their worst nightmare," he said in a terrible British accent. Softening his voice, "Except instead of being their slave, Spirit has other plans for you."

"Such as?" she said icily, feeling as if she wanted to back away from this man she had come to love.

Knowing what she was going through, he took no offense. "Only you can answer that one," he told her, his hands still firmly but gently cupping her face. "We... Are not trying to control the outcome. We don't have, or even want to for that matter, have control over--"

"But I thought that you wanted to transform the planet?"

Dropping his hands to hers, "That's different." he said, turning to begin walking again, "Yes, we want transformation to happen. But we don't want, really can't have, control over anything."

"At first, I couldn't see anything," she was telling him. "I almost thought I heard everyone else laughing at me."

"All your fears and doubts. And maybe some peripheral influences from outside as well."

Shivering suddenly, she said sheepishly, "I guess."

"And then... It happened. You began letting go and began being where we were. Opening up to your true Self once more."

Knowing that he was right, she was about to come back with another retort, but let it go. Fighting back the tears, "I just want it to be over. You know? The questions. The temptations to give in. I just want it to be over."

Putting his arm around her, she leans in as they walk. "I know."

"That's—"

"Their way," he said, with a mild disgust rising in his voice. "Control Now. Power Now." Stopping once again and turning to put his arm around her, he said gently in her ear, "We... Have a longer view.

"But for now," he said once again softly in her ear, tickling her in a very good way, "We have a shorter time to share together."

Leading her into the darkness of the thicker woods towards their secret grove, she asks, "Is this what I think it is?" the feeling of being a teenager coming to her now.

Smiling and saying nothing, Devon just led her further into the rich darkness of a simple night.

"So, what so we do? Where do we go from here?"

Reaching for her hand, he wanted to hold her so close to him. For the short time that they had left for now.

"For now?" he said once again softly in her ear, tickling her in a very good way, "We have a shorter time to share together."

"Is this what I think it is?" she asked, the feeling of being a teenager coming to her now.

Leading her into the darkness of the thicker woods towards their secret grove, "Let's leave everything else behind us for the rest of the night."

Once again walking hand in hand in the fragrant pines of the forest, Kat suddenly couldn't hold the questions any longer.

THIRTY-TWO

The next evening the entire Community was gathered both inside the Flight House, as well as outside with all of them outside sitting around a large bonfire as their numbers had grown so much that even the massive Inner Room could not contain them all. Now another sort of round was taking place, as the Energy swirled around the dome faster than horses ever could.

Kat had chosen to sit outside however, feeling the humming and building energy for the coming spiritual fire fight between the Cult and the Community of Light.

The Energy was gathering all around her, and she could feel it crackling through the air and reaching into the ground for strength and support from the very earth itself. Looking around with her eyes closed, she also saw that there were star-like bodies of bright light appearing among them to lend support as well. This was a turning point. A major turning point in the history of the earth.

As the assault finally approaches, she senses that when it does, it will be like a special effects Fourth of July of negative energy. With beings the likes of which she couldn't have even imagined a mere two weeks ago. Or was it only one week?

But she could also feel that the March of Destruction had also begun, marching its path up the hill that she and Devon had driven up in fear of attack just almost a week ago. *So much has happened since*, Kat thought.

Stretching her heightened senses out into that oncoming Darkness, she saw Monstrosities there much like she had seen in the plane which were searching for her before Boulder. Things that had obviously once been men at one point, but were now only twisted and huge caricatures of men, faceless, being driven by their Masters whipping them into their frenzy of destruction. These Creatures, unlike Frankensteins Monster, had no true consciousness anymore. They were merely tools, striding through the forest breaking and snapping ancient trees as if they were twigs. The Fire Lords were behind them, setting fire to everything that stood in their way.

Behind them, were tens of thousands of their Minions, eyes Black and reflecting the fires that were set surrounding them.

They were now as mindless as the Monstrosities, marching haphazardly as they moved to a fate that most were not even consciously aware of. They were merely Tools, as much as the Monstrosities were. Tools of Darkness, magic fodder waiting to die if their Masters needed them to.

Surrounding her outside this House of Prayer, Meditation and Power though, she could feel the hum of Power rising. She could first feel, and then see a glow forming around many of those surrounding her.

These were bubbles of Power forming around most of these anti-Darkness individuals. Even though her father had attempted to desecrate it, this space still hummed with positive Godly energy.

Slowly, she watched from inside, as these practitioners of Light finished forming their own shields against the Darkness. Many around her also began levitating in their personal bubble as well.

She could feel her own Power rising to meet that of the Others around her, building her own bubble and contributing to the energy of others.

Will there be enough of us? Kat asked Devon nervously and silently. This was a Gathering unlike any other the planet had experienced before, but the Dark Forces that she could sense coming, seemed to dwarf their number.

Not only were there the Mages and their beasts of burden, the Monstrosities, but also the thousands of Normals, unaware of their culpability in the Dark Evil that their lives had been in unconscious obeisance to, who were being held in unconscious thrall by those Mages. They were the cannon fodder that the Dark Overlords were dragging into their final assault on the Bearers of Light, intending on using them and then throwing them away like cattle to the slaughter.

I'm feeling their strength and Hatred pouring in our direction, Kat thought.

Yes. I feel it too. And I'm sure everyone here of any depth of learning is also feeling it as well, Devon responded.

Our Strength is not in numbers, Daughter, she heard The Ancient softly tell her. *You who have traveled to the Limitless Realm of the Infinite should know that.* Kat wasn't sure whether Angelus was chiding, or encouraging her.

It's not in the physical that we will beat back this Assault, Devon added. *Each one of the Oldest Lightworkers that we have here are more than a match for their hatred. You alone have bested the best of the Beast in your father.*

Reaching out to assure her physically, he reached gently through her bubble of Power, and with a soft grip of her hand told her, "Your time to fear is gone."

Squeezing back and feeling the love pouring out of him, Kat worked to brush away her fear. She remembered a line from a science fiction novel of the past, "Fear is the mind killer." She needed to tap into that experience she has experienced of dying and return to calming her fears. Of course they would win. They had the Infinite Being of Creation on their side. The Dark only had a perversion of that.

Fear not, and know that I AM with You. Whatever happens.

Godness wills It, she finished his thought.

Caressing her hand fondly, he gave her one last kiss on her cheek, and released her hand, settling into his meditation.

Closing her eyes, she worked on remembering that feeling of Power that she had felt, and the touch of the Infinite Presence when she had died. That she had felt in bringing her body back into physical form just a mere two days before

Her Fathers Dark Magic had shredded her body down to its subatomic particles and blown them to the wind. That should have been the end of her then. Killed and cast into the emptiness of the Void, beyond Light, she experienced a death that should have lasted an Eternity. But didn't.

And here she was among the living again, having conquered the death that her father had intended for her. She had proved her faith and power were strong enough to overcome anything.

Sitting in the deepening Silence surrounding her, Kat became aware of only the sound of the crackling fire in front of her. It was fed as much by the growing Energy of those sitting at her sides, as it was the wood that had been sacrificed for it. She now sat around a very different fire than that of the Red Circle.

So she let go of the need to be aware of her surroundings and her fellow Flyers in Spirit. She was both herself, and becoming Everything as far as her mind could fly.

Touching down gently on individual trees on the mountaintop surrounding them, she stretched out to feel the approaching Darkness coming for their destruction in the same moment. Expanding far beyond her *sense* of self.

Suddenly, she was brought back to her body as she felt the first encroaching tendrils of the Dark Enemy reaching out. Then she heard the voice of Angelus whispering to her, *We do not fight. We only seek to influence and encourage the Light within all beings to come forth.*

But still, with all that Kathryn had felt, and Seen, and done, she also felt that Fear rising up in her as well. That no matter how powerful Angelus and the members of the Community were -- it would still not be enough.

This is how They seek to influence, Angelus told her. *Be still and know that I AM with you*, she repeated.

As soon as Kat allowed the fear to melt away, the tens of thousands of fierce magic wielders melted away as well. What remained were those thousands being forced and coerced by the magic wielded by the true Adepts (who were far fewer than they made themselves appear to be).

They are Many, but they are no match for the strength and Power of the Light, Angelus whispered.

Kat calmed further and felt the peace and the Power flow into her that she had felt after returning from The End and her apparent demise. She began seeing a field of stars flowing down from Everywhere, strengthening the growing energy of the Community around her.

This was not an Armageddon approaching. This was a desperate attempt at dominating the world far beyond the physical illusion.

She saw now that it was doomed to fail. That indeed beyond the perception of the Darkness of space, was the Infinite Field of

Light. She felt her part in this drama, and felt an even deeper calm descend on her like that Help that had come from the deepest part of the All That Is that had saved her many times.

Then she saw a hundred or so of the giant Monstrosities, five or six times the size of normal men (like a certain green comic book character), but without any humanity left in them. They reminded her of the Monstrosity she had seen in her fathers plane, except that these were moving, like tanks crashing through the woods. They mowed down any tree that got in the way (and even a few of the mortal Minions). Except these were rage filled as much as the monstrosities of the plane had been pain filled. Or perhaps this rage only hid the pain deeper.

They were the front line offense, snapping aged trees like they were twigs. Even though these were Old Growth Pines and Redwood, her heightened senses heard the trees scream in pain as they were crushed aside.

Behind the Giants were the Adepts, driving their Minions ahead of them. These were now mindless Dark Power wielders, sending their negative energy out through their upraised hands. They were killing, burning, anything left alive that the Giants had not laid waste to in their wake.

Thousand of years of living beings on the mountain were

being torn and burned away by this unnatural fire of Dark Magic, just as if a forest fire were sweeping the mountain.

As if to say *Enough*, members of the Community now elevated in power, were rising like bright stars encased in cocoons of Light, moving off in the direction of the approaching hordes.

Stretching her heightened senses further out into that oncoming Darkness, she saw the Monstrosities there, moving crashing forward, screams of rage for all those that could hear being voiced.

But she knew just below the surface, that that wasn't the case. The air was humming with the crackling clear magic of the Light, preparing this place against death and destruction. As she and Devon joined the others in the Flight House expanding into their Light fields, she could feel the expectation of something great and wonderful developing in the psychic *air*.

Everyone was now feeling the approaching Minions and their Masters, burning the woods in advance of their push. Seeing the fires and putting them out as fast as they can be set, the members of the Community have extended their reach out as far as the advancing hordes. Seeking to subtly influence the human

Minions who were weakly tied to the Dark Energy, many were fleeing already, having found themselves deep in the mountains where they don't normally go.

But there were literally thousands of these, some fully knowing what they are working towards and a great many unaware of what they're doing. *There will be many shattered lives after this fight*, Kat thought, *as Many find themselves awakening to the Darkness which they had formerly served.* The Pitiful, awakening to their Darkest Nightmares, will be at a loss as to who they are.

Spreading into the woods Kat could feel the harrowing power of the evil intent that was focusing on her, bent on her destruction and that of the Community.

Many of the Community are ringing the deeply dark woods at dusk, Gathering Light as they walk, humming and building up bright globes of power between their hands.

She saw many of the Younger Ones getting caught in the first Dark Energy blasts. First their personal shields darkened and then began to shrivel and then their bodes inside, finally burning up and becoming cinders of ash floating on the wind before disappearing in a flash of Light.

The Other Practitioners, older Ones mainly (but not all), took in these blasts of Dark Energy and transmuting them, began glowing and sending out Waves of Light in all directions. This caused the Adepts to falter and acme begin fleeing. The Minions stumbling and waking from their Dark Dream, many began wailing in sheer terror when they found themselves far from home. Others would throw themselves onto the stumps of downed trees, impaling themselves.

Some of the younger Ones not killed by the Dark, swooped in and began herding these former Minions now Lost in the direction of the Community. These could be saved much like they themselves had once been.

In other areas, the more powerful and ancient Workers of Light were going here and there laying siege to the more powerful of the Dark Adepts; Kat and Devon were among these.

Going from Adept to Adept, Kat and the Others would absorb the Blasts of Dark Energy and return them to the diminishing power users of the former Darkness, who now began cowering when their Darkness was not sufficient.

Many of these Adepts fled at this onslaught, but those more powerful Ones began taking the waves of Light and mixing them with Darkness and returning them against the Lightworkers, some of whom died the deaths of the Younger Lightworkers, turning into ashen cinders to float away.

Eventually, the most Powerful of the Dark Adepts began to take over as their numbers began being freed of the Dark Control. Dark Fire clashing with transmuting Light, the forest was ablaze with cascading waves of Dark Energy and Light transmuting It everywhere.

Eventually the Dark Mages disappeared, one by one, until only the most Powerful on both sides were facing each other. By now most of the Minions had either fled, killed themselves or were released from Darkness and were being guided towards the sheltering welcome of the Community.

After sustaining the assault, the negative forces began retreating, returning in waves again and again.

The Light around the Community of Light was growing even stronger and began cascading in rolling waves of Light off the mountaintop.

If seen from above, the ring of Light cuts through the Darkness and infiltrates with veins of Light. As this happens, dark swirls explode and ascend all around the lens, as the Community of Light releases all of the built-up Energy of the

Crown Towers Cult coven into the Light.

"You will Lose," one of the Dark Mages roared, hurling bolts of fire at the remaining Lightworkers.

To which Angelus replied, "Your Night is done," and with a flash of LIght from her hands, this Mage was reduced to a groveling, defeated mere mortal man, bereft of his former Powers. "Your time is over."

In the end, the dark woods were glowing from within. The forest fires that had been raging, were now calmed to cinders. Many of the former Minions were wandering lost, in need of healing.

After sustaining the assault, the negative forces began their final retreat.

In the woods Kat could feel the harrowing power of the evil intent that was focusing on her, bent on her destruction and that of the Community.

Many of the Community were now minus their shielded bodies, Gathering Light as they walk, begin humming and—

As dawn was breaking in the East, most of the Forces of Darkness had either dispersed, were dead or were begging for mercy. The mercy of which of course, was given freely. "Your bondage has been broken. Your Dark Ways dispersed. Go now in peace, and as Someone once said, *And Sin no more*. You have been given a second chance. Do not return to your old Ways," Angelus told them.

After many of them had gone, Kat asked, "Can they be trusted to not return to their darkness?"

"Most of them, yes. Some will always be drawn back to the power of the Dark."

"And what's going to happen to us?"

"We will disperse to the winds. We have foreseen this moment for decades now. What will be will be, as Godness Wills it.

"There are other Strongholds of Light, scattered around this Country and the World, many far older than this one. This was, to use the modern perforative, on "the front lines" in this "battle" as it were, but the other Fortresses of Light will continue."

"But what am I supposed to do. I was only getting used to—"

"It is time, my dear, for You to disperse as well. This was only the first battle of many. Our paths will expand and converge. You will know what to do. Go Inward and the Council will always be there for you. The Darkness will not give up, The Beast has much to loose if **It** does."

Robin Chappell

THIRTY-THREE

Two mornings after the Assault on the Community — older cars and ancient busses from the 60's, which were once commercial and school busses — began to arrive to disperse the once thriving and now diminishing Community of Light. Tearful fair-wells and the scattering of the members of the Community began, as the number dwindled over that day.

It had been both a long week and a very short one later, as Kat was saying goodbye to what had seemed like such a strange place to her only a short time ago. She had grown used to the outer utilitarian nature of the place, craving those times in the Flight House with all the strange brothers and sisters she had met here.

The Community was like the home she had never known, and now here she was leaving it already. It didn't seem fair, she thought. *I should be able to settle down, for at least a year.*

Kat was being sent off to battle the Darkness, performing the same

413

task that Devon was doing—looking for those who could look to such as herself for help.

Devon was going off on his own errands for peace, and Kat was having to let him go too. These last few moments alone together were going to have to last for... Godness only knew how long.

"Will I ever see you again?" she asked, not sure she wanted to know.

"Yes. And at times when you least expect. And of course, I'll always be there with you in Spirit, Kat. If you need me, all you need do is think my name and let me know where you are."

"The Beast has lost a lot of Its — "human resources," shall we say. But they *will* come after us again. We have time before they do, but We will be long dispersed before they can."

"So... We didn't win."

"No," Devon smiled once again, but sighing. "That wasn't the object here. Changing minds, influencing viewpoints, elevating the Consciousness — that's our way. Helping to direct the course of evolution. Seeking to help those who are seeking to do the work of God. That's where we go from here."

"Sounds hopeless," Kat sighed.

"Only if we give up hope."

Looking out over this high landscape of trees and high clouds, she felt herself on top of the world. But she knew that she was going to have to go back into that World. She wished achingly that this man she

414

had so grown to love could go with her. She knew that for now though, that it was too dangerous for both of them to do so.

It had come time for Kat and Devon to say goodbye to Angelus. "Will I ever see *you* again either?" she asked Angelus

"Perhaps… But You are now in control. You do not need my help."

"But—"

Touching Kat on the forehead, the Older Woman told her, "All you need do is go inside at any time, and you will be connected with all of us. You know this. Physical distance is an illusion as is everything else in this life."

Closing her eyes, Kat began looking strangely disoriented, opening her eyes and focusing on Angelus. It was all so clear now. "My god," she said, her voice mixed with both reverence, awe and... Remembrance. She knew this woman before. "You were — are — Mary Magdalene."

Looking both far off in the distance and inside suddenly, Angelus spoke as if from a great distance. "I used to be called by a name similar to that." Returning to the present, she continued with, "And before that, Rachael. That was then, but this is now.

"The past is not important. Only the Now."

Touching Kat's head with her palm. "Go now in peace. You have yourself to depend on now."

On the verge of tears now, Kat was almost pleading. "But…"

"You are a very powerful woman, Kathryn Runyon. Never forget that. You have won a victory that many before you have failed.

"Your life is now very different from what was, but this Story continues. We have only won the first Battle of Many that have been, and will continue to be."

Kat returned to the waiting car containing the several others such as herself, going out to battle. Attempting to go in peace. Only time would tell.

Godness will it, she thought. At least she had a few days with her sisters and brothers of Light before she was off on her own. She didn't want to look back as the car was crunching the gravel on the road out, but she did.

Devon was no longer visible. And Angelus was fading off in the distance.

Go in peace, Daughter, she heard Angelus tell her in mind only. *You will do well.*

Godness wills it, Kat said mentally, bidding farewell.

The End (for Now)

About the Author

Robin Chappell is an Author and Fine Artist/Photographer living in Los Angeles. Originally from Missouri, he had lived the majority of his life prior to moving to LA, in Washington, DC. He moved to LA to work in the Film and TV Industry as a screenwriter and an actor. This novel is from the (already written) screenplay, "shadows and LIGHT."

He has a number of other books in "various stages of development," to be released over the next several years. He is also in development with his first television series (Title tba).

Once more, if you enjoyed this book please indulge the Author in leaving an honest Review on his Amazon Author Page. Your Reviews are greatly appreciated.

Also, if you would like to find out more about Robin and his Creative Output (books and art/creativity) you can sign up for Robin's monthly newsletter LA VIEU FROM VINCI by emailing him at robin@21stcenturydavinci. You can also opt out at any time. (Your email will never be sold.)

Robin Chappell

www.ingramcontent.com/pod-product-compliance
Lightning Source LLC
Chambersburg PA
CBHW061509020726
47502CB00006B/2001